P9-DXE-564

Angie Amalfi Mysteries by
Joanne Pence

COURTING
DISASTER

AN ANGIE AMALFI MYSTERY

JOANNE
PENCE

AVON BOOKS

An Imprint of HarperCollinsPublishers

AVON BOOKS
An Imprint of HarperCollins*Publishers*
10 East 53rd Street
New York, New York 10022-5299

Copyright © 2004 by Joanne Pence
Excerpts copyright © 1993, 1994, 1995, 1996, 1998, 1998, 1999, 2000, 2002 by Joanne Pence
ISBN: 0-06-050291-6
www.avonmystery.com

First Avon Books paperback printing: December 2004

Avon Trademark Reg. U.S. Pat. Off. and in Other Countries, Marca Registrada, Hecho en U.S.A.
HarperCollins® is a registered trademark of HarperCollins Publishers Inc.

Printed in the U.S.A.

10 9 8 7 6 5 4 3 2 1

To three special friends—
Peggy Staggs, Cheryl Maude, and Jane Jordan

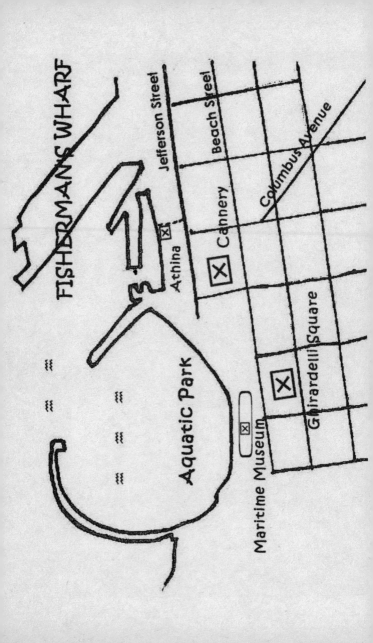

COURTING DISASTER

Chapter 1

 A fat, salty tear trickled down Stanfield Bonnette's narrow cheek. He pulled a Kleenex from its cellophane packet. The tissue tore apart and he ended up with half in his hand, the other half still stuck in the packaging. A metaphor for his life.

Real men don't cry. He'd heard that often enough from his father, and believed it, even as he fought to stop his tears while walking down the steep hills away from his top-of-Russian-Hill San Francisco apartment.

Real men especially didn't cry out of self-pity over losing girlfriends they never had who were engaged to men they didn't like. Men who were more macho, more sexy, and definitely more exciting.

They didn't even cry when they had a job they despised, a father who scorned them, and they received no respect from anyone, ever.

Another tear formed in the corner of his eye and he wiped it away, even more disgusted with himself.

Outwardly, he had everything—a well-paying

job at a bank, good looks, a nice apartment, and access to his father's money whenever he needed it. He was in his early thirties, single, slim, with silky brown hair, brown eyes, and boyishly handsome looks. Back in the days when Hugh Grant was young and wildly popular, people said Stan reminded them of the English actor. Now both seemed a bit dated.

As he crossed Union Street he faced San Francisco Bay and Alcatraz—old, solitary, and squalid, much the way he felt.

At the foot of Russian Hill, where the ground became level and flat, past the old red brick Cannery that had been converted into tourist shops and eateries, he reached Jefferson Street, the heart of Fisherman's Wharf. To his right were famous restaurants and tourist attractions, but where he stood the buildings were wooden, single-story, and windowless, with company names painted over doorways or garages, all a part of the real world of fishing boats, warehouses, and fisheries.

Many of the area's restaurants featured Italian food, yet another reminder of the woman he was mooning over, Angelina Amalfi. Okay, maybe it was true that they'd never seriously dated, and she'd never indicated that she felt anything for him other than friendship. But as she talked about her upcoming engagement party, he suddenly realized how much she meant to him. He had no doubt her engagement party—being planned by her mother—was going to be the biggest and most lavish ever held in the city of San Francisco.

If his mother were to plan an engagement party for him, it would probably consist of Kentucky Fried Chicken and Hostess cupcakes. To say his mother wasn't thrilled with him or the way he was living was an understatement. And her disappointment was exceeded only by his father's.

At times like this, he couldn't help but think his parents were right. After all, he'd lost Angie, and now he would never have a chance to convince her that their relationship might become more than friendship.

No, that wasn't exactly true, either. He'd tried. More than once. She'd never noticed. What did that tell him?

He sighed woefully. She would have been perfect for him, too. Beautiful, smart, ambitious . . . rich . . . and a great cook. He loved food. Loved to eat. Day. Night. Midday. Middle of the night.

Angie's kitchen was one of the Seven Wonders of the World. He could knock on the door to her apartment right across the hall from his, she'd invite him in, and he'd head for her refrigerator. It was like a magic box, filled with the most delectable leftovers the world has ever known.

And soon, once she was married, this wonderful, scrumptious, mouthwatering phase of his life would be over.

Tears threatened again.

Not that he cared about her only for her culinary skills. She understood him. She never nagged or pressured him, but just accepted him for what he was. Or wasn't. In fact, he had a longer relationship with her than he'd had with any other woman.

Maybe something was to be said for *not* dating women he liked.

With a heavy sigh he wondered what delicious feast Angie's mother would serve at the engagement party. At least he had that to look forward to.

For some unknown reason, still thinking about Angie, Stan turned down one of the small roadways off Jefferson Street that led back to the rough wharves where fishing boats were docked. It was an area where tourists never ventured and homeless people sought shelter—smelly and dingy, with gulls swooping overhead and salt water, oil spills, and worse at his feet.

A small building, separate from the others, caught his eye. A sign in Greek-style lettering proclaimed ATHINA RESTAURANT. One story with a flat roof, the once-white paint was now gray and peeling. The windows had scrolled bars over them in a pretty design, but bars nonetheless. In the window, a cardboard sign read FRESH FISH! GREEK SPECIALTIES SERVED HERE.

Stan stepped closer to the Athina and sniffed. A blend of lemon, cinnamon, and clove wafted over him. All his thoughts about Angie's kitchen had made him hungry. Perhaps a little nourishment would help allay his sorrows.

Angie Amalfi sat curled up on a petit-point sofa in the living room of her penthouse apartment. She was a petite woman with big brown eyes, and salon-added auburn highlights in short dark brown hair. Behind her, the picture window held a view that stretched from the Golden Gate to the Bay Bridge. At her side, the Yellow Pages were open to "Banquet Facilities." A phone was in her hand.

"Postrio. Can I help you?" The woman's voice sounded pleasant.

"Hello," Angie said cheerfully. "I'm wondering if you can tell me if you have a large party booked there for the evening of Saturday, May fifth?"

"A party? Let me check the calendar. . . ."

"It would be for somewhere between three and five hundred people, I'd imagine," Angie added.

"That's quite a group. Let me put you on hold."

Hold? Angie didn't get a chance to protest before the line went dead. How long did it take to look up a date on a calendar?

She didn't have time for this. Her engagement party was only nineteen days away—less than three short weeks—and she still hadn't found out where it would be held. That might sound strange, but it was true. Unfortunately.

When she agreed that her mother could handle the engagement party as long as Serefina would leave the wedding planning completely to Angie, it had seemed like a heaven-sent arrangement. All she had to do was come up with a guest list. She did better, and had an A list, B, and even a C list of invitees—and knew Serefina would add a bunch of her own.

Angie remembered how every one of her four older sisters had torn their hair out over Serefina's meddling in their wedding plans. With this arrangement, that wouldn't happen to her. She loved her mother dearly, but Serefina was an elemental force of nature. Tidal waves, tornadoes, and hurricanes had nothing on her. Unstoppable, when she set her mind to something you simply battened down the hatches and hoped to survive with minimal damage.

Also, at the time Serefina had made the suggestion, Angie was desperately trying to find the perfect dress for the party and was so frazzled she would have agreed to almost anything. She'd gone to nearly every store and boutique in the greater Bay Area, and was giving serious thought to a trip to Los Angeles or New York, when a beautiful Dior in a rich, deep buttercup yellow arrived at one of her favorite shops. It was floor-length, fitted and slinky, with a plunging V in front and back. It was sexy, slimming, and made her look almost tall. In a word, it was perfect.

She was prepared for an equal struggle to find a new suit for her fiancé, San Francisco Homicide Inspector Paavo Smith. The second one she picked out, however, he liked. She had to agree it was gorgeous, as were the tie, shirt, and shoes she chose to go with it. He was so easy to shop for he took half the fun out of it.

That done, she was ready to take on whatever came next, especially since she was currently between jobs. Actually, the way her career was going, it was more honest to say that when she did work, she was "between unemployments."

With nothing else of a serious nature to occupy her, every detail of the party suddenly loomed large in her mind with problems she needed, wanted, *ached* to solve. After much careful thought and hours of watching shows about engagement and wedding parties on the Lifetime Channel, she approached her mother with suggestions. She wanted a romantic setting, ice sculptures and champagne fountains surrounded by yellow orchids to complement her dress. As guests oohed and aahed, she would step onto the dance floor for the first dance of the evening. A small band would play something loving and emotional, like "I Will Always Love You" or "You Are the Wind Beneath My Wings." Paavo thought both songs were schlocky, sentimental, and overwrought, but she was sure she could convince him they were perfect for this.

She was bursting to tell her mother all her ideas . . . and that was when life as she knew it fell completely apart.

Serefina refused to tell her anything about her party at all. Instead, she planned to "surprise" Angie with the party arrangements—*all* the arrangements, including the location. Angie was surprised, all right. Not to mention flabbergasted.

"Hello." The woman came back on the line. "We do have a big party coming in that day."

"Great!" The word came out in a high-pitched squeal. This was a fabulous restaurant—one of Wolfgang Puck's. Angie breathed a little easier. How could she have dreamed her mother would let her down? "Your calendar shows that the party is the Amalfi-Smith engagement, right?" she asked.

There was a long pause. "I'm sorry, but we don't give out names. Are you invited to the party?"

"It's my party!" She'd have to remember not to use that line again. It reminded her of a Leslie Gore song that she hated. "I'm Angie Amalfi."

The woman's voice changed from friendly to sneering. "And you don't know where your own party is being held?"

"Well ... uh ... my mother is making the arrangements, and—"

"So, it's a surprise, and you want to ruin it!"

"I didn't say that!" Angie answered heatedly. *How had the woman guessed?*

"It's pretty sneaky of you to go behind your own mother's back this way, Miss ... Amalfi, is it?"

Now Angie was irritated. Who was this person, to lecture her? Especially since she didn't know Serefina. Only those who knew her could understand why Angie needed to make sure all the details were being handled correctly. "Listen, I was just asking—"

"*You* listen! If this was the Amalfi party, which it isn't, I'd cancel it right now."

Mouth agape, Angie stared at the phone. The dial tone sounded.

She crossed that place off her list of possibilities.

She was about to dial the next number when a better idea came to mind.

Inside the Athina Restaurant, the décor was basic "American diner." Booths hugged two walls, wooden tables and chairs filled the center, and posters extolling beers and wines plus mandatory aerial photos of the Acropolis and Athens were the only wall decorations. A black clock with green fluorescent hands and the words MILLER TIME along the top hung in a hard-to-see corner.

"Here's a menu." The waiter, a young blond-haired man with a mustache and a sharply angled face, handed Stan a plastic-covered sheet. "You want something to drink?"

"Chablis," Stan replied, scarcely looking at him, but studying the menu.

"We have ouzo, Greek wines, American beer. What do you want?"

"A white Greek wine, then. Something like chablis."

The waiter scrunched his thin mouth and walked away.

"What's good today?" Stan asked when the waiter returned with a glass of Malvazia white. Stan had never heard of it. He took a sip. It was definitely different from California whites, but it would do.

"Fish is our specialty, cooked Greek-style. The owner and the cook are fishermen. You can't find any fresher in this city. Octopus cooked in wine, Greek-style, is popular. So is our sea bass. If you don't like fish, *souvlaki* is a specialty."

Stan thought about the exotic food. He had no idea what *souvlaki* was. "Do you serve gyros?"

The waiter sneered. "Every Greek restaurant can put together a sandwich on pita bread."

"I'll have one. With chicken."

The waiter gave another of his disdainful looks and walked away.

When Stan left the restaurant, his belly full, the sky had turned gray and the wind was strong. The fog, rolling in through the Golden Gate, felt thick and sharp against the skin. Out on the bay a mournful foghorn blared.

He stood wavering on the sidewalk, not yet ready to go home to his lonely apartment. He wasn't sure when the apartment had become lonely. For years it wasn't. In fact, he'd always thought of it as a neat bachelor pad. Maybe he would again, once he got over this funk about Angie.

Right now, though, he didn't feel like being alone with himself. The gyros had helped a little, but not enough.

With his jacket collar turned up and his hands in his pockets, he continued down the side street. The restaurant was the last building. Just past it the street ended. There, stretching in both directions like the top of a T, ran the wharf—a broad, asphalt-paved area with boat docks all along the water's edge. The restaurant had a side door that opened directly across from one of the berths. Stan remembered the waiter saying something about fresh fish.

The wharf itself had been built to sit some six or seven feet over the water. Railroad ties had been placed to stop cars from rolling off it into the bay, but that was it. There was no railing. Jutting up every so often were metal handrails attached to ladders that dropped straight down to reach any boats that were docked.

Stan headed for the water, enjoying the dark, chilled air that so well matched his mood. A number of boats were moored, all rocking slightly from the tide. His peaceful solitude was broken, however, by the sound of raised but muffled voices.

His waiter berated a woman who sat on a rough-hewn, backless wooden bench at the water's edge. His face was hard, his expression intense, and she was shaking her head, not looking at him, but staring out at the water as if it hurt to hear his words. Her feet were propped up on a railroad tie. A hooded rain parka, the cheap kind that was basically a sheet of heavy green plastic worn by slipping it over the head, covered her hair. The way she sat scrunched on the bench, the parka draped her body like a tent.

The waiter bent close, grabbed her shoulder, and said something straight into her face. She turned her head away from him and the hood slipped down. The waiter then straightened and strode away. She reached out her hand toward him, but he didn't turn back. She raised her chin, apparently struggling to hold her emotions in check.

She wasn't a beautiful woman. In truth, she seemed a bit plain, but something about her held Stan's gaze. Loose wisps of dark brown hair blew about her face. Her skin was pale and flawless, her nose high and rather long, almost Roman.

She must have sensed him staring at her, for she turned his way. She wore no makeup, making the contrast between her fair skin and dark eyes even starker. Her eyes were large, with nearly black brows winged at the temples. As she gazed at him curiously, what captivated him most were her high cheekbones and full, lush mouth.

Being caught staring, he had a choice of either brazening it out or averting his eyes from her altogether. For some reason, he didn't want to turn away, and so he grinned, giving a little shrug and lift of his eyebrows as if to say, *Okay, you caught me—a guy looking at a woman. So shoot me already.*

She gave a small tremulous smile in return, then looked away.

How had he thought she wasn't beautiful? When she smiled, rather shyly it seemed, her face brightened. A long strand of hair blew across her mouth, and she brushed it back from her face.

She wants to be alone, he thought. As much as he would have liked to say something to her, he couldn't bring himself to speak.

He headed toward the main street. He'd taken less than a dozen steps when he stopped. How much of an idiot was he? She was obviously hurting. That obnoxious waiter had been rotten to her about something, poor woman, upsetting her terribly, yet when she saw Stan, she'd smiled. Shouldn't he at least try to talk to her? Offer help? Consolation? Maybe he could cheer her up a bit.

He should give her a friendly hello and see how she responded. If she ignored him, okay, he'd understand. If she answered, who knew where it might lead?

With that thought, he hurried back to the wharf.

The bench was empty.

Chapter 2

On sunny days, sunbathers and swimmers filled Aquatic Park, a public area with a broad lawn, concrete bleachers, and a small beach on the north shore near Fisherman's Wharf. On cold, windy, fog-filled days like this one, people strolled along that beach or walked out onto Municipal Pier, which circled and protected the shoreline, or simply sat on the bleachers watching the curious mix of humanity that made up the city. Always it seemed, day and night, the area attracted those seeking rest and relaxation.

But not today.

Yellow crime scene tape cordoned off the beach. A crowd had gathered to watch the police at work. They all knew what had happened. Something like that couldn't be kept a secret in this busy part of the city, and especially not when the person who made the discovery stood in the middle of the crowd and talked about it, repeating his story over and over to newcomers as they approached to check out the commotion.

The bushy-haired, big-bellied fellow told how

he swam each morning in the cold salt water, convinced of its beneficial effects on the circulation, spiritual well-being, and blood cholesterol. He'd been standing in the water at mid-chest level when he saw something with a pinkish gray cast on the beach under the pier closest to Fisherman's Wharf. The tide was low and when the water ebbed, he could see the object clearly.

It was fairly large. At first he feared it was a shark, but he soon realized it was no fish—it had limbs. Curious, he waded toward it. As he neared, he told himself it was a mannequin, a department store dummy. Soon, though, he had to accept that it wasn't a mannequin at all, but a human. A male. And he looked very dead.

The man let out a small shriek. He knew he needed to contact the police. First, though, he pulled the body farther up onto the beach, afraid a big wave might come along, catch it in the undertow, and suck it out to sea. He described to the mesmerized listeners how the shirt, shoes, and socks were gone—probably sucked off by the churning waves, how white and jellylike the skin appeared, and how distended the stomach.

In fact, he expounded on this with more authority than any coroner San Francisco Homicide Inspector Rebecca Mayfield had ever heard. She tried to ignore the know-it-all, but couldn't. The loud, authoritative voice kept breaking her concentration.

Rebecca was in her thirties, single, and so physically fit most of the other Homicide inspectors looked weak and flaccid in comparison. She wore black slacks and a black-leather jacket over a cream-colored turtleneck. Her shoulder bag had a special compartment where she kept her service revolver secure under a Velcro band, but easy to pull out if needed. She wore little makeup and her shoulder-length blond hair was held back in a barrette at the nape of her neck. She managed to look competent and professional—although that may have been as much because of the square-shouldered, long-legged way she walked and her take-charge, brook-no-nonsense demeanor than anything else.

She was the only female Homicide inspector on the force.

Her irritation grew as speculation about the death bounced back and forth between members of the crowd. One person opined that a shark had killed the victim. Since more and more sharks were spotted in the ocean off San Francisco Bay, why not inside the bay as well? Another said it was the work of the devil.

Rebecca caught the eye of her partner, Bill Never-Take-a-Chance Sutter, on the road to retirement and more interested in the scenery along the way than in any of their cases. As a result, Rebecca handled on her own just about everything the "team" got. Loyal, she defended her partner even though she'd love to wring his lazy neck.

She was sure he'd immediately come along with her on this case, rather than waiting an hour or two, simply because of its location. Sutter loved the beach, despite the day's chilling breeze. He often said he might retire to one, if he could find beachfront property cheap enough. Rebecca suggested Tierra del Fuego off the southern tip of South America.

The two detectives surveyed the scene and waited for the CSI to complete their work. The ME had already come and gone. She'd be doing an autopsy, no doubt about it.

The fog thickened, making the air colder and damper, but it didn't deter the crowd from continuing to offer strident opinions, each more outrageous than the last, and to argue with each other about them.

Rebecca could stand no more. Coming face-to-face with death brought out strong feelings in people, and the way things were going, she was going to be faced with another homicide if they didn't disperse. She marched into the crowd. "Go home, everyone. There's nothing more here for you to see."

"You got no right to tell us to leave," one pontificator yelled. "What happened here is an abomination! What's wrong with the police? People getting killed on a public beach! Why can't you keep us safe?"

Rebecca just stared, hard, at the man. He swallowed the rest of his words and faded away. The others soon followed, and the beach grew quiet except for an occasional foghorn or the clang of a cable car bell at the nearby end-of-the-line turntable.

Once the crowd left, she pushed aside the sheet that covered the body and crouched down. The deceased was a white male, probably in his late thirties, early forties, with a mustache, beard, and long brown hair pulled back in a ponytail. Something about him seemed eerily familiar.

She asked her partner, but Sutter had no idea.
He was busy studying the sand—looking for evidence, he said. The fact that the CSI team was
there doing the same thing didn't faze him.

Once back in Homicide, she'd ask Paavo Smith,
who was clearly the best inspector on the force.
Not to mention the best-looking. All right, she
might be a cop, but she was also a woman—
healthy, single, and unattached. Unfortunately,
Paavo was engaged to someone else. Of course, if
his love life ever went south . . .

She turned back to the victim. Wearing rubber
gloves, she lifted his shoulder to inspect a small
entry wound in the man's back. It had created a
large exit wound on his chest. The CSI would do
what it could to canvass the area for the bullet, but
she didn't give them much of a chance for success.

Standing again, she covered the body. This was
actually a very clever setting for a crime. Most of
the evidence had been washed out to sea.

Angie buttoned her MaxMara cherry-red jacket and
leaned into the sudden harsh wind as she made her
way toward the marbled grandeur of the Fairmont
Hotel high atop Nob Hill. The wind whipped her
hair from one side to the other, and the fog stripped
away the curl and turned it to frizz. Bursting
through the hotel's heavy front doors, she took a
deep breath, ready to readjust her jacket and attempt
to smooth her hair, when a voice called, "Angie!"

Startled, she turned to find herself face-to-face
with her nemesis.

It wasn't that she hated Nona Farraday, not even

that she was jealous of her . . . well, maybe just a little of her tall, slim, blond, patrician good looks and her job as restaurant reviewer for *Haute Cuisine* magazine. The fact that she made Angie feel like the product of short, dumpy peasant stock with a do-nothing, going-nowhere job (when she even had a job) wasn't pleasant. That's all.

"Hello, Nona," she said through gritted teeth as the two air-kissed. "What a surprise to see you here!"

Nona flicked back her long silky hair. She looked stunning, not a thread out of place, while Angie felt as if she'd just gone ten rounds with an eggbeater. "I had lunch with a *Gourmet* magazine editor," Nona said. "He's only in the city two days, but found time for me . . . of course."

Angie's gritted teeth started to grind, her smile more forced. "Of course," she repeated. "I won't keep you."

"Lunch is over, though I do have to get back to the office. Deadlines, you know. But what are *you* doing here?" Nona's lashes fluttered.

"Oh, I'm just . . . um . . ."

Nona's eyes suddenly bored into her. "This doesn't have anything to do with your engagement party, does it?"

Angie feigned shock. "My mother is handling the whole thing."

"Right." Nona folded her arms. "Your mother's invitations were so *darling* telling us how she wanted to keep *everything* except the time and date of the party a surprise to you. She won't even let the guests know where the party will be held until the day before! It's such a . . . cute idea."

"Cute? Well, yes. . . ." Actually, Angie had another word for it, but she wasn't about to let Nona know how much her mother's "surprise" irritated her. It was her engagement party, for pity's sake! She had a right to know the details of it.

"I can understand why your mother is doing it this way," Nona said smugly.

Angie's lips stretched into a fake smile. "You do?"

"If your mother told us, you'd find out for sure. Then you wouldn't be surprised." Nona began to chuckle.

Angie joined in, but her strained laughter was even more fake than her smile.

"Lots of people will come just to see if Serefina can pull it off." The more Nona talked about it, the harder she laughed. Angie, on the other hand, no longer even pretended amusement. She fumed.

Her laughter over, Nona's gaze traveled over the lobby's high ceilings, the dark mahogany and red velvet furniture. "You don't think she'd . . . No, of course not. No way!"

"What are you talking about?" Angie asked, pouncing on the implication.

"I'm wondering if you're here because you found out she was planning on using one of the banquet halls in the Fairmont. Someplace like . . . oh, the Crown Room, for instance." Nona shuddered. "She wouldn't do that to you."

"What do you mean?" As a matter of fact, Angie's first choice for her party would have been the Crown Room. Reached by an outside glass elevator to the top floor, it was elegant, romantic, and offered a panorama of the entire city. "It's a beautiful space," she said, hoping her voice didn't sound as thin and hysterical to Nona's ear as it did to her own.

Nona gave her a piteous look. "True . . ."

Angie waited, then couldn't stand the suspense. "But?"

After a long, anguished sigh, as if she were a martyr being tortured by an Inquisitor, Nona said, "It's just that the last engagement parties I went to were *all* either at the Top of the Mark or the Fairmont's Crown Room. I thought your party would be more original than that."

"They were?" Angie wracked her brain. She hadn't been invited to any engagement parties in the Fairmont. The Mark Hopkins, yes. Who did Nona know that hadn't invited Angie? Who was stiffing her? She swallowed.

"Don't you remember?" Nona's eyes went wide with surprise, then softened with sympathy. "Oh . . . you weren't there, were you?"

Angie bristled. What an actress! "I remember now," she cried jovially. She, too, could act. "I had other plans. Sometimes it's difficult to juggle one's social calendar."

"Isn't that the truth? Speaking of which, I've got to run," Nona said. "Take care. And if your party is at the Crown Room, I'm sure it'll be lovely. They have *lots* of experience."

As Angie marched toward the special elevator to the top of the hotel, she wouldn't have been surprised to learn that the ends of her wind-tossed hair had singed from the hot steam pouring from her ears.

Chapter 3

Chin in hand, Stan sat hunched over Angie's kitchen table early the next morning, glum, hungry, and once again uninspired about going to work. He held the dubious title of Assistant Director of Supply Maintenance at Colonial Bank, where his father was one of the largest stockholders. Stan figured that as long as the bank had a hefty supply of pens, forms, and paper, he had no reason to sit at his desk waiting for someone to run out. Every so often, he went to the office and looked at the supply database on the computer. Occasionally, he even stuck his head into a supply cabinet. Then, job done, he'd leave.

As Angie gave him some coffee, she'd railed about her encounter the day before with Nona.

The sad part was that she'd actually been relieved to learn her mother had *not* booked the Crown Room for the party. What was wrong with her?

Her experiences had taught her one thing: that although banquet halls and restaurants wouldn't give you the names of the parties who had booked

21

them by phone, when you went there in person it was easy to stand close and read the names on the reservation calendar yourself.

Now all she had to do was go to those few of her mother's favorite restaurants capable of handling a huge party, and check for Serefina's reservation. Nothing to it.

Normally, Angie's best friend, Connie Rogers, would accompany her on such a search, but Connie had a gift shop to run. Besides, she thought Serefina's approach was correct, and said that if Angie were to learn anything at all about the party, she'd monopolize planning the whole affair.

Angie had no idea why anyone would think such a thing. All she wanted was to make sure the restaurant was one that both she and Paavo liked. He was the groom, after all, and should have some say in this. She also wanted to make sure the food was prepared the way she preferred, since, as a Cordon Bleu–trained gourmet cook, she had the right to expect perfection in the food at her very own engagement party.

Besides that, she'd like to know that the party favors were something she could be proud of, the decorations done in colors she liked and that wouldn't clash with her dress, that parking was plentiful in the area, that seating arrangements were such that people who hated each other wouldn't be placed side by side, that the band would play music she enjoyed—if there *was* a band, which she hoped there would be—and that all the myriad little details so easy to forget about would be taken care of.

What was so bad about that?

Sheesh! Connie had sounded as if Angie went

around acting like her mother or something. A shudder went through her. She couldn't possibly . . . no, she was nothing like Serefina.

Stan offered to join her on her quest to Fisherman's Wharf, an area filled with a number of Serefina's favorite restaurants. Angie was glad for the company and even offered to buy him lunch as a thank-you. Although he could drive her crazy with his lackadaisical attitude about work, career, and making something out of himself, he was always there when she needed a friend or a shoulder to cry on—both before she met Paavo and after as she'd struggled to convince Paavo the two of them were meant for each other. As a result, she always tried to be a helpful friend to Stan as well.

Not that he ever took her advice, but that was another story.

They started out at Alioto's Restaurant. No Amalfi party was being held there. Fisherman's Grotto Number 9 was next.

"It isn't like you," Stan said, "to let your mother take over this way."

"How was I to know she'd be so sneaky?"

"Sneaky?"

"I thought she'd simply handle the arrangements—not keep them a secret from me!"

"Maybe she thought that was the only way she *could* handle them."

Shades of Connie. Angie scowled. "That's not true!"

"The invitations were clever," he began.

If he laughs, I'm taking him back to his apartment right now.

Stan smirked. "Serefina knew that if the invitations told where the party was, you'd figure out a way to get Connie to tell you. She's never been able to keep a secret from you."

Angie put her hands on her hips. "Why should I go all the way across town to see Connie? One sniff of my lasagna and you'd sing like a bird!"

"Why get pissed off at me?" he asked, hurt. "It was your mother's idea, not mine." He grinned. "And the day before the party, when I get the special-delivery letter telling me the location, you can come over with lasagna. No problem."

"You wouldn't find it so funny if the fate of your party was in the hands of the U.S. Post Office! It's going to be a disaster. I just know it."

After Fisherman's Grotto they worked their way through other large restaurants along the wharf until it ended at Aquatic Park. They found no Amalfi party.

"Now what?" Stan asked.

Angie paused a moment, arms folded, peering down Jefferson Street at the shops, restaurants, and milling tourists. "I was sure she'd pick Fisherman's Wharf. I suppose I can just forget about it," Angie said stoically.

"Sure, like Columbus could forget about discovering America, or Einstein forget about the theory of relativity, or—"

"Oh, shut up!"

The two walked past the cable car turntable. Up ahead was Ghirardelli Square, the red-brick one-time chocolate factory, now a tourist mecca.

"I wonder if she could have rented Ghirardelli Square," Angie mused. "All of it."

"It takes up an entire city block," Stan pointed out. "I'd say it's a little large, even for your family."

"I wouldn't be so sure about that."

They went into the Maritime Museum to warm up from the chilling wind and fog, and to use the public restrooms that were few and far between in the area.

Outside, the museum looked like an ocean liner with curved ends, portholes, and decks. Inside, painted ship figureheads, mast sections, jutting spars, artifacts, photos, and documents from the early days of West Coast seafaring were spread over the three floors. Colorful WPA murals adorned the walls.

"I've always loved this place," Angie said as she studied a sextant. It was an oddly shaped one, and she couldn't figure out how it worked. "Remember when I was becoming quite the expert on San Francisco history?" She moved on to a model of a schooner. "I always enjoyed that. I should go back to studying it again."

"I was never into ships," Stan said. "I get seasick." He picked up a brochure that advertised renting out the entire museum for large parties and was going to hand it to Angie, but she had already stepped out onto the balcony. He put it back and followed.

She stood beside a statue created by San Francisco artist Beniamino Bufano. "What am I going to do, Stan? I'm making myself crazy."

"You need to ignore it. You made a deal with your mother, now forget about it. Just be thankful it's your mother and not your father who's planning the party."

"Very funny," she said. She had to agree, though. To say her father wasn't happy about this marriage was like saying Bill Gates had a little money.

"Maybe you need a job to distract you," Stan suggested.

She shook her head. "How can I concentrate on a job when the one and only engagement party I'll ever have in my entire life is in my goofy mother's hands?" Angie clutched the railing tight. "I haven't given serious thought to a job since I became engaged, except for that stint with a TV soap opera not long ago. Too bad it didn't pan out, as they say. It might have made me famous."

The two exchanged looks, recalling all too well Angie's recent brief and unsuccessful foray into television and, as one, turned to stare glumly out at the bay.

San Francisco Homicide Inspector Paavo Smith was a big man, six-foot-two, with broad shoulders and a hard face with icy blue eyes known for making tough guys cower, known for making just about anyone cower, in fact, except his fiancée.

He was at his desk, Rebecca Mayfield in the guest chair at its side. The desks in the Homicide bureau were set in two rows and surrounded by overflowing file cabinets and cluttered bookshelves. Homicide was a part of the Bureau of Inspections, located in San Francisco's Hall of Justice building. The homicide inspectors' beat covered the entire city and county—all forty-nine square miles of it, minuscule by most city standards.

"I thought I had a floater," Rebecca said, as she told Paavo about her case that morning. "But now it's pretty clear he was shot on the pier—we found blood spatter—pushed off, and then the body didn't travel far at all."

"What do you mean by 'travel'?" Paavo asked.

"I'm figuring that if the tide was high when he hit the water, whoever did it might have seen him sink and hoped he'd get pulled out to sea. He didn't, though."

Paavo nodded. Now it made sense. "Any ID yet?"

"Nothing. I'm running his fingerprints, but in the meantime, something about the guy is familiar to me. Never-Take-a-Chance disagrees, but I'd like you to take a look a him."

"Sure." Paavo had heard a bit about Rebecca's journey to Aquatic Park that morning already. It was the most interesting new case in the bureau at the moment. He'd been doing paperwork for the DA's office on one of his cases that was going to trial, and he was more than happy for the interruption.

She placed four photos of the corpse, one by one, across his desk. They'd been taken that morning. The first photo startled him, and the later ones only confirmed that his initial reaction was correct. "It's Sherlock Farnsworth III."

"Is that his name, or a joke?" Rebecca asked.

"His name. You probably know him as Shelly Farms—it's what he liked to call himself, and what the press called him."

"Shelly Farms—the homeless advocate?" she asked. Paavo nodded. "If I'm remembering right, wasn't he educated as a lawyer, and spent all his time fighting city hall to help the poor?"

"That's pretty much true, but also keep in mind that Farnsworth belonged to a law firm that specialized in class-action suits, so he had his share of enemies. He kept pretty quiet about it, and you had to dig to find out. The press was on his side in most of his fights, so they weren't about to blow the whistle on his big moneymaking sideline."

Rebecca frowned as she gathered up the pictures. "If he was a lawyer, I'm going to have my hands full." As one, she and Paavo both glanced up at Bill Sutter, who was sitting at his desk, feet up, eating Cheetos and flipping through the pages of *Travel and Leisure* magazine.

"He must be taking a break," Paavo said.

"If you've got some free time now and then . . ." Rebecca began.

She didn't have to ask twice. "Anytime, Rebecca. In fact, I'll call a couple of guys who worked with Farnsworth right now. I'll ask what he was up to."

She smiled. "Great, and I'll start pulling up his vitals."

Just then, Paavo's phone rang. Rebecca went back to her desk as he answered.

It was one of those women-from-Venus-men-from-Mars type phone calls from Angie.

After he hung up, he put his head in his hands.

His partner, Inspector Toshiro Yoshiwara, tossed aside his pen and swiveled his chair in Paavo's direction. Like Paavo, anything that could take him away from report writing was welcome.

A big man, nearly six feet tall and stocky with pure muscle, Yosh liked to say his family was from the "sumo wrestler" part of Japan.

"Headache, Paav?" he asked. An aisle separated his desk from Paavo's.

"A five-foot-two-inch headache." Paavo groaned.

Yosh didn't need to ask who. His full, round face broke into a mischievous grin. "What's Angie up to now?"

"I have no idea. Something about finding a job, ruling out Fisherman's Wharf, Nona Farraday, and sextants."

"Nona Farraday?" Luis Calderon's head popped up over a stack of homicide folders. The piles of papers atop the bookshelf behind his desk practically formed a wall between him and the inspectors behind him. Calderon was in his forties, with a mustache and heavily pomaded black hair worn in an Elvis-style pompadour. For Calderon, men's hairdos had reached perfection in the days of "Love Me Tender."

"Did you mention her and sex?" he asked with a shudder. "Talk about a ball-buster!"

In one of the most bizarre episodes in a peculiar string of them, at one time the lithe and sophisticated Nona Farraday decided she had a crush on bellicose, belligerent, and bristly Luis Calderon. Although at first he was flattered by the attention of such a beautiful woman, Calderon soon found her irritation at the long hours he worked, his need to cancel dates when someone had the bad taste to get murdered while he was on duty, his poor choice of places to take her to, and her constant nagging about his clothes and hair more than he could abide.

To Nona's shock, he dropped her and refused to answer her phone calls. Nona had never been so insulted in her life. What added even more insult to her already injured ego was when Calderon began dating a muscle-bound, Harley-driving female shoe repairperson.

That relationship didn't last long, either, however. Everyone suspected it was because Calderon didn't like dating someone who was meaner and tougher than he was.

"She's not coming here, is she?" Calderon asked nervously, as if expecting Nona to swoop down on him like the wicked Witch of Endor.

"No. Angie ran into her yesterday and now she's all upset."

"Gee, Nona has that effect even on women, does she?" Calderon shook his head miserably.

"Look on the bright side," Yosh said to Calderon with a smirk in Paavo's direction. "At least you aren't engaged to her and forced to go to an engagement party planned by your future mother-in-law."

"The bright side is I'm not engaged to anyone!" Calderon jumped up and put on his jacket. "I'm going down to Nick's for a beer. Got to calm my nerves. I'd invite you guys along, but since you're the ones who've given me a bellyache, I'd rather not have anything more to do with you."

"We love you, too, pal," Yosh said. "Just like Nona."

Calderon gave a one-fingered salute, then turned

to Rebecca. "Want to join me? I can give you point-
ers on your case. You've never had a floater before,
have you? Wait till you hear what salt water does
to the body, plus all the little creatures that live in
the water. They're pure eating machines. It's
gross."

"Screw that," she said, and went back to her
computer.

Calderon shrugged and left the room.

There was silence as Yosh eyed his friend and
partner sympathetically, then Paavo said quietly,
"I don't even want an engagement party. I didn't
know such a thing existed until Angie's mother
mentioned it. I expected Angie would have a zil-
lion bridal showers, but grooms never show up for
those. I figured I'd have a stag party for the gang
and that's it."

"Too bad she won't elope," Yosh said, commis-
erating.

"Elope? Hell. We still haven't settled on a date
or place for the wedding. I know it'll be more than
a year off. She'll need that much time to prepare."
Paavo looked grimly at his partner. "Yosh, tell me.
Is this the biggest mistake I've ever made in my
life?"

Yosh laughed. "The secret is, pal, try to ignore it.
Nancy loved it when we got married—all the
planning and the decorating. The biggest problem
came when she had to decide who was invited to
the wedding and who wasn't. That's when things
got really vicious. The trick, I learned, is to just say,
'Yes.' Whatever Angie comes up with, whatever
she says, you respond, 'Yes.' That way, you don't

get in trouble if anything goes wrong; you don't
get irritated when she changes her mind; and you
don't think about it. Period. Got it?"

"Just say, 'Yes'?" Paavo sounded skeptical.

"Exactly."

"Maybe we need to get a beer at Nick's, too,"
Paavo said.

"*Yes*," Yosh replied. "There. See how easy it is?"

Paavo grinned. Neither of them ever drank
while on the job.

Just then, his phone rang. When he answered,
all thoughts of parties, laughter, and fun flew from
his head.

The caller was the man who detested him more
than anyone he'd ever known, including hardened criminals he'd sent to the big house for murder. Paavo had no idea why he was calling. He
never had before; the two barely talked when in a
room together.

With more than a little trepidation he listened to
the voice of Salvatore Amalfi, Angie's father.

"Paavo was no help at all." Angie dropped her cell
phone into her purse as she walked beside the
beach at Aquatic Park toward Fisherman's Wharf
for Stan's long-overdue lunch.

"He knows it's in good hands," Stan said. "Why
should he get involved?"

"Why?" Angie couldn't believe the question.
"He should be enthusiastic and curious about his
party. He's engaged, too!"

"I know a good spot for lunch," Stan said,
clearly not wanting to comment on Paavo and en-
gagements. "A Greek place called Athina. I just

discovered it yesterday. The owners are fishermen and the fish is the freshest in the city . . . or so they say."

"Don't they all?" Angie murmured. "But I love trying out new restaurants."

As they walked, Angie continued to plot and scheme about ways to discover more about the engagement party. She had only eighteen days left.

Stan tuned her out as they neared the restaurant. He didn't know why, but his steps grew lighter. It couldn't be the beautiful woman who—he hoped—worked there, could it? He wondered if she was still troubled and upset. He understood feeling that way. He could offer help, advice, sympathy—whatever she wanted, come to think of it.

Angie didn't look thrilled as they turned down the ugly side street. "No wonder I never noticed the restaurant."

Not only was the building small and dingy, but Stan now realized the windows could use a good scrubbing. Of course, the area's constant barrage of fog, car exhaust, and seagull droppings meant that keeping the windows clean required almost constant vigilance. Maybe that was why the owners had apparently given up and stopped washing them some years ago. Why bother?

Stan could appreciate that.

Inside were two other customers.

The waiter, the same young mustachioed fellow who had served Stan the day before, led them to a booth. Stan glared at him. What kind of monster was he, treating a woman so badly?

The waiter basically ignored him and gave

Angie a long discourse on Greek wine. She opted for ouzo at the end of the meal, served Greek-style over ice with a splash of water. The waiter looked well pleased.

Stan ordered a Bud Light.

Angie studied the menu. "If the food is good, I should write a review of it. Maybe *Haute Cuisine* will publish it as a change of pace from Nona's vitriol. She never met a meal that pleased her. No wonder she's so skinny."

The waiter brought Stan his beer, and Angie a San Pellegrino. "I couldn't help but overhear," he said with a cocky waggle of his head. "You're a restaurant reviewer?"

"Yes." She flashed him a wide smile. "Freelance."

"How great." He sounded impressed. "What's your name? Maybe I've read some of your columns."

"Angelina Amalfi," she said. "It's been a while since I wrote anything, however."

"Too bad. Will you critique this restaurant?"

Angie tried to look woeful. "Now that you know me, I can't. It would give the cook an unfair advantage."

He threw up his hands. "Pretend I never said a word!"

"Don't worry about it." She laughed. "I'm not sure I'll go back to reviewing, anyway. It can get rather tedious."

"I'd read any review you wrote," he said, ogling Angie and doing all he could to ooze charm. "Just observing you here for a moment, I can tell you're a person of good taste."

Stan was ready to barf.

"Why, thank you." Angie was pleased by the compliment. "That's very nice."

"If you write a review, be sure to mention that Tyler Marsh is the best waiter in all of Fisherman's Wharf. By the way, you can call me Ty."

Stan didn't care what the sleazy, unctuous jerk's name was. He only wished he'd go away.

"Maybe I should simply write a review of the wait staffs in the area," Angie said with a smile, "and forget the restaurants."

Tyler glanced at the stout, gray-haired man sitting on a stool by the cash register and glaring at him. He must be the owner, Stan thought. If so, he should tell his employee to get back to work.

"I know a number of small but excellent restaurants in the city that would do well with a little publicity from someone like you." Tyler leaned near Angie with a cock of the head toward the scowler. "Just don't tell my boss that."

Stan turned away from the mutual admiration society and looked around the restaurant, wondering if the woman he'd seen on the dock the day before was working here now.

"Are you ready to order?" Tyler asked.

Angie ordered a light lunch of dolmades—grape leaves stuffed with rice and lamb—and a salad of feta and kalamata olives. She couldn't pass up baklava for dessert. Stan ordered chicken gyros. Tyler lifted an eyebrow, obviously remembering his same order the day before.

Their lunch was almost ended when Stan looked up and saw a brown-haired woman. Her back was to him, and she was wiping down a recently vacated table to ready it for the next patron.

Her hair formed a thick braid down her back, and it seemed to be the same shade as the woman's on the wharf. Was she the one he'd been waiting for?

He put down his sandwich and stared, his heart doing handsprings.

She'd just about finished when, whether out of curiosity or because she felt his gaze on her, she peered over her shoulder.

It was her. He smiled.

Her returning smile brightened her face, just as it had the day before. He didn't know when he'd ever seen anyone more radiant. She was breathtaking, with sparkling eyes and full lips spread wide.

He was vaguely aware that Angie's head swiveled in the waitress's direction even as she continued chatting to him about possibly writing up some restaurant reviews, but he didn't care.

This time, he promised himself, *this time I'm going to talk to her.* Determination filled him, and he felt ready to burst with anticipation.

Then she turned around.

The smile dropped from his face when he saw her body. Only because her shoulders, arms, and even legs were thin had he not noticed from behind, or out on the wharf when she was covered with that tentlike parka: she was pregnant.

Considering how slender she was, and how round her belly was, she was not only pregnant, but *very* pregnant. Like . . . ready-to-give-birth-any-moment kind of pregnant.

She wore no ring on her left hand, but then, she might not wear one considering the kind of work she was doing.

A frown touched her brow at his shocked reaction, and at the same time, her gaze jumped to Angie, who was still talking. The diamond engagement ring on Angie's finger sparkled.

Just then, a Mediterranean-looking fellow in his late thirties or early forties, medium height and build, with curly black hair, hazel eyes, and olive skin, stepped out of the kitchen. He wore an apron that reached from his waist to his knees, and was wiping his hands on a blue-striped rag. His dark scowl met that of the waitress. She saw him, and hurried to finish wiping off the table.

One last time, the waitress glanced at Stan, questioning and troubled, before she scooped up the tray of dirty dishes and hustled back into the kitchen. The fierce-looking man in the doorway placed a hand against her back as if to hurry her along, his eyes making a penetrating sweep over the dining room before he followed.

Stan realized she must have thought he was engaged to Angie, yet eyed and smiled at other women. But then, she was pregnant, so where was the man in *her* life? Was it the waiter she'd argued with? Or maybe the cook who had touched her so possessively? Or someone else? If so, why had she smiled that way at *him*? She had some kind of nerve, to look disdainfully at him considering her circumstance! What was wrong with the woman?

And what was wrong with him that he felt so disappointed, as if all the sunshine had gone out of his life?

"Stan?" Angie called. "Stan, are you listening? I try to think about other things, but my mind keeps reverting to the engagement party! I just don't know what to do anymore."

"Let's go, Angie," he said, so flummoxed he forgot that she was the one who promised to take him to lunch, and he threw money on the table. "You need to get home so you can concentrate better."

"Maybe you're right. Wait, what about my ouzo?"

He didn't answer as he helped her from the chair and hurried her out of the restaurant, leaving Angie to wonder what in the world had come over him.

Chapter 4

The next morning, Angie was sipping her morning coffee and reading the newspaper about the murder of Shelly Farms, who she was shocked to learn had really been named Sherlock, when the phone rang. As she reached for it, she couldn't help but think anyone named Sherlock probably would grow up with either great compassion for those who had misfortunes from birth, or would become a serial killer.

"Hello, this is Diamond Pastry," said a very slow-talking woman with a high, nasal voice. Angie was about to laugh—it had to be her friend Connie imitating Ernestine the Operator: *One ringy-dingy.* Before she could say anything, the woman continued, "Is this the Amalfi residence that ordered the purple cake?"

Angie's throat closed so tightly she could barely squeak out the words. "Purple cake?"

"Uh . . . sorry to bother you, ma'am, but we're here at Diamond Pastry—"

"I know, I know. Tell me about the cake. Is it a

big cake? Like . . . an engagement-party-size cake?"
*Please, God, don't let Serefina have ordered a purple
cake for me.*

"You see, ma'am, the lady who ordered, the
phone number got wiped out when a big blob of
chocolate frosting dropped on the order form. Not
that we usually toss around chocolate frosting . . .
well, sometimes. But I don't want you to get the
wrong impression of our bak—"

"Don't worry about it!" Angie jumped to her
feet, clutching the phone tight. "Is the cake for a
party on May fifth?"

"Uh . . . oh. You won't believe it, but the other
baker just found what we need. Everything's okay
now. I'm so sorry to have disturbed you, ma'am."

"Wait!" Angie shrieked. But the connection had
already been broken.

It couldn't have been Serefina, Angie told herself as she paced back and forth across the living
room. There were lots of Amalfis in the city. Oo-
dles of them. Some weren't even relatives.

Any one of them could have ordered a purple
cake for a variety of reasons . . . couldn't they?

She pressed a hand to her forehead. What if her
engagement cake was purple? What if the entire
décor for the party was purple? Her beautiful Dior
dress was yellow.

Yellow and purple together would remind people of Easter—and she'd end up looking like a
baby chick!

She collapsed onto a chair, stricken. The only solution was either to find out what color her cake
was, or to change the dress to be on the safe side.

Using the caller ID feature on her phone, she

saw that the pastry shop was listed as "PRIVATE."
Odd. Nevertheless, she hit the redial button and
got the same slow-talking woman. "Diamond
Past—"

"This is Angie Amalfi. Can you tell me—did my
mother, Serefina Amalfi, order the purple cake? Is
she your customer?"

"Uh . . . I don't know. I don't think I can tell
you, anyway."

Angie really hated this privacy mania. "Can
you tell me if it was for a cake on May fifth?"

"I'm sorry, ma'am, but I just don't remember
the date. I can tell you that it was a big cake. Real
big. And it has big yellow flowers on it. They take
time with all the petals—"

Angie hung up. Yellow flowers? Her worst fears
were coming true. The good news was that the
flowers would match her dress.

The bad news was that her party was going to
look like a giant Easter egg hunt.

Paavo walked into Moose's Restaurant. Slightly
upscale and with Italian cuisine, it was on Washington Square in North Beach, catty-corner to St.
Peter and Paul's Church where Angie went to
mass.

The maître d' asked if he was there to see Mr.
Amalfi, and when Paavo answered in the affirma-
tive, he was led to a private room in the back. Either Salvatore didn't want to be seen with him, or
didn't want to be seen, period.

He had no idea what this meeting was about.
More than once, a bribe to break the engagement
crossed his mind. He hoped he was wrong.

"Sal," he said, holding out his hand.

Angie's father stood, and the two shook hands warily. Sal was nearly six feet tall, but thin and somewhat frail due to a heart condition. His hair was gray, and he had a small gray mustache. His eyes weren't the dark, rich chocolate brown of Angie's, but were lighter with flecks of green. When he spoke, he had a slight Italian accent. "Thanks for coming," Sal said. "Sit. I told the chef to bring out a few of his specialties. Whatever he thought was good. Is that okay with you?"

Paavo could see that Sal didn't want to waste time ordering. "Sure," he replied.

"Wine?" Sal asked.

"No, thanks. I'm on duty."

Sal scowled. "What, you don't drink?"

"Not when I'm on duty," Paavo repeated.

Sal beckoned the waiter. "A bottle of a nice chianti, *per piacere*. And?" He glanced at Paavo.

"Water's fine," Paavo replied.

"Perrier?" the waiter asked.

Paavo nodded. Sal looked disgusted.

As the waiter turned, Sal called, "I said I want wine that's 'nice'—not the most expensive." He glowered in Paavo's direction. "I'm the only one in the family who knows the value of a dollar."

Paavo's jaw tightened. Was this going to be about money? How he didn't make near enough to support Angie in the style to which she was accustomed? "Angie and I have reached an agreement about money," he said firmly.

He had to wait for Sal's answer as a different waiter brought out sourdough bread and salad, and then the first reappeared for Sal to okay the wine choice.

When they were alone again, Sal said, "Yeah, I know you and Angelina don't talk about money—you got nothing to talk about, right? Anyway, you got it wrong. I didn't ask you here to flap my gums about the two of you. There's nothing more to say. You both made that clear to me. I'm just the father. Why should I count, long as I pay the bills, right?"

Paavo chomped down hard on his tongue, but was rapidly losing the battle with himself.

"Anyway, you treat her good, keep her happy," Sal said, "and we'll be all right." Despite the words, his tone dripped with doubt over Paavo's ability to do that.

"Fine." Paavo's word was clipped and cold.

"This is something else," Sal continued. "Police business. Eat, then we'll talk."

The meal was silent and tense. Paavo recognized that the veal scaloppini and pappardelle with porcini mushroom sauce were excellent, but they could have been cardboard and fell in a lump in his stomach. Sal only nibbled at his food, finally pushing the plate aside. "Look, Smith, I got a problem."

Paavo put down his fork, ready to listen.

"I guess Angelina told you I have managers to run my stores nowadays. I'm president of the family corporation, so I go check on them from time to time."

"Angie's told me," Paavo said. He knew all about Sal's string of shoe stores in shopping malls and downtown areas throughout northern California.

"I got a problem with one of my managers." Sal dropped his gaze.

When he didn't continue, Paavo considered the situations that result in "police business," as Sal called it. "Are you talking theft? Embezzlement?" he asked.

Sal shook his head. "I wish. It's worse. Lots worse." He caught Paavo's eye. "It's love."

Paavo felt the blood drain from his face. "You aren't saying that you and this manager—"

"No! God, no!" Sal exclaimed. "Hell, I never even liked her all that much." He took a sip of wine. "She called me, one, two times, with questions about the store. So, I answered. Then she says she wants to meet about the store—ways to improve profit. Her store's doing fine, but what's wrong with making more money, right? I had lunch with her a couple times. Then they started."

Paavo's brows crossed. "They?"

"Phone calls, letters."

Paavo studied him, trying to figure out exactly what this was about. "So this employee, a store manager, has a crush on you?"

Sal nodded. "I have to break my goddamned neck every day to get out to the mailbox before Serefina does."

"Serefina doesn't know?"

"Hell, no! And I don't want her to, understand?" He glared, then folded his hands, his discomfort at having to tell this to Paavo evident with every painful gesture.

"Tell me about the woman," Paavo said.

"Her name's Elizabeth Schull. When she first called, it was kind of flattering—I'm an old man, been married over forty years. She's a young woman. Well, young compared to Serefina. Or me." He drew in his breath. "But she's making my life hell. Serefina wants to know why the line goes dead so often when she answers. I told Elizabeth to stop calling. When she didn't listen, I said I would fire her." His voice dropped low. "She said I wouldn't dare."

"A threat?"

Sal nodded, watching, expectant.

Others had gone to Paavo with similar stories about threats. They never liked what he had to say. He knew Sal would be the same. "It's not illegal to threaten people. There's nothing the police can do about it. Your attorneys can come up with a good case to fire her, though. She's harassing you. Why not just do it?"

"Nothing you can do?" Sal took the napkin from his lap and tossed it on the table. His words dripped with disgust. "I listen to some woman threaten me, my family, and you say I'm supposed to handle it myself? I thought you were a strong man, some big macho guy that swept my daughter off her feet. Now I see the truth."

Paavo had just put up with more than he'd ever taken from anyone else. "Look, Sal," he said, his voice a calm cover over a cauldron about to blow, "she hasn't committed a crime. I'll see what I can find out about her, talk to her, whatever. But I won't be doing it as a cop. Is that clear?"

"Clear as mud!" Sal bellowed. "Don't you want to know what she said?"

"Of course I do." Paavo's jaws were beginning to throb from the gnashing of his teeth.

"She said, 'I know what Serefina's up to, and I know all about your youngest daughter's engagement party.' Then she described Serefina's day to me, and Angelina's apartment building. She's watching them both."

Paavo was astonished. "You actually think she might harm Angie or Serefina? That's a hell of a lot more serious than an employee having a crush on you."

"Don't swear at me, Smith!" Sal said.

Paavo had had just about all he could take, Angie's father or not. "You've got to tell them. Warn them about her."

"No!" Sal was firm, unmovable. "She won't touch them, but she can still make trouble. The last thing I want to do is ruin the happiness around my little girl's engagement party, even if it is to . . . Well, forget it. If we do this right, Serefina and Angelina won't have to know anything about it."

Paavo leaned back in his chair, focusing on Schull and not on Angie's father's obnoxious personality. In his judgment as a professional police officer, not as a future son-in-law, he didn't like seeing this kept secret, and his cop instincts told him that Sal was being neither open nor honest about it. However, if the woman was as off-balance as he made her sound, she had to be kept away from Serefina and Angie no matter what Sal's problem actually was. He nodded, his lips tight. "I'll help."

The North Beach area's Fior d'Italia had no Amalfi party, nor did the Washington Square Bar and Grill. The next restaurant for Angie to check on was Moose's. As she passed St. Peter and Paul's Church, she went inside to light candles and say a prayer for loved ones and those seeking guidance about engagement parties.

As she stepped out of the dark church, the bright sunlight made it hard to see. She stopped and blinked, looking up and down the street a moment.

Parked at the corner was a car that looked amazingly like her father's. Sal Amalfi was the only person she knew who still drove a 1969 four-door red Lincoln sedan with red leather seats and a huge red steering wheel. Sal loved the car. It was the first one he ever bought straight off the showroom floor. It had everything he'd ever wanted, and he'd babied it completely. It ran like a dream, eight miles to the gallon. It used to get better mileage before the California Air Resource Board pressured him into adjusting it to take unleaded gas, but their computers went berserk every year that it came up for a smog check.

Every so often Angie or Serefina would take him out to test drive a Mercedes or BMW or even a Jaguar. He declared them all garbage—flimsy, poorly made, death-trap tin cans. Nothing compared to his own personal Sherman tank.

Maybe he'd like a new Hummer.

Angie eyed the car as she walked toward it. It had to be his. If so, what was he doing in North Beach? Her parents lived south of the city in the wealthy peninsula town of Hillsborough. Because of his heart condition, Sal rarely left home, and it was even rarer for him to drive anywhere, especially into San Francisco, one of the most congested cities in the nation.

Serefina, on the other hand, enjoyed driving her Rolls-Royce. If Sal was riding with her, however, he clutched the dashboard the entire time. As a result, they often hired a chauffeur to get them from one place to the other. That way they didn't have to worry about parking or Serefina's driving.

Angie stood beside Sal's car. He liked Moose's Restaurant. Perhaps he was there having lunch with a friend.

She should try to find him. Wouldn't he be surprised!

She was a few feet from the entrance when her father stepped onto the sidewalk. She waved and smiled. To her amazement, Paavo appeared right behind him.

Both men awkwardly watched her approach. They seemed to be leaning away from each other, which she dismissed as a weird perspective, or uneven sidewalks. She gave each a quick kiss. "What a nice surprise! My two favorite men right here together. . . ." She stopped talking, expecting them to tell her why they were there.

Instead, Paavo said, "What are you doing here, Angie?" His voice sounded strangled, as if he were under some great strain.

She didn't want Sal to know what she was up to. "Just shopping, a walk in the park. Nothing special. What about you two?" She kept the smile on her face, difficult though it was.

All of a sudden, to her amazement, Sal wrapped a stiff arm around Paavo's broad shoulders and yanked him close, then patted his back hard. Very hard. "We've decided it's time to get along even better than we have been."

Angie gawked. Paavo pulled free, yet kept a sickly smile pasted to his face as he said, "That's right. Bury the old hatchet." He gave Sal what looked like a friendly tap on the shoulder. Sal staggered back a couple of steps.

The two men eyed each other, stiff as lampposts, smiles spread wide, teeth clenched. What in the world was going on? "I'm so glad to hear it," Angie said nervously.

"Yes," Paavo said, his gaze hard as ice.

"Right," Sal murmured, returning a smoldering glare.

"How nice," Angie added, trying to get them to remember she was there.

"Excuse me, Angie." Paavo faced her. "I've got to get back to work, I'll call you later." He made a ninety-degree turn toward Sal with as much finesse as a tin soldier. "Good lunch, Sal. Thanks."

The two stiffly shook hands. Both looked positively miserable.

"Me, too." Sal also backed up. "Got to get home. *Arrivederci*, Smith. Angelina, *ciao*!"

The men darted off in opposite directions as she stood rooted to the spot.

Angie watched them go. The Tyson-Holyfield bite-off-an-earlobe boxing match had nothing on those two.

Chapter 5

Friday night with nothing to do.

The only good thing about it, Stan thought, was that it wasn't Saturday night. Although, to be honest, he couldn't remember the last time he'd been excited about a date for a Saturday night. Were the women getting worse or was he growing choosier? Or just not interested in disrupting the placid but dull life he was living?

Saturday nights, more and more, meant renting movies from Blockbuster. Sometimes he'd call up a buddy from work and they'd go barhopping to meet women. The right women, though, were always already taken.

Like Angie.

He needed to get out of this funk. If he was being completely honest with himself, he'd admit that Angie never was and never would be the woman for him. For one thing, she was too bossy with him. He noticed she never bossed Paavo. That told him a lot.

The last thing he wanted was a girlfriend who acted like a drill sergeant. He wanted someone sweet and pleasant. Malleable wasn't bad, either, come to think of it. Someone who idolized him, found no faults, praised his virtues. The perfect woman.

Angie had mentioned a few times that the women who worked at *Haute Cuisine* magazine would go to a bar after work on Fridays. Whenever she had an assignment with them she'd go along to schmooze with the editors so they'd remember her if a staff position ever opened up.

Unfortunately, Nona Farraday already occupied the only staff position she really wanted—restaurant reviewer. Angie was sure if the woman died she'd take the job with her just so Angie wouldn't get it.

Stan's remembering Angie's story was either because it had so impressed him or was a measure of how desperately lonely he'd become.

At four o'clock he left his apartment and took a cable car, then two Munis across town to the Blue Unicorn. He didn't own a car. Didn't see the need for one in the city crisscrossed with bus and cable car lines. It was nearly six o'clock before he reached the bar, which wasn't as bad as it seemed when you considered that a person driving could easily waste an hour trying to find street parking.

On the way home he'd splurge and take a taxi. Maybe.

Standing near the bar, laughing and chatting with a couple of women, was the aforementioned Nona Farraday, beautiful as ever. Stan worked his way nearby and ordered Cutty on the rocks. Drink in hand, he turned, caught her eye, and feigned surprise. "Nona," he said.

She didn't respond as she eyed him from his Helmut Lang sports jacket to his handmade Santoni loafers. He owned a few expensive clothes, bought mostly for going to dinners and events with his parents in Beverly Hills. Since his parents didn't have much to do with him, the clothes were hardly worn.

Apparently finding him acceptable, Nona gazed archly. "Have we met?"

"I live across the hall from Angie Amalfi." He held out his hand. "Stan Bonnette."

"Mr. Bonnet." She shook his hand. "How could I have forgotten?"

"That's Bon-*nette,* accent on the last syllable. It's French. But you can call me"—he lifted an eyebrow—"Stan the Man." It was an old line, but one that worked.

Actually, come to think of it, maybe it didn't.

She chose to ignore it. "So what are you doing in this area? Far from home, isn't it?"

"I'm meeting a friend nearby for dinner and I'm early. It's good to see you again, Nona," he said. "Angie often mentions you."

Interested now, she turned her back on her girlfriends. "Does she? Were you *very* good friends with Angie? Before her engagement, of course."

"No. Never. She isn't my type. A little too busy and neurotic for me."

Nona raised her eyebrows at his description. Angie was hardly neurotic, but since Nona was, or so he'd heard, he expected she'd eat up hearing Angie described that way.

"Not that she didn't spend months inviting me

to dinner, bringing over desserts, and what have you." He gave a woeful shake of his head. "It was something."

"You didn't like the attention?" Nona asked, head cocked.

"I liked the food . . ." He smirked.

She gloated. "You make her sound pathetic."

"No, Angie's just fine." He took out a slim solid-gold cigarette case and lighter. The set had been his father's until Howard Bonnette gave up smoking. "I know there's no smoking indoors, but if you'd like one we can step outside."

"That's a beautiful case." She took it from him. He could see her scrutinizing it as if to make sure it wasn't merely gold-plated.

"What do you say?"

She handed it back. "I don't smoke."

He tucked everything back into his jacket pocket. "Me neither." He glanced at her drink. "Refill?"

Her enticing blue-gray eyes were large and widely spaced. "Whiskey sour." Her voice took on a smooth, velvety quality that reverberated in the pit of his stomach. He couldn't answer, so afraid was he that his own voice would come out with a squeak. He placed the order.

"Why don't we find a table?" he suggested.

She headed for one in a corner. A dark, intimate corner.

He gawked at her, his mouth hanging open. She actually seemed interested!

As suavely as he could, he followed, although passing the happy hour hot hors d'oeuvres spread

was almost his undoing. Angie had frowned at
him many times after he'd piled a plate high with
free food, and called such behavior "gauche." That
was the last thing he wanted to be around Nona.
He ran his fingers through the lock of hair over his
brow.

Her perfume reached him—subtle, with a light
floral scent. It made him want to move closer, but
he suspected sticking his nose against her neck
wouldn't sit well.

When they reached the table, he raced to the
side she chose and pulled out a chair. She looked
surprised but sat. He tried to slide it back in but
was too late and she was too heavy. After a shove
or two that did no good, he sat in the chair opposite. She looked only slightly annoyed as she slid
her own chair closer to the table.

He quickly discovered that she enjoyed nothing
so much as talking about herself, telling him all
about her success in the magazine industry. She
acted as if Tina Brown routinely sought her advice.
He'd half expected her to do the old vaudeville
routine of talking while drinking. Still, he could
scarcely believe that Nona Farraday was paying
any attention to him at all. He wondered what
Angie's reaction would be if he dated Nona. Would
she care? Would she be sorry that she'd treated him
as no more than a friend? That she'd spurned his attention over all the time they'd known each other?

Strangely, though, when he thought about asking Nona for a date, it wasn't Angie who clouded
the picture. It was the intriguing, long-haired gyp-
sylike creature he'd seen at the Athina.

She had a wholesome look to her, an innocence

that he found appealing. That was the type of woman who interested him. The more Nona chattered, the more she seemed too modern, too career-oriented and sophisticated. He wanted someone gentle, kind, like . . .

Why was he doing this to himself? He had no business thinking of the woman at the restaurant. She was pregnant, probably married or at least living with some guy.

Yet he couldn't help but wonder why her big brown eyes had searched his face the way they did, why her mouth had tilted upward in a warm smile. He needed to talk to her. That was all there was to it. His mind had conjured her into some exotic mystery woman, which was ridiculous. If he spoke to her instead of rushing away whenever he laid eyes on her, he'd learn to get over her the way he had all other women who crossed his path. Heck, she probably had BO and cackled when she laughed.

Tomorrow, he'd go back to the restaurant and—

"It looks like my friends are leaving," Nona said, causing Stan to snap out of his reverie. "I promised I'd have dinner with them tonight . . ." She waited. He made no reply. "I should go now."

He jumped to his feet. "I'm so sorry. I don't mean to keep you." He helped her up, reminding himself that she was Nona Farraday and she sounded as if she wanted to see him again. "I . . . I'd like to call you sometime, if that would be all right."

She lifted her chin. "I'd like that." She slid a business card from her handbag and gave it to him. "I've got a few days free here and there."

"Great," he murmured. "I'll call. Soon."

As she strutted toward her friends, she glanced back and gave him a coy little wave with her fingertips.

He'd call soon. Maybe.

While Rebecca was chasing down leads Paavo had suggested on Sherlock Farnsworth, III, he turned to the situation Sal Amalfi had given him.

Sal had faxed him Elizabeth Schull's five-year-old job application and résumé with her background information, full name, and birthdate. Sal said she still lived in the same apartment building, which happened to be one that he owned.

Paavo asked why the résumé's information only went back eleven years, and Sal said it was because before that she'd been married and had nothing to show on it. Sal had believed her.

Paavo began his investigation by looking to see if she had any kind of criminal record. She didn't, which wasn't a surprise, since he couldn't imagine Sal Amalfi not checking on such a thing before making her a manager. He found her driver's license number, and nothing was of interest there, either. Not even a parking ticket.

She'd written that she was born in San Francisco. He put in a birth certificate request—and there was nothing.

The red flag that first struck when he'd looked over her résumé began to wave furiously when he investigated her credit history and Social Security number and found that all that information, as well, began eleven years earlier. It was as if she hadn't existed before then.

He went to a database he'd rarely used and keyed in Elizabeth Janice Schull. A few searches led him to an interesting discovery. Eleven years earlier, she had legally changed her name from Janice Eleanor Schullmann.

Under her birth name, he found a court case listed, a civil suit that was settled before it went to trial. On several occasions, he'd worked with one of the attorneys involved, so he phoned him.

"Sure, I remember Janice Schullmann," Barry Connelly said. "She hoped to take my client to the cleaners—he was her employer and it was a sexual harassment case. The trouble was, the whole case was a pack of lies. When her attorney realized the only witnesses he had were ones she'd convinced she'd been wronged, but who'd never witnessed anything firsthand, and when it also came out that she'd been phoning and sending love letters to my client, he dropped the case. She hasn't killed anyone, has she?"

"Not that I know of," Paavo said, perplexed.

"Well, since you're in Homicide and all . . ." Connelly added. "It wouldn't surprise me, frankly. She's delusional, and lives in her own little world. That's why she's so believable. I think she truly believes everything she says is going on. It's scary to talk to her. She makes you want to believe it, too."

"Thanks," Paavo said. "I owe you."

"I know." Connelly chuckled. "That's fine with me. Oh—for you to owe me even more, get your hands on the records at Langley Porter."

With that, he hung up.

Langley Porter was a mental hospital in the city.

Their records were tricky to get at, and usually impossible without a court order.

Paavo phoned Sal on his private cell phone and told him what he'd found out.

"So that's the way it is," Sal murmured, then spoke more loudly. "Okay, I'll talk to her. Let me know what else turns up."

"You'll what?"

"I'll deal with it."

"Wait," Paavo said, "all I've told you points to her being dangerous."

"I know." Sal hung up.

Paavo stared at the phone uneasily. He didn't like the sound of that.

Chapter 6

When Angie tried to fall asleep, she couldn't stop her mind from racing. Finally, she sat up and worked crossword puzzles and jumbles until her eyes would no longer stay open.

The first problem had been her dinner with Paavo. He'd seemed agitated, but wouldn't explain himself, and no matter how much she hinted at it, he gave no details about his lunch with her father. Finally, she asked him about it straight out.

He said they'd run into each other and decided to have lunch, to talk, to get to know each other a little better.

Fine, except that it was pie-in-the-sky, Fantasyland BS. The idea of Paavo and Sal resolving their differences would have been wonderful, except for one thing. It was impossible.

Her father didn't approve of Paavo becoming her husband. End of story, because Salvatore Amalfi was nothing if not stubborn. He wanted his youngest daughter to marry a man who was a mover and shaker, one who had either inherited or earned lots of money. Hadn't he sent her to Paris's Sorbonne for a year? To the Cordon Bleu? Hadn't she lived in Rome? She had education, good taste, looks, talent, was an excellent and knowledgeable cook, and now Salvatore expected her to *do* something with those qualities. To simply marry a man who moved murderers into prison and caused crooks to quiver and shake wasn't what Sal had in mind.

Angie tried hard to make something of herself, to make her parents proud of her and her accomplishments. It hadn't happened yet, but she wasn't about to give up. In the meantime, was it really so bad that she had fallen in love with a man of limited wealth?

The irony was that Paavo Smith was more like Sal Amalfi than any lawyer, investment banker, or CEO Angie had ever met. Both men had started out with nothing and had gotten ahead through their own hard work.

Salvatore's mother had died when he was young. After his father remarried, he and his older brothers never felt a part of the family the way his half-brothers and -sisters were. Each of them left home early, set out on their own, and rarely looked back.

After marrying, he supported his young wife by working in a shoe store.

Serefina knew how to save money, and soon encouraged Sal to open his own store. Deep in debt, with young daughters, Sal and Serefina worked long hours side by side, seven days a week to make the store profitable. All profit made went back into the business or real estate. A second shoe store was bought, and then an apartment building. Who would have expected San Francisco real estate to flourish the way it did, or that Sal was even better at real-life Monopoly than he was at selling shoes?

Sal was a self-made, hardworking man—with more than a little help from his wife.

Angie hoped to be a help to Paavo as well, although given his career she couldn't work beside him the way her parents had. On the other hand, she had helped him solve a murder or two.

Like Sal, Paavo had grown up without the support of a large, loving family. He considered himself unloved and unlovable except for the elderly Finnish man, Aulis Kokkonen, who raised him. He'd always assumed his mother had abandoned him after drugs or alcohol got the better of her. Not until recently did he learn who his father was or why his mother left.*

He'd led a fairly wild life until he went into the Army. It straightened him out and taught him a lot about himself and responsibility. The discipline and order he'd enjoyed in the Army made police work attractive. He liked what the force stood for and what it meant to do the job well. Working hard, taking criminology classes at San Francisco State, and with a talent for analysis, he quickly rose to the position of Homicide inspector.

Angie could readily see the similarities between Sal and Paavo, even if they couldn't.

---

*For Paavo's story, see *To Catch a Cook*.

Both men were driven to succeed in their chosen fields.

Both didn't suffer fools.

Both hid their emotions with a gruff exterior over hearts soft as marshmallows.

And if need be, each would give his life to save hers.

She'd rarely met men of such strength, courage, and resilience.

Now, if only they could get along. . . .

The second problem was Serefina. Her mother had phoned to ask if she thought it would be best to serve basic sushi or if the more exotic types would be better as appetizers.

Angie nearly had palpitations. She didn't want raw fish at her engagement party. What was her Italian mother doing spouting names like *unagi*, *ikura*, or *ama-ebi sushi* anyway? Angie liked Japanese food well enough. After a bottle of warm sake she'd even eat chewy but tasteless raw octopus tentacles. But it was hardly engagement party fare—at least, not *her* engagement party.

Purple cakes, yellow chicks, and raw fish.

The party from hell. And now she only had two weeks left to straighten it out!

After a restless night's sleep, the situation appeared no less bleak when she awoke. She phoned Connie Rogers to lament, but her dear friend actually had a customer who seemed interested in buying more than a buck-fifty greeting card. She had no time to talk.

Angie didn't think things could get any worse when Nona Farraday phoned. To Angie's amazement, the conversation was actually interesting.

Soon afterward, Stan knocked on the door.

"If you're sitting around moping about your party," Stan offered, eying her robe and slippers, "I thought you might want to go to lunch."

"I'd like that," Angie said. "We can talk about what we've *both* been up to."

"How about the Athina?" Stan suggested. "I've got a yen for Greek food."

"Don't talk to me about *yens*." Angie shuddered. The word for Japanese currency brought her back to sushi, which brought her back to her party, which made her depressed. "You surely do like Greek food all of a sudden. It's one of Nona's favorite cuisines, by the way."

He stared at her, stunned. "She phoned you?"

Angie just chuckled.

"Welcome to Athina. I'm the owner, Eugene Leer." The rotund, gray, jowly fellow Angie had noticed during her prior visit greeted them. He'd obviously remembered her and Stan as well. "I'm glad to see you like my little restaurant." He led them to a booth near the window.

"The food's quite good, very authentic." Angie studied his chubby face and wide forehead and nose. "I must say, the name Leer doesn't sound Greek."

"I'm not, but my cook is. Michael Zeno. You'll have to meet him. I understand you're a restaurant reviewer. Miss Amalfi, is it?"

"That's right. I'm sorry to say I haven't written any reviews lately." She fingered her engagement ring. "I've been distracted."

"Congratulations." Leer glanced from her to

Stan. "No wonder you aren't doing reviews." He handed them menus. "My waiter will be with you in a moment." With that, he bowed and walked away.

"I guess he's disappointed," Angie said to Stan. "No free publicity." She stopped talking as the friendly and garrulous Tyler Marsh arrived to take their orders. Fresh-caught bass baked in a tomato, wine, and garlic sauce called *spetsiotiko*, with egg-lemon soup for Angie and chicken gyros again for Stan. Tyler rolled his eyes.

"There's something about that guy I just don't like," Stan muttered when he and Angie were alone again.

He proceeded to tell her about meeting Nona, but the entire time he searched for the mysterious waitress. He knew he wasn't an artistic man, knew that much of the beauty around him went right over his head unnoticed and unappreciated. And yet, he felt like Michelangelo discovering the face for his Pieta. He couldn't get enough of looking at her.

She wasn't in the dining room. He had no idea if that meant she wasn't working or if her duties kept her in the kitchen. He tried to concentrate on Nona and to work up some enthusiasm. Nona was not only gorgeous and stylish, but she was clearly interested and available. She wouldn't have phoned Angie about him if she wasn't.

And yet . . .

"Sounds like she's not your type," Angie said, studying Stan. "It surprises me. I thought you two would be a perfect match."

"So did I," he said, his mind contrasting take-charge Nona with the soft winsome woman he'd seen on the dock. "Once."

Stan watched Angie head toward the parking garage. She would have dropped him off back at the apartment, but he didn't feel like going home yet. Nothing waited for him there.

Even here on Jefferson Street, nothing interested him. He hadn't seen the waitress. She was probably home with her husband. Maybe with her new baby as well. Everyone seemed to have someone but him.

And Nona.

He sighed, trying to decide what to do with himself, when he glanced down the side street to the wharf. Although it made no sense, his steps turned in that direction. The backsides of restaurants had never interested him before, nor had staring at the water or at fishing boats. They always looked dirty. He suspected fish guts lurked in every corner. He hated untidiness in anything, and flicked a speck of lint from his cashmere sweater.

The dock closest to the restaurant was empty, just as it was the last time he'd been there. Boats lined other docks, tied to thick moorings. He wondered what it would be like to own one of those boats, to sail out to sea away from all this. The only problem was *he'd* be there—boring, same-old-same-old Stan.

He stood with his toes along the edge of the wharf, hands in the pockets of his slacks, and looked down at the water. Today it had a greenish tinge, like pea soup. He never much liked pea soup.

Behind him, he heard a soft, "Hello."

Startled, he turned to see the woman who had captured his thoughts. She wore a long trench coat. It wasn't buttoned or belted and where it gaped open her stomach protruded.

He stepped back.

"Be careful!" She started, reaching her hand out toward him, then looked embarrassed by her action. "There aren't any railings. You don't want to tumble into the bay, do you?"

Her voice was gentle and light, much as he'd expected it might be. For sure, she'd never cackle.

He moved away from the edge.

"I didn't mean to startle you," she said, "I'm sorry." She looked chagrined, yet her eyes sparkled as if she were laughing at his discomfort.

He stood straighter. "What are you doing out here?" he asked.

"It's my lunchtime. I came out to see if a friend was here, a homeless man who calls himself Shelly Farms. He usually hangs out around the docks and used to check in with me regularly. I haven't seen him for a week and I'm worried."

Stan looked around. Except for the two of them, the area was empty. "Sorry, it's only me here."

She smiled. "That's fine, too. You can also be my friend."

He liked that.

She moved toward the bench she used the first time he'd seen her and sat, unwrapping her sandwich.

He'd followed as surely as a puppy on a leash. "What is it?" he asked, hovering near.

"Tuna. The smells make everything around here taste fishy. It isn't an area to try to eat baloney, for instance. Or peanut butter."

Stan winced at the thought.

She chuckled. "Luckily, I like tuna."

He nodded. "Me, too."

"Why don't you sit and talk to me while I eat?" She patted the bench. "You seem like a nice fellow."

"I do?"

"Yes." She twisted open a bottle of Aquafina. "And you have a beautiful fiancée."

"Fi—? Oh, you mean Angie. She's not my fiancée. We're just friends. Neighbors, actually." He nodded and fidgeted; nervous, shy, and unable to believe he was finally talking to her. As she ate, he tried to fill the silence. "She's marrying someone else, and I just go along with her now and then for moral support. Her mother is planning a big engagement party for her, you see, and the two made a deal that Serefina would stay out of the wedding plans if she could handle the engagement, but then she took it a step further and is keeping everything a secret from Angie, so now the whole thing is driving Angie crazy and she's going all over San Francisco asking restaurant owners if they have a party scheduled for May fifth, and . . ."

The woman's brows kept rising higher and higher as Stan talked, as if nothing he said made sense to her.

"I know," he admitted with a small smile. "It's weird."

"Someone else is your special girlfriend, then?" she asked, continuing with her sandwich.

"No. No one."

She looked at him curiously. "I'm surprised."

He felt his cheeks redden. His lack of companionship wasn't anything he liked to talk about. "Tell me," he said, changing the subject, "when is your baby due?"

"Yesterday," she replied, and then burst into laughter at his stricken expression. "Not really! I've got three weeks yet." She had a beautiful laugh, warm and hearty. Her slight shoulders shook with mirth. Everything about her was a delight. He didn't understand this strange reaction at all.

"Should you still be working?" he asked. "I mean, shouldn't you be lying down? Or in the hospital or something?"

"I'm fine. Everyone says it's okay to work up to one or two weeks before the due date. Anyway, I need the money. It's going to be hard after the baby is born. I'm trying to save for that."

As much as he didn't want to know, he had to ask. "What about the baby's father? Are you married? Doesn't he work?"

She shook her head. "He's no longer involved." Her eyes clouded and she looked away.

"Once, I saw you and the waiter arguing," Stan said.

"It's over," she murmured. And that, in itself, told him everything he needed to know about that relationship. She continued, "He was a mistake, nothing more. Maybe—" Her voice caught. "Maybe the baby is, as well."

"No, don't think that," Stan said vehemently.

Their eyes met. "I don't, at least not most of the time. But to be alone at a time like this, it isn't easy."

An unfamiliar feeling stirred in Stan's breast. What was wrong with him? He tried to ignore it. "You've got a hospital and doctor lined up, don't you?"

"My social worker has lined up a birthing clinic for me."

"Social worker?" he asked, confused.

"I'm poor," she said with a sad smile, then lifted her arms as she looked down at the cheap clothes and shoes she wore. "Or hadn't you realized that?"

"I'm sorry." The realization swept over him of how incongruous it was to be having such a conversation with a woman he knew absolutely nothing about.

He found himself studying her. Her frame was slight yet solid, her jaw firm, her hands strong and capable-looking with square, polish-free nails. He liked everything about her. "I'm concerned, that's all."

Dark eyes held his. "Why?"

Her question puzzled him because he had no answer. He gazed out at the water. "You're right. I should keep my mouth shut." He glanced at her again. "But you do have people who'll take care of you, don't you?"

She smiled shyly. "I know some who might help."

He didn't like the sound of that. "Look, if they don't help enough, call me. This is my cell phone number." He took out a small leather-bound notebook and wrote out his name and number. It took him a moment to build up the courage, but then his chest swelled and he blurted out the words, "I'll help you."

"Stan." She whispered the name as she read it, then carefully folded the paper and put it in her pocket. "You're very nice, Stan." She crumbled up her sandwich's waxed paper and threw it and the empty water bottle in a trash barrel. "I've got to get back inside. My lunchtime is over. Thanks for sitting with me."

He stood as well. "Thank you."

She started to walk away. "Come back again. I'll see you another time, I hope."

"Okay," Stan said, watching her as she used a key to unlock the back door to the restaurant and go inside. "Hey, wait! What's your name?"

The door shut behind her before she answered.

Chapter 7

Paavo stood on the cement walkway above the beach at Aquatic Park. The sun was going down over the Golden Gate, and he watched the waves roll onto the shore. At sundown the changing temperatures over the water caused a chill wind to blow into the city. He turned up the collar of his sports coat.

Just above the beach the Maritime Museum looked down upon the scene. He knew it was one of Angie's favorite "old San Francisco" spots. She often talked of how, when she was a little girl and her older sisters were in school or busy, she and her mother would walk to it from their Marina-district flat. She'd learned a lot about San Francisco history there, insisting that Serefina read descriptions of the displays over and over. Afterward, if the day was warm, she'd play in the sand; if cold, they'd walk out onto Muni Pier and check on the fishermen who dropped their lines into the water.

A chill rippled down his back and he put his hands in the pockets of his slacks. Thinking of that reminded him of how troubled he was over Angie and the situation Sal had confronted him with. He and Angie had vowed never to lie to each other. Up to now he'd pretty much kept the vow. Although she stretched the truth—or forgot it now and then—she'd never out-and-out lied to him.

Yet he'd lied because of Sal, and disagreed with Sal on top of it. He hated being in this predicament but, despite their dreadful lunch, it was a chance to form some sort of bond with his future father-in-law, and he didn't want to ruin it.

From the time they were introduced and Sal took one look at him and decided he wasn't good enough for his daughter, there'd been tension between them. As far as he could tell, the whole problem centered on money and position, though he wasn't sure of that, either. Sometimes he felt Sal thought of Angie as a prize who should go to the highest bidder. No, that was harsh. He knew Sal loved his daughter, but the man's insane devotion to the idea that it would take money to buy her happiness was childish.

Now he wondered more than ever about Sal's judgment. Given proof that Elizabeth Schull had been involved in a false sexual harassment claim and the suggestion she'd been in a mental institute, the last thing Sal should want was to face her alone. The idea of it made Paavo suspicious. Just what was Sal up to?

Paavo forced his concentration back to the murder case as he left the walkway for the beach where Farnsworth's body had been found. Whenever he was in any way involved in a case, Paavo visited the scene of the crime. As much as it might be a cliché, the crime scene often did, in fact, give a sense of what might have happened, and sometimes why.

Paavo wanted answers to both questions.

People argued constantly over whether Farnsworth was a saint who worked among the poor and homeless and gave them help and advice when he could, or a sinner: a scam artist who used the homeless for his own purposes to make money at his law firm. Paavo thought he was a little of both.

Farnsworth had been practicing law when for some reason—probably no one would ever know exactly why—he underwent a spiritual conversion. He believed it was necessary to do good works in this life, and Spirit, as he called his god, led him to the homeless. But Spirit also knew that Farnsworth needed to provide for himself or he'd end up just like the people he ministered to, so he kept up his law practice. He did everything except appear in court—that, he left to his partners.

Paavo, frankly, had liked the guy. They'd worked together a few times on murders of homeless people. Those were cases that got little attention from the press, and usually little from the district attorney as well. Leads were few, and finding anyone who would talk to a Homicide inspector was next to impossible. That was when Farnsworth stepped in. He—like Paavo—believed every man's death diminished him, homeless or not, and murderers should pay the price.

Now he was the victim. Paavo would see that justice was done.

* * *

Angie picked out a Spode "English Garden" cup and saucer and placed them on the counter. She was in Everyone's Fancy, her friend Connie's gift shop, located across town from Angie's apartment in a busy neighborhood shopping area on West Portal Avenue. Unfortunately, the activities in the area rarely extended into Connie's shop, despite Angie's attempts a while back at helping her upgrade her merchandise.

The mainstay of Connie's business was greeting cards. Hers were all either extremely mushy or extremely funny. She left the in-betweeners to grocery store racks. Nevertheless, it took a lot of card sales to pay rent.

Buying something expensive was one way for Angie to get Connie to pay attention to her and her troubles. Several days had gone by and Angie was no closer to finding out the location of her engagement party.

Connie eyed the china suspiciously. She was a few years older than Angie, blond, and with a round figure that caused her to constantly diet—or think about dieting—to avoid drifting from curvaceous to plump. Blue eyes pierced her friend. "Is this a bribe?"

"Whatever are you talking about?" Angie asked innocently. "I'm going to give my mother a present for all the hard work she's doing."

"Keeping your engagement party a secret from you?" Connie put her hand on her hip. "The woman's lucky you don't give her poison. I know you, Angie Amalfi, and I know she's driving you nuts."

"I wouldn't put it quite that way." Angie picked

up the Spode, pretending to study it. "She loves pretty cups and saucers like this one."

"Fine." Connie rang up the sale, then got out a box and gift wrap. "But don't waste your time being coy. I have no idea where the party is."

"Really?" Angie asked, disappointed.

"And if I did know, I wouldn't tell you."

As Angie watched, she remembered the call about the cake. "Don't use purple gift wrap, please. I've developed a sudden aversion to the color."

"Purple? You're kidding." Connie reached for pastel green.

"Oh, Connie!" Angie wailed, sudden tears in her eyes. "You don't know what I've been going through. First some baker calls about a purple cake, then . . . then a stripper called about jumping out of it! What is my mother thinking? She's gone crazy! I've got to stop her."

"Don't cry, honey." Connie walked around the counter to pat Angie's back and hand her a wad of tissues. "That doesn't sound like Serefina to me," Connie continued. "It's got to be a mistake or a joke."

Angie wiped her eyes. "Who would joke about such an important occasion?"

"It's a mistake, then. Someone's got your name mixed up with another Amalfi, that's all. Someone who likes strippers and purple cakes." Connie grinned. "Someone like your Cousin Richie, maybe."

Even Angie had to chuckle at that. Richie was one of those people who no longer surprised her with the crazy things he was up to. "Maybe you're right."

"Have you ever mentioned to Serefina the type of party you hoped for?" Connie asked.

"Sure. The wedding will be serious and beautiful, so the engagement party should be a bit whimsical. Romantic, of course, but also fun. A time for me, Paavo, friends, and relatives to get together without stress. Weddings are always stressful, no matter what. I'd like to avoid that."

"Whimsical?" Connie asked skeptically.

"Yes. Good food, lovely clothes, but something a little different. I know it won't happen. We'll probably end up at a wonderful restaurant, but still . . ."

"Where would you like it to be?" Connie asked.

"I don't know anymore! Oh, well, why think about that? My mother will most likely come up with something very traditional and lovely, right?"

"I didn't have an engagement party before my first marriage. Next time, I'll do it right," Connie said dreamily. "An elegant restaurant with white linen tablecloths, crystal goblets, gold-rimmed white china . . . that's what I'd like. If, that is, I marry a Rockefeller or some other tycoon. If not, my friends and I will probably gather at Pizza Hut. Beer and pizza on the house!"

"And everyone would love it," Angie said.

Connie nodded. "Maybe someday . . ." She went back to the counter and began to tape the gift paper in place. "I take it you had no luck checking restaurants."

Angie shook her head. "It didn't work, and now I've only got thirteen days to go. I'm at my wits' end."

"Well, if I hear anything that might help, I'll let you know," Connie said as she unfurled a long length of green ribbon and then began to wrap it around the package. "Although I can't imagine anyone better than 'Stan-the-Man' at sleuthing out a place where food will be served."

"Puh-lease!" Angie said, studying a figurine of three clowns in a hot tub. She didn't get it, and put it back on the shelf. "He was lots more interested in going to a shabby little Greek restaurant than helping me."

"And that surprises you?" Connie asked.

"I know he loves to eat, but once there, he just picked at his meal. He only livened up when he was making eyes at a pregnant waitress."

Connie was so surprised by Angie's words her hand slipped and the bow she was making unraveled. "Pregnant? You don't think Stan . . . ?"

"No way. He could never have kept that a secret. Shoot, he even tells me when he's having intestinal troubles. Give me a break!"

Connie shook her head and went back to creating a bow. "So, who is she?"

"That's what I wonder. I asked Stan and he said he didn't know. The funny part is, I believe him."

Connie's eyes lit up. "Maybe we need to find *that* out."

"Say, you don't sound half so curious about my party," Angie remarked. "Why is that?"

Connie said nothing as she concentrated on creating a beautiful bow.

* * *

Stan was awakened from a sound sleep by a shrill ringing. He picked up the phone by his night-stand. "Hello?"

A dial tone sounded.

The ringing continued.

He sat up, confused.

The sound came from the cell phone on the bureau beside his wallet and comb.

By the time he picked it up, it had already switched to messaging. Instead of listening to the message, he simply hit the caller ID—it showed pay phone—punched "call back," then laid back in the bed. The call was probably a mistake, he thought, as he listened to the ring.

He peered at the clock radio . . . 1:45 A.M. . . . and groaned.

"Hello?" A woman hesitantly answered.

"This is Stan Bonnette. Did you just phone me?"

"Stan . . . oh, Stan." Her voice broke as if she were going to cry.

"Who is this?" he asked, sitting up.

There was a pause. "It's me. Hannah. From Athina."

Hannah. So that was her name. His heart clenched.

"Stan, I'm scared. You said you'd help me. I'm not sure where else to turn."

Although he'd convinced himself that the only smart thing would be to stay away from her and the Athina, hearing her voice he tossed such intentions aside. "What do you mean? Where are you?"

"I'm in the all-night Safeway near Fisherman's Wharf. In a phone booth. My . . . my water broke.

Labor pains started. Stan, I need help. I don't know what to do."

He was silent a moment, then got out of bed and began to pace. "Is it safe there? Are there people around?"

"It's safe."

"Can you get a taxi? Your social worker set you up someplace, right? Can you get there?"

"No. I can't go there."

"What do you mean?"

"I can't! Trust me in that. I need to get out of the city. Help me, Stan. Please." She was crying.

He rubbed his forehead. "What about San Francisco General? They'll take you."

"I can't." The hysteria in her voice rose. "You . . . you said you'd help me."

Me? He had said that, hadn't he? He stopped pacing, bewildered. *How can I help?* "How often are the labor pains coming?" He didn't really know what he was talking about. All he knew was frequent was bad, infrequent good.

"I'm not sure. Every fifteen minutes or so, I guess."

Was that frequent or infrequent? His heart pounded. He had no idea what to do. "You should be home, in bed, not in some grocery store."

"You aren't listening to me." Her disappointment reached across the phone lines. "I'm sorry. I shouldn't have called—"

"Wait!" He didn't want her to hang up. "I'll come. I'll call a cab and be right there. Wait for me at the big main entrance on Bay Street. We'll get you to a hospital."

"I . . . I don't have any insurance."

That stopped him a moment. How much could it cost to have a baby? People seemed to have them at home and in taxicabs all the time—basically for free. "Don't worry about it. Just don't move . . . except to be somewhere that I can find you when I arrive."

Stan called for a taxi, then threw on khakis, a T-shirt, shoes, and a sports jacket. He was pacing outside in front of the apartment when the cab showed up less than ten minutes later.

As promised, Hannah waited at the grocery's main entrance. She was wearing the rain parka. Her thick dark hair, loose and full against her shoulders, made her face appear small and white as death. She tried to smile when she saw him, but her eyes were limp with fear.

He sprang from the cab but paused as the enormity of his action, of the depth of his involvement, struck.

"Stan," she whispered. "You're here."

Her simple words spurred him forward. "Come on." Steadying her with his arm around her back, they hurried to the taxi. A pain gripped her, forcing her to stop a moment. It wasn't too strong, she said. To him, though, it was horrifying.

He eased her into the cab.

"Not SF General, please," she murmured, clutching his hand. "Please. Somewhere else. Somewhere on the peninsula, maybe. A small hospital. A place no one would think of to look for me."

"You're hiding from someone?"

She nodded. Stan didn't like that. He had

planned to insist she go to SF General. With a
baby ready to pop out, it wasn't as if she had a
choice. But if she was scared and hiding . . . He
hated making decisions. Lately, he'd always gone
to Angie to help him make them. Maybe he
should phone—

"Hey," the taxicab driver shouted, "I don't want
no kids born in this cab. Let's get goin' or I want
you both out of here."

"All right," Stan said, his anxiety growing.
"Head north. Marin General in Greenbrae, just off
Highway 101. You know it?"

"Yeah, I know it. Hang on tight. I don't like the
way she's moanin'."

They practically flew across the Golden Gate
Bridge. Twenty minutes and one contraction later
they reached the emergency entrance. Stan ran inside to get help. He came back out with a wheelchair.

"Good luck, you two," the cabdriver said, then
sped off.

Stan noticed the relief on the man's face as he
left them. He would have liked to leave as well—
to go back home, back to his nice comfy bed. How
had he gotten caught up in this, anyway?

He didn't say a word as he pushed Hannah
into the emergency ward, preferring to concentrate on getting her into a doctor's hands and out
of his own.

Emergency was fairly quiet, as he expected it
might be in this area. The nurse approached. "So
this is our mother-to-be," she said. Stan and Hannah both nodded. "We have some paperwork
first." Stan inwardly groaned.

"Name?" The nurse asked.

Hannah looked so scared, shy, and over-whelmed that Stan answered for her.

"Hannah," he replied.

"Last name?"

"Uh . . ." He glanced at Hannah, and the nurse gawked at him.

"Jones," Hannah said, slightly dazed.

The nurse's mouth twisted skeptically as she wrote. "Address?"

Hannah gave the address of the Athina. Stan also learned she was twenty-three years old and could name no living relative. She'd been raised in foster homes and never knew her parents. She refused to give any information about the father of the child. Somehow, as the nurse continued the questions, Stan found himself holding Hannah's hand tight, doing his best to give moral support.

When the nurse pulled out yet another form, Hannah doubled over with a contraction. Perspiration flowed from Stan's forehead. He was sure she'd give birth right there at the front desk.

"Can't we hurry?" he wailed. The contractions seemed to be only about five minutes apart at this point.

The nurse was unmoved as she asked about insurance coverage. Because Hannah didn't have any, Stan went through a lengthy song-and-dance during which he agreed to pay basic, everything-goes-like-clockwork costs, capped at $12,000. That it could cost so much to have a baby stunned him. Fortunately, his father had plenty of money.

"We're going to send you up to the maternity ward," the nurse said. "You don't need to be in emergency, the baby's got a while yet. They'll take good care of you up there." She then handed copies of the paperwork to Stan. "Give this to the receiving desk on the fifth floor."

"Me? But . . ." He gazed longingly over his shoulder toward the exit.

"The elevators are to your left."

Before he knew it, Stan was not only on the fifth floor, but waiting outside the examination room. Everyone seemed to assume he wanted to stay with Hannah. Rather than argue, he went along. After making sure she was all right, he planned to go straight home.

His own nervousness surprised him, a ridiculous state to be in over someone he'd just met. Someone whose last name he didn't know because whatever it was, it certainly wasn't Jones. She was a stranger to him. Nothing more.

When Dr. Linda Jedlicka peered into the waiting room, Stan jumped to his feet. "Is she all right?"

"She's fine." The doctor gave him a reassuring smile. "The baby's heartbeat is strong. I expect things will be happening in the next hour or two. She's asked for natural childbirth, so we'll move her into a very nice delivery room set up to look much like a bedroom. If anything goes wrong, though, it's just steps away from a full operating room. You can wait for her in number twelve on the right. When the nurse wheels her in she'll show you a button to press if things start happening more quickly than expected."

"Me?" Stan felt woozy. "But, you see, I . . ."

Dr. Jedlicka's eyes were kind as she rubbed his

shoulder. "Don't worry. She'll be just fine. And so will you."

As Stan sat in the delivery room with Hannah, he again considered calling Angie. She should take over here for him. Women understood these things. He didn't. Not the slightest bit. Hannah seemed to find comfort by his presence, though, and he decided to wait a while. Big mistake.

When "things" started to happen, as the doctor put it, all hell broke loose.

All Stan could remember was that he'd tried to leave, he really had, but Hannah was holding his hand so tight his knuckles were squished together, and the nurse gave him a fierce glare as she said, "You aren't going to leave her alone *now*, are you?"

He edged closer to Hannah for protection.

Before he knew it, he'd been tied into a gown like a sausage, and the dictatorial nurse was instructing him to tell Hannah when to breathe.

"Breathe?" His voice cracked. That was the only word he managed to get out of his mouth when the nurse told him exactly what she thought of men who didn't bother to attend Lamaze classes. He was too dumbfounded to speak up for himself, especially when Hannah went into the most violent contraction he'd ever seen.

He took a moment to thank God he wasn't a woman.

The nurse coached him on how to coach Hannah, and he found himself growing increasingly light-headed as he huffed and puffed along with her through the contractions, and wiped sweat from her brow—and his own—in between them.

After what seemed like an eternity, the doctor announced that the crown of the baby's head was visible.

Up to this time, he'd stayed near Hannah's head, her legs draped with a sheet. Now, though, at the excitement Dr. Jedlicka and the nurse displayed, curiosity got hold of him. He peeked. He thought he'd feel like a Peeping Tom, but he didn't. The sight was too overwhelming for there to be anything the slightest bit sexual about it.

Birth, right there, in front of his eyes.

He felt weak in the knees, but he couldn't turn away. He couldn't miss it. He gripped Hannah's hand, and for the first time, smiled at her. "Soon, Hannah. Everything will be fine."

She was surprisingly stoical. He could tell when the pain came hard, but she never cried out. In fact, between contractions, he heard her thanking him for staying with her. Between her thanks and the nurse's frowns, he'd been frozen to the spot.

And scared. Every little order the doctor gave to Hannah or the nurse was like a stab to his heart. *What's wrong?* He'd wanted to shout. *Is something wrong?* But he'd been too afraid to ask for fear that the doctor would say yes.

Now, though, now . . .

His head was swimming when the doctor said, "Here it comes."

Stan held his breath as the baby's entire head emerged, and then watched the doctor ease out a shoulder. He had no idea a baby's bones were so gelatinous.

The hospital room began to spin. The baby was coated with some whitish, reddish gunk. Once the head and shoulders were out, the rest followed so quickly, Stan couldn't believe it.

"It's a girl!" The doctor announced.

A girl? His eyes welled with tears.

"She's beautiful," the nurse said, smiling at Hannah.

"Take the scissors," the doctor ordered.

From a deep fog, Stan tore his gaze from the baby and realized he was the one the doctor was speaking to. The nurse handed him huge shears.

"Cut," Dr. Jedlicka said.

The umbilical cord.

Stan moved the scissors where the doctor indicated and pressed down. The cord was much harder than he thought, and as he pressed, he realized that this was living flesh . . . *alive.*

Black and purple spots danced in front of his eyes. He wondered if he'd ever forget the sound of the scissors against the cord, the way it felt as he cut through it.

The nurse was cleaning up the baby, he guessed. He wasn't aware of much of anything except that Hannah was no longer in pain. He was watching the doctor, trying to regain his composure, to be cool, suave Stan once again, when the afterbirth came sliding out of Hannah's body.

And that was when Stan-the-Man fell over in a dead faint.

Chapter 8

Angie was ready to give whoever was pounding at her door before eight o'clock in the morning a good piece of her mind, but her annoyance vanished at the sight of Stan, unshaven, disheveled, exhausted, and babbling like a madman.

His story about helping some woman he barely knew give birth was a half sentence from total incoherence. Angie realized it was the waitress, but still, why would some stranger want Stan Bonnette with her at such a time? No one could be that desperate.

He was going to sleep for a while, he said, and asked if she'd drive him back to the hospital later to meet Hannah and the baby. Of course she agreed. She'd never seen Stan in such a state—troubled, confused, and overwhelmingly elated all at the same time. She had to find out what this was all about.

She thought he'd sleep most of the day, but at noon he was shaved, nattily dressed in a sports jacket, knit pullover, gabardine slacks, and loafers,

his hair perfectly coiffed, and ready to head for
Marin General.

"How did this happen to me?" Stan asked,
wringing his hands as he sat in the passenger seat
of her Mercedes. "I just *smiled* at the woman. Next
thing I know I'm watching her have a baby. I
mean—oh, my God!"

"It doesn't make any sense to me," Angie admitted.

"I'll say, though, it was lucky for her I went
along," he said proudly. "I kept a clear eye on the
doctor and nurses. Made sure they did a good job.
At the same time, I kept Hannah calm. The birth
was much easier for her because of that, you
know."

"Is that so?" Angie looked at him as if he'd
taken leave of his senses.

"Still"—he gave a weary sigh—"I had no idea
my smile was so endearing." He rubbed his eyes.
Deep bags were under them. "I may never smile at
a strange woman again."

They soon reached the hospital. At the nursery
window, Stan pointed out Baby Jones to Angie.
"She's seven pounds, nine ounces," he said. "With
all her fingers and toes. You know, Hannah really
did check them. She's a good, healthy size. The
doctor said we should have no problems with
her."

Angie was surprised to hear the note of pride in
his voice, as if he had something to do with it. "I
can't wait to meet Hannah, Daddy."

"Don't start, Angie," Stan warned.

Hannah was dozing when they reached her

room, but woke at the sound of footsteps. At the restaurant Angie had thought her to be a plain person, the type a judicious use of makeup might help. But when Hannah smiled at Stan, her face took on a warm glow that made her almost beautiful. He hurried toward her, then stopped, suddenly shy. She held out her hands, and he gripped them tightly as he bent down and kissed her cheek. "You've come back," she said.

"Yes. And . . ." He gestured toward Angie in the doorway. Only then did Hannah seem to shrink again into shy plainness. "Hello," she said, her voice soft.

Angie introduced herself. "Your baby is beautiful."

"She is," Hannah said proudly.

"Are you all right?" Stan asked. "Comfortable? You aren't still in any pain, are you? Can I get you some water? Juice?"

"No need, Stan, relax," Hannah said with a soft chuckle. "They're taking very good care of me. I'm fine, and it's all thanks to you."

He stared at her, his Adam's apple bobbing as if he needed to swallow but couldn't, then he gave a quick glance at Angie, and finally the floor.

"Have you named the baby yet?" Angie asked.

"Kaitlyn," Hannah said. "Kaitlyn Emily." She looked again at Stan. "Since everything went well, Stan, we'll be released tomorrow afternoon. I'll pay you back for all this. It'll take a while, but I will."

"Don't worry about it," he said. "Will you go back to your apartment, then? Will there be anyone around to look in on you?"

She shook her head, her mouth firm. "I can't go back to it. I'll get a room for a week or so. After that, I'm not sure. Perhaps Los Angeles. I know some people there."

"Los Angeles?" Stan was horrified. "You can't take a newborn to Los Angeles. The smog will kill her. A person has to become acclimated to a place like that! You need to stay in San Francisco." He frowned. "What kind of a room will you stay in? Do you have money for a good room? There are so many dives in this city. You can't take Kaitlyn to a dive."

"Don't worry, Stan," Hannah said. "We'll be all right."

"Maybe you should stay with Angie," he suggested.

At Angie's stunned and annoyed glower, he quickly added, "Or with me. I've got room. And my apartment is healthy. I keep it clean."

"I can't accept that," Hannah said. "It's too much."

"You can trust me." Stan turned to Angie. "Tell her. She can trust me. I'd never impose myself. Not that you aren't a beautiful woman, but . . . you're a mother." The last word he spoke so reverently that both Angie and Hannah had to smile.

The nurse brought in a tray with a light snack. "The doctor says you're undernourished. You need to build up strength," she told Hannah, then eyed her visitors. "And rest."

Stan went to the notepad and pen beside the bedside telephone and scribbled something as he talked. "We'll be here tomorrow," Stan said, "to help when you're discharged. We'll figure out what the best place is for you to go to at that time, okay? I wrote down Angie's cell phone number since she'll drive." He glanced at Angie. "You will, won't you?"

"Sure," she said, wide-eyed at this new and decisive Stan.

"Angie's number is in case my cell phone isn't working. She's got a Mercedes," Stan continued. "It'll be a safe car for the baby to ride in."

Angie knew Stan's cell phone didn't work well because he'd been too cheap to pay for a good one. That had been part of his character, but if he'd paid for a hospital room for a relative stranger, his metamorphosis was even greater than she'd thought.

Hannah frowned with worry, but then she nodded.

As Angie and Stan walked down the hall, Stan paused at the nursery. "Let me take another quick look at Kaitlyn."

Baby Jones was sleeping, but that didn't stop Stan from waving and making comical faces at her. "Can you believe I actually saw her being born? Being born! It was like . . . so amazing!"

He stood so straight and stepped so high as they walked down the hall, Angie was surprised he didn't bump his head on the ceiling.

"I'm so glad you called me, Hannah. I was worried about you." Dianne Randle's matronly face was lined with concern. A woman of about fifty-five, she added no color to her short gray hair, and no makeup detracted from the piercing blue of her eyes. Her plump figure gave her a motherly air that Hannah, as well as many other young women, found comforting.

"Thank you for coming," Hannah said.

"I checked all the files I could about the young man you told me about. Mr. Bonnette has no record that we're aware of at Social Services, and I asked one of my contacts in the police department to check as well. He seems all right as far as that goes, but still, are you sure you can trust him? Not every sicko comes with a warning label, you know. Sometimes, they don't have any until it's too late."

The social worker's question gave Hannah pause. Over the past month, Dianne had become a friend as well as the one who had guided her through the government blitz of paperwork needed to take part in California's MediCal program. The sole benefit to Hannah's low salary was access to free prenatal care, hospitalization for the baby's birth, and afterward, Aid to Families with Dependent Children benefits.

Hannah had first learned about the help Social Services gave to unwed mothers through her friend Shelly Farms. Shelly was a strange man— he dressed like one of the homeless, but he was smart, and knew a lot of good people. She'd gone to him when things started to go badly between her and Tyler, and he suggested she go to Social Services.

When Tyler found out, he'd been furious. He insisted he'd take care of everything, but she'd grown wary of him. If it hadn't have been for Shelly, she didn't know how she would have gotten through this period. Lately, though, he'd stopped coming by the restaurant to visit her. She wondered why. He told her he'd always be there to help her, but he wasn't. It both worried and confused her.

Now Dianne was raising questions about another man Hannah had put her trust in.

"Maybe you're right," she said. "I should know by now not to trust my judgment."

"Don't write this new one off completely yet," Dianne advised. "He might be exactly what you need. I take it your boyfriend Tyler knows nothing about this?"

"Former boyfriend, and no, he doesn't."

Dianne frowned. "We're going to have to have a serious conversation about your life and where it's going."

Hannah didn't want to hear it. "Have you heard from Shelly lately?" she asked. "I haven't seen him for days."

Dianne looked startled by the question. "You don't know—" She stopped abruptly, then smiled and said, "You don't know where he is and neither do I. Perhaps he's simply out finding some lost souls to send me." She stood and patted Hannah's arm. "And I'm glad he does. Now, don't worry so much. Forget about everything but you and that baby. No newspapers, hear? No TV unless it's a comedy or love story. No depressing news stories, okay?"

Hannah smiled. "Okay."

"Everything will be all right," Dianne said, her eyes strangely sad. "I'll be back tomorrow."

"Thank you," Hannah said.

* * *

Angie spent the entire evening from the moment Paavo picked her up until halfway through the dinner speculating about Stan, Hannah, and their relationship. She could tell he was becoming bored, and she didn't blame him. Stan was one of his least favorite people, especially when he came to believe that Stan would have preferred to be the one engaged to Angie. She had to laugh at the idea of her and Stan, but Paavo was serious.

He was a lot more interested in her story about a purple cake and a stripper. To her surprise, he was especially intrigued that both callers were women. He seemed lost in thought at that point, and hardly offered any commiseration as she talked about her poor luck at finding the restaurant or banquet hall where her party would be held.

None of this, however, was the reason she'd wanted to go to dinner with him tonight, and it certainly wasn't why she'd chosen Moose's. The only problem was, she wasn't sure how to get to what she really wanted to talk about. She decided to take a diversionary route.

"What kind of engagement party have you always wanted?"

He had just taken a mouthful of food and nearly choked on it. "Do you know how many engagement parties I've been to?"

She shook her head.

"None. Does that tell you anything?" She must have looked disappointed because he quickly added, "The only party I care about is ours—after the wedding is over. Engagement parties, bridal showers, the wedding reception, even a stag party—I'd gladly do without them. I want you to be my wife, Angie. The rest is so much . . . what's the word? Frippery."

She swallowed hard, unsure whether to cry or to hug him.

He took her hand and spoke. "Being engaged is, for me, a time to show the world that a beautiful, warm, loving woman has agreed to be my wife. I know you want a fancy party and a big wedding. They're important to you, and for that reason alone, they're important to me. But to tell you the truth," he said, and she saw the smile in his blue eyes, "I'll be glad when they're over."

What more could she ask for? She half stood to reach him for a kiss. "You're right," she said when she sat back down. "I shouldn't get so wrapped up in . . . fripperies."

"That's not what I said at all," he protested. "You should, because that's part of what makes you the charming woman I love. But that doesn't mean I should as well. Being engaged, being married, doesn't mean we agree on everything, or are in lockstep, it means we respect each other's opinions, and our differences. You love parties; I barely tolerate them."

She nodded. "That's the way my parents have always been."

"That's right." His mouth turned down. "Your mother welcomed me with open arms; your father hates my guts."

"Even after you had lunch with him?" she asked. "Didn't that help?"

"We're working on it," he said. "But don't put

much hope there. If you can think of anything I should be doing, let me know."

"Become Italian," she quipped.

He wasn't in the mood to laugh.

"I don't think there is anything," she admitted, "because the problem isn't you. When I was still living at home, I'd have a new date almost every week, it seemed, and the only ones he ever approved of were a couple of guys who were sons of friends of his. In both cases, I didn't go out with either fellow a second time."

"So, it's hopeless," he murmured.

"No, not at all. Mamma says he'll come around in time. He already admits, to her, that I'm happy with you and that's what matters most. He even admits, to her, that you're a good man. The next step is to get him to admit those things to us. He's a stubborn old coot, but his heart is in the right place."

"I suppose," Paavo admitted. "But he's an expert at hiding it."

Chapter 9

 "Wake up. Get the baby. We're leaving."

Hannah opened her eyes to see Tyler Marsh standing over her. Fear gripped her. "What are you doing here?"

"Let's go," he said.

"I can't just walk out of the hospital." She clutched the blankets as if they could protect her from him.

"Sure you can. No one's able to hold you against your will. Is the kid a boy or girl?"

She studied him, trying to determine if he was lying. If he'd looked in the nursery, he would have seen pink ribbons on Kaitlyn's crib. Or didn't he care enough to look for his own child? Of course not. Why should that surprise her?

She hated him even more than she thought possible. "It's a boy."

"A son. Good. Don't just lie there. Move."

"I'm not going," she said.

"Yes, you are." He grabbed her arm and dragged her from the bed. "Where are your clothes? Get dressed!"

She yanked her arm from him and backed away until the wall stopped her from going farther. "The baby can't leave. There's something wrong with his lungs. He's in an incubator. He was very small."

His eyes narrowed as if trying to decide whether or not she was lying. "You said everything was going well, that the baby would be strong and healthy. Hell, woman, you got big as a house. How could the brat be a runt?"

She felt tears threaten. How had she ever loved this man? "He'll be fine as long as the congestion clears up and it doesn't turn into pneumonia. He needs to stay in an incubator a few days." She prayed that what she was saying made sense.

He gripped her shoulders, lifting her to her toes, his face too close to hers. She turned her head, sickened by the sight of him, by the memories of all he'd once meant to her. "You're lying again, aren't you? We're wasting time." He shoved her, and she sprawled onto the bed.

She scrambled over the mattress, trying to get far from him. "It's not a lie. Believe me. The baby will be all right. In a couple of days we'll go with you."

He paced, running long fingers through his hair. "What are you doing here anyway? Why aren't you at that birthing clinic you talked about or SF General? How can you pay for a hospital like this?"

"The maternity ward at SF General was full. They moved me here."

"Why didn't you phone me?"

"It . . . it happened so fast. I didn't think I was in labor. I went to emergency because I felt sick, and they told me. How did you find me?"

"You didn't want me to, that's for sure," he growled.

She sat up straight, taking deep breaths and trying to bring some semblance of sanity back to their relationship. "I was going to call as soon as the baby was healthy enough to leave."

"Sure." He leaned toward her. "That's why I had to call all over the city to find you, and couldn't until I remembered that you often told people your name was Jones. Then I figured that if you were using a fake name, you'd probably left the city. On my third call, I found you." With a quick movement, he clutched a handful of her hair, jerking her head close and forcing her to look him in the eye. "Now, why don't I believe that you planned to tell me where you were?"

Tears filled her eyes. "Of course I was going to tell you. Where else would I go?"

He gave a hard tug on her hair, hurting her. "We made a deal. Don't ever forget it. All this makes me very suspicious of you, Hannah."

"I'm not backing out of anything," she cried, desperate for him to leave her alone. "Maybe the baby will be all right tomorrow. Come back then. I'll talk to the doctor about letting him go home."

"Good girl." His voice was low, almost a growl. "Very good girl." Then he put his hand under her chin and tilted her head. He met her lips with his in a soft kiss, a loving kiss, the kind he used to give her when they first dated.

Stunned, aching for the warmth and gentleness from him she'd once adored, she allowed it until she realized what a sick, lying bastard he was and pushed him hard away from her.

He put his hands on his hips and smirked. "You'd better not be lying to me, Hannah. Remember that."

With the unspoken threat hanging in the air, he turned and swaggered from the room.

Angie was sitting up in bed trying to figure out a word for YNNNAGOI when her cell phone rang. She should have been asleep already, but her conversation with Paavo had kept her awake. Once again, she'd turned to crossword puzzles and word jumbles in the newspaper. They helped her clear her mind of other things. They also had a tendency to make her sleepy. She was turning to them more and more these days.

As she reached to answer the late-night phone call, the answer struck: ANNOYING.

"This is Hannah," a soft, timorous woman's voice said.

Hannah? She didn't know any Hannah. Why would someone . . . Then she remembered. Stan's friend. It was twelve-thirty in the morning. Had something happened to the baby? Why call her and not Stan? "Yes?" she said.

"Angie, help me."

Angie tucked Hannah's long brown hair under a blond wig. They were in the women's room near the emergency entrance. Angie had parked her car there, rather than by the main door.

Hannah wore one of Angie's loose-fitting rain-coats. The baby was under it, held by Hannah's right arm while the left one was wrapped in paper towels. From a distance, it would look as if Angie were wheeling out a patient with a broken arm. The broken arm could explain the odd way Hannah sat in order to hold the baby against her.

The head nurse had been unhappy about releasing the baby, but she had no choice when the mother demanded to leave.

"I had no idea you were so clever, Angie," Hannah said as she looked at herself in the mirror.

"That's not all." Angie took out a pair of lightly tinted sunglasses and put them on Hannah. "In the dark, they'll look like they're for distance."

"No one would ever recognize me," Hannah exclaimed.

"That's what you said you needed," Angie replied doubtfully.

"But what about you?" Hannah asked. "You've been to the restaurant. Tyler will recognize you."

Angie could have kicked herself. Here she'd prided herself on her fast thinking ever since getting Hannah's distraught phone call, yet she'd forgotten something so basic. "I know!"

In a supply room, she found a white cotton towel, wrapped it around her head to cover her hair, and pinned it against the nape of her neck.

"Okay, we're all set," Angie said. "But before we leave the hospital, I want you to tell me why you're so afraid of Tyler."

Hannah chewed her bottom lip. "I've told you. He's crazy."

"He didn't appear at all crazy to me, Hannah," Angie said. Something about Hannah bothered her. She wanted to trust the woman, and yet—

"I don't want him to ever touch me or my baby!" Hannah cried.

"My God! You think he might hurt a baby? Why?"

"I can't . . . I don't want to go into that." Hannah pressed her hand to her forehead. "It'll be better for everyone if you don't know." She turned pleading brown eyes on Angie. "He'll be back tomorrow. I've got to leave. Stan offered his apartment. If I could stay there just a day or two, that's all the time I need. No one would find me there. I don't want to go to LA with a baby this young."

When Hannah called, she said she'd contacted Angie because if the baby's father was watching and Stan showed up in a taxi, Tyler would see who she left with. But he would never dream she was leaving in a Mercedes. With Angie, she and the baby would be safe.

Angie had pondered a long time over calling Paavo or Stan about this. The more she thought about it, though, the more she believed that the two women could more easily leave the hospital unnoticed than if either man were with them.

She didn't know if she was doing the right thing or not, but Hannah had convinced her she'd leave the hospital that night with or without help.

Angie hunched over, head bent, and pushed the wheelchair out of the hospital.

Although the parking lot had a number of dif-

ferent exits, they all funneled onto the same road-
way. On that street, Angie noticed someone sitting
in a parked car, a dark, older American car of
some sort.

A shudder went through her as they passed it
on their way out, and despite her better judgment,
she headed toward the freeway faster than the
speed limit allowed.

Paavo was tossing and turning in bed, unable to
sleep as his conversation with Angie at dinner
kept replaying in his head. He lived his life using
logic and reason, and couldn't stand her father's
stubbornness about him. It was both illogical and
unreasonable. In short, it pissed him off.

He threw back the covers and sat up. Sal's
words about taking care of the problem himself
had troubled him all day. Maybe that was why he
dressed, picked up his car keys, and left the house.
For someone logical and reasonable, it was neither, but he drove in the direction of Elizabeth
Schull's apartment.

As he neared her building, he could see, parked
across the street from it, an old red Lincoln that
took up half the block. *Damn!* he thought.

He stopped and pulled into a parking space,
then shut off his headlights. As his eyes adjusted
to the dark, he could see that the Lincoln wasn't
empty. Sitting in it was none other than Sal
Amalfi, watching the apartment. What was he up
to?

Paavo sighed. It was going to be a long night.

* * *

When Stan opened the door to his apartment, the sight of his unexpected visitors vanquished any trace of sleepiness.

Without a word, Angie shoved past him. Hannah, in a blond wig, gave him a wobbly smile and followed with the baby in her arms.

"Hannah?" He gaped. "Why aren't you still in the hospital? Angie—what's going on?"

Angie tossed the complimentary hospital bag with formula and diapers onto the sofa. "It's a long story."

"What's that?" His head swiveled from one woman to the other, and then to the strange paraphernalia on his sofa.

Hannah looked ready to drop.

"You need to lie down." He held her arm to steady her. "The bedroom's this way."

Angie was already ahead of him. While he stood in the doorway, holding Hannah's arm, she found fresh sheets and remade his bed, then pushed a nightstand out of the way and shoved the bed against the wall. "That should do it," she said.

Stan gaped at his rearranged bedroom.

"This is wonderful." Hannah looked at him with adoring eyes. "I don't know how to thank you."

"It . . . it's nothing," he said stoically. "I'll make up the couch for myself."

Angie sent Stan out to find an all-night grocery to buy basic supplies for a baby, while she helped Hannah set up a couple of bottles of formula.

It was near dawn when Hannah, wearing one of

Angie's nightgowns, sank into Stan's bed, exhausted, and Angie headed back to her own apartment.

Stan still hadn't returned from the store.

Chapter 10

As soon as Angie woke up the next morning she was on the phone with Paavo to tell him about her adventurous night with Stan's strange new girlfriend. He warned her to stay away from Hannah and her troubled relationship. Every cop knew that domestic disputes, even if the couple wasn't married, were potentially the most violent and the most dangerous.

Connie was much more interested, and she had news for Angie as well. She'd donated her hot tub clowns and a few other items to the public TV station's week-long annual auction to raise money and pledges, and while at the KQED studio, she learned that the station had gotten a number of the city's biggest restaurants to donate dinners for four. The auction director had planned to have the restaurateurs share the TV camera to promote their restaurants and the event.

As soon as Connie said that, Angie knew it was a disaster waiting to happen. Connie affirmed it, saying jealousy ran rampant, with each owner demanding peak audience time and more minutes on camera than any other owner. The whole concept was threatening to fall apart.

While Connie spoke, Angie thought about the restaurateurs all gathered in one spot—owners of the type of place Serefina would likely choose for a party. She barely had a week and a half left. Maybe she'd gone about this all wrong and needed to talk to the owners themselves.

Just then an idea sprang to mind. It was the answer to her prayers—and maybe KQED's as well.

Paavo got himself a cup of French roast, black, at the South San Francisco Starbucks, then took a seat at the table across from Sal. He'd called him that morning, planning to discuss face-to-face the foolishness of sitting outside Schull's apartment. If she saw him, she'd have a case against him that Johnnie Cochran wouldn't be able to get him out of.

To his amazement, Sal showed up wearing what looked like a doctor's white jacket.

"What's that getup?" Paavo asked.

"When you called this morning," Sal said, "I realized you'd be the perfect foil. Let's go."

"Go? Go where?" Paavo's voice rose. "We need to talk."

"We'll talk in the car."

Sal headed out the door, and Paavo followed, fuming. Now he knew where Angie got her one-track mind.

"Do you want to drive?" Sal asked. "Or shall I call a taxi? I'm not sure of the way, and I don't like driving in strange neighborhoods."

"The way to what?" Paavo asked.

"The Langley Porter Psychiatric Hospital."

After much arguing, which did no good, Paavo decided to drive them himself in hopes of convincing Sal to change his mind. His hope was in vain.

"May as well park in the doctors' parking," Sal said.

Paavo went to the general area. "It's not going to work," he warned.

Both men got out of the car. "Come along and find out," Sal answered, clipping an ID badge to his breast pocket. The badge had his photo and was from San Francisco General, which worked closely with the city's mental health facility. "It's amazing what a little money can buy," he said, patting the badge.

"You'll get caught."

"*Dio!* You're like the Voice of Doom," Sal complained. "The same thing over and over. Relax! You'll be there to arrest me if I do anything wrong. I just want to look at her records. It's not as if I'm going to rob the place!"

"Sal, it's illegal." Paavo said the words as slowly and forcefully as he could.

"So is jaywalking."

He headed for the hospital, Paavo at his side.

"Excuse me, nurse." Sal strode up to the woman at the reception desk. "Where can I find the archived medical records? I need to look up something right away that's a good twenty years old."

She looked him over quizzically. "I'm sorry, but do you belong here?" she asked.

Here we go, Paavo thought.

Sal lifted himself up to his full height, his voice quivering with indignity. "I'm Dr. Salvatore Amalfi. Who do you think I am?" He peered down his nose at her.

"Oh, of course . . . I'm so sorry," the nurse murmured. Then, stronger, "You'll need to go to the basement. Keep to the right when you get off the elevator. It's all the way at the end of the hall."

"Thanks."

Paavo breathed deeply as they took the elevator.

They got a few surprised looks as they passed a couple of orderlies and a doctor and walked through the basement corridor, but no one questioned them.

They went through the file cabinets until they found the one with her records, listed under her original name, Janice Schullmann.

Sal pulled it out and read, Paavo peering over his shoulder.

She'd been engaged to be married, and one week before the wedding, she learned that her fiancé had run off to Reno and eloped with another woman. When he returned, she tried to run him over with her car.

She accepted a stay in the mental hospital, and in return the ex-fiancé didn't press charges.

The diagnosis in layman's terms was "a psychotic episode brought on by extreme jealousy."

"A very scary woman," Paavo murmured.

Sal nodded, his face a little pale.

Hannah padded barefoot into the kitchen, where Stan sat at the table reading the *Chronicle.* Her face was still wan and tired, and she was bundled in a thick terry cloth bathrobe from Angie.

"You're awake," he said, jumping to his feet.

She was already asleep when he finally made it back from the grocery last night, or, more accurately, this morning. He rarely went grocery shopping. Trying to shop for a woman was bad enough, for a baby was impossible. He read labels until his eyes went all bleary and finally a female store clerk took pity on him and helped him out.

He'd slept on the sofa in his clothes, not wanting to disturb her by going into the bedroom to get his pajamas.

"Are you sure you should be up?" he asked as he dashed around the small table and pulled out a chair for her. "Sit, please."

"Thank you, but—"

"Would you like some coffee? Tea?" He darted from the table to the Mr. Coffee on the counter.

"Coffee is fine," she said.

Coffeepot in hand, he looked at her seated at the table. "Oh, a cup." He put down the pot, dashed to the cupboard, pulled out a cup, studied it, put it back, and took out another, finally settling on a third with a matching saucer. He hurried back to the pot and poured, then set it in front of her.

She asked for milk and sugar. He'd bought milk, and found some rock-hard sugar cubes in the back of a cupboard.

"I don't want to put you to any trouble," she said.

"You're no trouble." He sat again, watching her, and pushed his newspaper aside.

She took a sip, then put down the cup. "I'll figure out where to go and what to do soon. I just
never expected . . ."

"It's all right. You're welcome here. Oh! You
must be starving." He jumped up and opened the
refrigerator. "We've got Egg-Os, Jimmy Dean
sausage breakfast"—leaving the door open, he
turned to a cabinet—"instant Quaker Oats, Pop-
Tarts, and I'm not sure what else," he said deject-
edly as he couldn't remember what else he'd
bought. Maybe nothing. "What would you like?"

"I don't know," she said, her head swiveling fast
as he rushed about. "I'm not very hungry."

"Well . . ." He wasn't sure what to do. Was he
supposed to decide for her?

"Just some toast, please," she said finally.

"Toast . . . toast." On top of the dinner plates he
found the long loaf of Wonder bread. Glad he
bought it, he took two slices and was about to drop
them into the toaster when the baby let out a cry.
The bread flew from his hand and onto the floor.

As Hannah left the room, he tossed the
dropped bread into the garbage and put more in
the toaster, then sat again, feeling a bit weary himself. He turned back to his newspaper, unsure
where he'd left off.

She soon returned. "Baby's fine. Took a little of
her bottle and went right back to sleep."

He folded the newspaper shut, then studied her
a moment before saying, "Angie said this is about
the baby's father."

She gripped the cup with both hands. "It's a
long story. Not one that's easy to talk about."

"She said you're afraid of him." The toast popped from the toaster and the sound made him jump as well. He never ate toast—not his own, anyway. He put it on a plate, then found the butter and remembered that he'd even bought some strawberry preserves. Slowly, as he perused his once-neat-and-bare cupboards, the horror that was last night's shopping adventure came back to him. He'd never seen such a huge food bill in his life. "How did he find you? Wasn't the name you gave fake?"

She nodded. "My real name is Polish, or so I've been told. It's pronounced Jan-ick, but spelled D-z-a-n-i-c. Weird, huh? Sometimes it's easier to simply use Jones. It isn't as if I knew any Dzanics anyway. I'm the last one in the whole world, it seems." She paused a moment, as if to quell the somber effect the words had on her. "I'd forgotten that I once told him I sometimes use Jones. If I hadn't been in such a state when we got to the hospital, I might have come up with something more original."

"He called the hospitals?"

She nodded.

"Why? I thought you said he was out of your life. It doesn't sound like it."

"There's nothing between us but hatred."

Her words were so stark, her expression so unhappy and troubled, Stan wasn't sure what to say. Obviously, there was a lot more to the story or she wouldn't be hiding.

"Here's the newspaper," he said, placing it beside her plate.

She shook her head. "My social worker said it's too depressing. She wants to make sure I don't get any more upset"—she used her napkin to wipe her eyes—"than I am. I'm so sorry to be so much trouble. I didn't mean to intrude." Sniffling, she buttered her toast. She didn't touch the preserves.

He stood. "Guess I'll take my shower and get dressed now while you're out here. I didn't want to disturb you earlier."

"You wouldn't have," she said.

He went into the bedroom and quietly got some clean clothes. Whenever the baby made any sound, he froze, not wanting to wake her. Her cry was surprisingly loud. He remembered how red and wrinkled she was the first time he saw her, and now, only thirty-six or so hours later, she looked quite human. It was all very amazing.

Under the shower the hot water beat down on him like needles as he tried to make sense out of all this.

He wasn't the type of man that women and children—or anyone—turned to for help. Having a woman and child show up on his doorstep was more than strange. He'd given Hannah his bed, yet had no idea who she was or what was going on in her life.

He soaped his body, scrubbing hard.

For all he knew, Tyler Marsh was insanely jealous and was loading a shotgun at that very moment. If he found her at the hospital, could he find her here as well?

Why did I let her come here? Stan asked that question over and over as he poured shampoo in his hand and began to lather his hair. She was nothing to him. None of this was his responsibility. He added more shampoo.

A glob of soap bubbles slid down his forehead into his eyes.

Eyes stinging, he groped for a washcloth. Why did this strange woman raise such a sense of responsibility in him? Finally, hair clean, eyes clear, he turned the temperature lever down to cold to clear his head and his emotions.

Chapter 11

After talking to the auction director at KQED, then dropping in on Stan and Hannah to make sure everything was all right over there, Angie went shopping.

Some people might say that was a frivolous thing to do in the midst of her neighbor's predicament and her own questions about her engagement party. But she had good reasons.

She was going to be on television, for one.

And Baby Kaitlyn had none of the things all babies need, for another.

It took her no time to find a Jil Sander plum-colored jacket, a knit scoop-necked blouse, and gold accessories that would look tasteful and elegant on television. She also bought matching plum slacks, even though she'd be seen only from the waist up.

Next, she headed for the baby department at Macy's.

Little girl outfits, even for newborns, were so adorable she couldn't resist buying lots more than she'd expected, as well as receiving blankets and booties. She remembered her sisters extolling the virtues of Target. Once there, she loaded her cart with diapers, formula, bottles, Desitin, baby soap, wipes, plastic sheeting, and whatever it seemed Hannah might need.

Angie saw no choice but to do this. Stan was clueless about babies, and Hannah had confessed she didn't have anything ready. Had she imagined the baby was just a fantasy or what? A mother not preparing for her own child was inconceivable. It only added to her conviction that something very strange was going on.

"Here I am," Angie said as she walked into Stan's apartment with four shopping bags of goodies. Stan was appalled by the mass of equipment, supplies, and clothes dumped on his living room floor. He had no idea such little creatures could need so much stuff. He was even more appalled when she handed him her car keys and sent him down to the garage to get the box that had been wedged into the back seat—a changing table. He'd never heard of such a thing.

Hannah was speechless and teary-eyed as she opened packages filled with adorable baby clothes. When Stan returned carrying the big box, Angie said, "You'll have to put it together so Hannah can use it."

"It's not put together?" he asked.

"Of course not. Just follow the directions."

As Stan puzzled over the nuts, bolts, and myriad pieces of wood and plastic that fell from the box when he opened it, Angie noticed that Hannah was growing increasingly pale. Although she'd been trying to stay up so as not to make Stan think she was a "burden," as she put it, Angie sent her straight to bed.

She then went through Stan's kitchen and made a long list of basics that he still needed to buy—things like eggs, lettuce, salad dressing, fresh vegetables, soups, rice, and pasta. No wonder he was always eating at her house! He had nothing in his cupboards but junk food and packaged mixes. She'd have to explain to him that not everything came ready-made.

When she handed him the grocery list, he gawked at it. "Sanitary napkins?" he asked, his voice strangled. "You don't mean . . . *women's* stuff, do you?"

"Kotex—that kind of thing, you know," she said.

"She needs that *now*?" he cried.

"Right after having a baby, of course!"

"I have to buy it?" His voice was so high it squeaked.

A short time later, while Angie pulled him away from the instructions he was puzzling over to show him where she was putting the baby things she'd bought, the doorbell rang. Stan answered.

"Diaper service," the man said. He was big, burly, and bald, and stood before Stan, his chest pushed out, with two enormous sacks of diapers in one hand and a plastic bucket under his arm. "Where'dya want 'em?"

Stan's mouth dropped and he turned to Angie. "Do I want them?"

"Of course! You can never have too many diapers. Put them by that wall," she instructed the deliveryman. He handed Stan the bucket and did as told.

"Okay," he said, filling out the bill and handing it to Stan as well. "I'll be back next week ta pick up the dirty diapers and give ya clean ones. We'll figure out if you're gettin' too many or too few. See ya next week."

"Next week?" Stan, the bucket still in hand, turned to Angie after the man had gone. "I'm supposed to keep dirty diapers here for a week?"

"She's just a baby," Angie said. "Go put the diaper pail next to the toilet. You simply shake them clean in the toilet, and then put them in the bucket. Some of my sisters liked the disposables, others swore by Di-dee-wash. Now you have a choice."

"Goody," Stan muttered.

When Angie left for her apartment, Stan was still trying to figure out how to put the changing table together. She had no idea brand new motherhood was so tiring, she thought, as she lay down to take a power nap.

She became wide awake, however, when a FedEx deliveryman arrived with a package from the Acme Wedding Supply Company.

She tore it open. A message inside said, "As ordered for engagement party."

When she looked at the contents, she knew it was time for a serious discussion with her mother. Surely she could come up with a simple, nonconfrontational—okay, sneaky—way to find out exactly what Serefina was up to because this had to stop.

Inside the box were one hundred papier-mâché doves—all painted black.

* * *

Hannah was driving him insane! How could she have disappeared this way?

Tyler nearly tore Marin General apart looking for her, as well as the administrator's office. He told them he was the baby's father and demanded information about the child's whereabouts. But since Hannah had left his name off the document, he had nothing to substantiate his claim. The fact that the administrators had to inform him the child was a girl and not a boy, didn't help his credibility any.

Even threats of lawsuits wouldn't get them to open their records to him.

He went to San Francisco General to see what their records showed, only to learn she'd lied about going there.

The little slut had no money for a nice hospital like Marin General. That meant someone was helping her. Who could it be but that slick character she'd been mooning over? The one with the fifty-dollar haircut and casual clothes that cost more than any suit he'd ever owned.

He couldn't remember ever hearing what the guy's name was, but the woman with him shouldn't be so hard to track down—the onetime restaurant reviewer, Angie Amalfi.

"I'd like to speak to you about an acquaintance, Miss Janice Schullmann, who is also known as Elizabeth Schull," Paavo said, showing his badge to a middle-aged woman working nights in the appliance sales department at Sears. "You were listed on a job application as a reference of hers."

"I haven't seen her in years," Lorraine Santiago said.

"This was an old application. Is there someplace private we can talk?"

Santiago told her co-worker she needed five minutes and led Paavo outside. She immediately pulled a pack of cigarettes from her pocket. "What's this about?"

"I've got a complaint about her that I'm investigating," he said.

Santiago lit a cigarette. "Not a man, is it?"

"It is."

"Look, I'm not her friend, all right?" She blew a long stream of smoke. "We hung out together for a little while when we both worked shoes at Mervyn's. She was always falling in love with guys who weren't interested. That's as much as I know."

"You say the men weren't interested, but I've heard she's an attractive, intelligent woman. What was the problem?"

Santiago puffed a couple more times before answering, as if trying to decide how much to tell him. "From what I saw, the guys she picked were always taken. You know, married, or engaged. She'd throw herself at them, calling, practically stalking. Then they'd get mad, and she'd play the victim."

"This has been a pattern, you say?"

"For as long as I hung out with her."

"Was she ever dangerous?" Paavo asked.

Santiago looked wary, and then almost relieved by the question. "It's funny you should ask," she said. "I've always wondered about that myself.

Nothing that can be proved, if that's what you mean. I will say, though, some of the women these men have loved have had weird accidents. And once there was even a fire. I can't say Elizabeth set it, and I hope she didn't, but it was always in the back of my mind." She dropped the half-smoked cigarette and crushed it. "Like I said, I don't see her anymore."

"Why not?"

"She started calling my husband when I wasn't home. Soon after, I found a slow leak in a tire—one that would have probably gone flat when I was out on the freeway at night, and that can be pretty dangerous. Luckily, I noticed the tire looked odd before I left work and went over to the tire center to ask if they thought there was a problem. They found a weird hole in the side—not like a rock or nail might have caused, but one from an ice pick or something sharp, hammered in, then pulled back out. It scared me. I transferred to another department at work, we changed our phone number and sent back all her letters as undeliverable. After a while the letters stopped coming. I always supposed she found someone else to torment."

"Now, remember," Angie told Connie as she drove from Connie's shop to the Athina, "we don't say a word about Stan or Hannah, but we talk to Tyler and try to figure out what the situation is between him and Hannah."

"How interesting," Connie said. "I'm pretty good at figuring out people—their emotions, their deep, dark secrets—so you can count on me,

Angie. Mum's the word. I can't wait to learn something about this bizarre Hannah myself."

After Angie stopped biting her tongue, she had to agree. "She's a mystery, all right. And what's even more curious, I've never seen Stan so quick to offer his help or mine to anyone."

"How long will she stay at his place?" Connie asked.

"I have no idea. Neither does Stan. Not that it matters. He's bewitched."

"All I can say is Stan had better watch out," Connie warned. "If Hannah's had to hide the baby from her father, that must mean he still cares about her and the child. To get between a man and his child isn't smart."

That might have been the case once, Angie thought, but these days it seemed a lot of fathers couldn't care less about their illegitimate children.

They reached the Athina Restaurant.

"You've been eating here?" Connie sounded shocked. They stood on the shabby side street that led to the restaurant and the wharf beyond. The area was bad enough, the outside of the restaurant worse.

"The food is good," Angie said. When they entered, Tyler Marsh was on duty. As soon as she saw him, Angie pinched Connie's arm as a signal that he was "the one." Connie squawked. Angie had been a little too enthusiastic.

Tyler gave them menus and Angie introduced him to her friend.

"How nice to meet you," he said. "I hope you enjoy the restaurant as much as Angie and her fiancé."

"My—" Angie was momentarily confused until

she realized his mistake. "My goodness! You think Stan is my fiancé? We're just friends. Nothing more. My fiancé is a Homicide inspector."

"A Homicide inspector." Marsh took a moment to absorb that. "I see. Very interesting. Maybe we should ask him to look into something here."

"What do you mean?"

"Our kitchen helper hasn't shown up for a couple of days and no one can reach her. We're all doing double duty."

Angie caught Connie's eye. "Do you think something bad has happened to her?"

"The others think so, but I don't." Marsh frowned. "I think she had her baby and took off, that she's planning to live off welfare and not bother to work anymore." With a grimace, he walked away to give them time to study their menus.

"He means Hannah, doesn't he?" Connie whispered.

Marsh abruptly turned and stared at them. It was probably a coincidence, but Angie told Connie to lower her voice even more.

When Marsh came back to take their orders of *bourekia*, meat and vegetables rolled in phyllo, and *spanakopita*, a spinach and egg pie, he began flirting with Connie, who subtly indicated she wasn't interested. To Angie's eye, the fellow wasn't even good-looking.

Still, he was gregarious, with a good sense of humor, and not in the least put off by Connie's rebuff. Angie soon got sucked into their conversation, and even found herself telling him about her upcoming stint on public TV. As they talked, the cook stood in the kitchen doorway, watching and listening.

Tyler then asked if Connie was Stan's girlfriend, and they explained that he was simply Angie's neighbor. He said the cook, Michael Zeno—he then gave a nod toward the fellow in the doorway, who turned and reentered the kitchen—had commented on the way the missing waitress had been caught staring at Stan a few times, and that he'd also seen the two talking out on the dock. He asked if Angie or Connie knew anything about that.

Angie said no, and Connie said nothing until Angie kicked her under the table. She yelped, then murmured, "Me neither."

"Tell me about this waitress." Angie hoped she'd been sly and subtle about inserting Hannah into the conversation. "Is she married? Do you know the baby's father?"

Just then, an attractive woman with black hair and an olive complexion stormed from the kitchen. "You're taking your sweet time!" She glared at Angie and Connie, then grabbed Tyler's arm and spun him toward her. She wasn't a large woman, but she was obviously strong—and very angry. "How long does it take to write down an order? I was talking to you!"

He jerked his arm away. With a quick glance at Angie and Connie, he tried to keep his voice low as he turned her toward the kitchen. "Olympia, I'm working."

"The hell with your work!" she screamed. "I know all about it, and I don't care. I'm tired of your lies."

He took her arm and tried to lead her into the kitchen. "Go inside!"

She shoved him away, causing him to topple backward. A table stopped him, but made a loud, clattering sound as it knocked against the chairs around it. "You can go to hell!" she cried. "I'll see you there. Believe me—*I will see you there*!"

With that, head high, she left the restaurant.

Tyler straightened himself out and walked to Connie and Angie.

"Old girlfriend?" Angie asked, wide-eyed and curious.

"She's the daughter of Eleni Pappas, a waitress here. Have you met Eleni yet?" Tyler asked, clearly trying to slough off the ugly scene. "Very nice woman. Usually works nights. Her daughter is a little . . . emotional."

"She seemed quite smitten with you, for all her harsh words," Angie said, pressing.

"Maybe so. I don't understand women. I never will."

He walked away. Angie never did get her questions about Hannah answered.

Chapter 12

At nine the next morning, while Angie pondered ways to get her mother to tell her about her party, she heard a knock on the door. It was Stan with Kaitlyn. Behind him was a man with a big box on a dolly.

"A crib, Angie?" Stan cried. He was unshaven, with bags under his eyes, and wore a sweatshirt and sweatpants. Baby drool was on the sweatshirt. "I don't have room for a crib. I've got my Bowflex in the bedroom, and that diaper-changing thing I spent all day yesterday putting together."

"Put the Bowflex in the living room," Angie suggested.

"Do you know how big it is? And how crowded my living room is already with baby stuff?"

"The baby needs a crib. That one is beautiful." She'd been out with Paavo the night before and they passed a baby goods store. She went in to pick up a few more things for Kaitlyn, and when she saw the crib, she bought it. "Where's Hannah?"

"Since we were up at four-thirty this morning with Kaitlyn, she's gone back to bed. I should, too, but the baby started fussing, so I picked her up for Hannah to be able to sleep, and then this guy came knocking at the door."

"Can I put this down while you two chitchat?" the deliveryman snarled.

"The crib will have wheels, right?" Angie asked. When the deliveryman nodded, she had him wait while she went to the linen closet and got sheets to protect her carpets, then told him to set it up in her living room, and they'd move it in place later.

Soon the deliveryman was cutting the box open.

"Let's go into the den," Angie said to Stan.

"How about the kitchen? I'm starving. Do you have anything to eat?"

Was he joking? "You bought groceries. Didn't you and Hannah eat?"

"I made us TV dinners last night," he said. "But they weren't very filling."

Angie took the baby from him. Kaitlyn immediately started crying. "What's the matter, sweetheart?" Angie cooed.

"Let me take her," Stan said wearily. As soon as he took the baby back, she quieted. "She started this yesterday. I don't get it." Stan dropped onto a chair, then slid down as if he didn't have the strength to sit upright. "I can't get more than three hours' sleep at a stretch before the baby wakes up, hungry and crying. I had no idea babies were so much work! The days and nights run together. I'm almost as tired as Hannah. I even wished I could go to work, just to get away from all this. So . . . what do you have to eat?"

"Before you worry about food, the baby needs her diaper changed," Angie said.

"I know." Stan rubbed his nose. "Nobody ever

told me babies were such smelly little creatures, either. I didn't want to wake up Hannah, though. I'll just keep her downwind while I eat. Want me to check out the fridge? See what's good in there?"

"You can't leave the baby that way," Angie exclaimed. "You'll need to change her."

He looked stricken. "Me? I've never changed a diaper in my life!"

"Go get one and I'll show you how to do it." With all her sisters' children, she'd had lots of experience.

Knowing he'd get no peace until he complied, he ran back to his apartment. When he returned, Kaitlyn in one arm, a box of Pampers in the other, Angie sent him back for Desitin, baby powder, and baby wipes.

The deliveryman had pieces of the crib spread all over the living room.

"You've seen Hannah do this, haven't you?" Angie asked as she placed a bath towel on the kitchen table.

Stan shook his head. "I've always left the room. There are some things I really don't want to get up close and personal over."

Angie put her hands on her hips. "I can't believe she didn't make you learn."

"Maybe she's not bossy," he murmured under his breath, laying the baby on the towel.

Her head snapped his way. "What did you just say?"

"Maybe she's too *fussy*. I really don't want to do this, Angie."

"Nonsense." Angie pointed out the sticky tabs on the sides.

Using just his thumb and forefingers, he tried to

lift off the Pampers tabs. They were stuck better than Krazy Glue. He pulled, tugged, and finally had to use all fingers and thumbs to grip them firmly and tear them open. Immediately he ran to the sink to wash his hands.

"Stan!" Angie shrieked. "You can't walk away from a baby and leave her on a tabletop like that! Once she learns to roll over, she could kill herself!"

"I'm so sorry." He darted back, his hands dripping. He wiped them on his sweatshirt. Luckily, the newborn hadn't gone anywhere. Gingerly, he lifted off the diaper. "Eeooouuuww!" he howled.

"Oh, for pity's sake!" Angie cried. "It's just baby poop."

"It looks like mashed lima beans!"

"Stop moaning." She handed him a baby wipe.

His mouth dropped. "You don't expect me to . . ."

Angie nodded.

His eyes flitted from Angie to the baby, as if trying to decide which was scarier. He apparently decided it was Angie, because he did as she said, muttering his new favorite expression, "Ee-yew," the entire time.

She helped him slide the clean diaper under the baby and then, in a cloud of baby powder from his overzealous shaking of the can, she told him to fasten it with the tabs while she knotted the plastic bag with the dirty diaper.

"I did it," Stan said. He lifted the baby.

The baby rose. The diaper slid right off her bent legs.

"What's wrong with it?" he cried. "That never happened when Hannah put it on her."

Angie lifted the diaper. The tabs were stuck to

the very edges. It could have fit Baby King Kong. "You've got to tighten it around her," Angie said.

"I thought it came in her size!"

"Try again."

"Uh-oh. Something feels warm." He put the baby back on the table and looked at the front panel and sleeve of his shirt. They were wet. "Oh, my God!" he shrieked.

"What is it?" Angie cried. "Stan, what's wrong? Are you bleeding?"

"It's baby piss." He held his arms straight out.

Kaitlyn began crying. Stan almost did as well. "Now you've upset her," Angie scolded.

With finger and thumb, Stan plucked the wet parts of the shirt from his skin. "I thought she liked me!"

"She's probably hungry, poor kid," Angie murmured, then glared at him. "And embarrassed about her diaper. Go get her a bottle. Hurry!"

He ran back to his apartment. The crib was still in a thousand pieces. He needed Hannah.

Stan returned, panting, with a bottle of formula and wearing yesterday's shirt since it was still in the living room, albeit crumpled, and he didn't want to rummage through his closet or dresser while Hannah was trying to sleep. He might have to think about moving his clothes out of his bedroom.

As soon as he returned, Angie thrust the squalling baby into his arms. Kaitlyn immediately stopped crying once more.

"She just wants you," Angie said, taking the bottle.

"I wish grown women found me half so desirable," he murmured.

"I know what'll help." Angie left the kitchen, soon to return with something that looked like a sling with straps. "I bought this for Hannah, but I think you could use it." She adjusted the straps wide. "It's called a Snugli. Put it on your shoulders, hook it behind your back, and it'll hold the baby against your chest, but leave your arms free."

Stan gaped in horror at the bizarre contraption. "Angie, please tell me you're joking."

At the same time, Rebecca Mayfield slowly cruised Fisherman's Wharf's Jefferson Street, avoiding jaywalking tourists and concentrating on her next action.

Her investigation of the death of Sherlock "Shelly Farms" Farnsworth was going nowhere. She'd managed to account for most of his activities the day he was killed. A couple of people said he'd seemed distracted by something, but when they asked him what it was he refused to answer. They'd wondered if he wasn't looking into something that might become another case for his law firm.

The last anyone saw of him was the evening before his death, on Jefferson, heading toward Aquatic Park. He'd been dead about twelve hours before his body was discovered.

People mentioned him being concerned about a pregnant woman, but no one knew who the woman was or what he found so worrisome about her situation. One man thought he was on his way to see her when he died, but even that fellow had no idea who she was or where she could be found.

To Rebecca, it made no sense to canvass the

wharf looking for pregnant homeless women, but she was desperate enough to consider it.

She kept Paavo informed of her lack of success, and he seemed as puzzled as she was.

Paavo was also in his car, but heading in the opposite direction from Rebecca. He was going to the Stonestown Mall, where Elizabeth Schull managed Amalfi Shoes. He had looked into her credit cards and found nothing of note; in fact, she either lived a sterile life or used cash for everything. Her phone records, however, contained a number of calls to the Amalfi residence and several to Angie's. That worried him.

He decided it was time to check out Schull firsthand, and he braced himself for the mall. He hated malls. Hated being in them, or having anything to do with them.

He also hated department stores and boutiques, truth be told, but he hated malls most of all. He hated the windowless design most of them used that made it impossible to know if it was day or night and which way was east, west, north, or south; the mazelike structure that made it hard to find anything without at least two wrong turns that supposedly would lead to the discovery of new must-see shops; the too-bright lights; the giggling packs of adolescent girls; and the glazed flat expressions of weary shoppers.

He wondered if in some distant future people would excavate these often one- or two-story buildings with their endless corridors and warrenlike small shops and wonder about the strange use they'd been put to, much as we wonder today about the peculiar cliff dwellings of the Anasazi and other Indians in the Southwest.

In the store a young blond salesgirl greeted him with a big smile. "Is Elizabeth Schull in?" he asked.

"She's the manager," the clerk said. "I can help you. We have some great selections in men's shoes. All our Italian leather boots are on sale."

"I need to speak to Miss Schull," he said pointedly.

"Oh." Her face fell. "I'll get her." She disappeared behind a heavy curtain that separated the front of the store from the storage and office areas.

The woman who stepped out to see him was far different than he expected. She appeared to be in her early fifties, tall and statuesque with wide shoulders, hips, and waist, and a hint of a double chin. Her eyes were blue, and her blond hair worn in a dated French twist. Her dress and shoes were black.

She held her hands clasped at her waist, her chin high. He noticed a spark of recognition in her eyes even before he showed her his badge. "Can we talk privately?" he asked.

"Paavo Smith. I'm not surprised." She turned her back on him and headed for the curtained-off area. "Follow me."

A tiny office stood in a corner past rows of shoebox-laden shelves. Windowless, it held a desk, file cabinet, and two chairs.

"Please have a seat, Inspector Smith." She gestured toward the guest chair as she stepped behind the desk and sat. "Congratulations on your engagement."

"Have we met?" he asked, sure they hadn't. He didn't sit.

"Never." Her tone was prim, her voice haughty. "And Sal isn't one to wave your picture under his employee's nose. Do you have any idea how upset he is about your upcoming marriage, Inspector?"

That she made no effort to hide her interest in his and Angie's life was not a good sign. "You've been down this road before, Miss Schull," Paavo said. "You know you need to stop bothering Mr. Amalfi and the rest of his family. You do understand, don't you, Miss Schull? And it is Schull, rather than Schullmann, that you prefer, correct?"

She didn't seem the least bit troubled that he'd found out about her past, and simply folded her hands, peering up at him with a steady gaze. "You have the wrong impression, Inspector Smith. I don't know what Sal told you, but it was obviously not the whole picture."

"There are laws against stalking, Miss Schull."

"And the question is, who's stalking whom?" She leaned back in the chair, a Cheshire cat–like smile touching her lips. "I'm just an employee. What can I possibly do to upset my boss? He, on the other hand, has quite a hold over me. I'm single and close to an age where it's difficult to find work. This job is a good one for me, comfortable. There aren't a lot of openings for experienced shoe store managers out there. So when Sal expressed his . . . interest in me, I couldn't afford to rebuff him."

"I don't believe you, Miss Schull." Paavo looked

at her as if she were beneath contempt. "You've gotten away with it in the past, but you aren't going to any longer. Do you understand what I'm saying to you?" His last question wasn't a threat. He seriously doubted her hold on reality.

"My life is lonely, and Sal is both a wealthy and an attractive man." She held out her wrist and smiled broadly. "He gave me this bracelet."

Paavo had learned enough about fine jewelry around Angie to know a quality gold and diamond bracelet when he saw one. If someone who didn't know Sal were to encounter Elizabeth Schull, she would be easy to believe. But he knew Sal. He couldn't say he liked the man, but Sal hadn't lied to him. Hidden something, yes; lied, no. He ignored the bracelet. "How did you recognize me, Miss Schull?"

She seemed surprised by his question. "Why, I've seen you with Angie, of course."

"And where did you see Angie?"

Still smiling, she stood up. "Those are enough questions for today, Inspector Smith. I have work to do. Maybe we'll have dinner together sometime—you and Angie, me and Sal."

"Where did you see Angie?" he repeated.

"Everywhere, Inspector Smith. I see her everywhere."

Chapter 13

Hannah had just gotten up from bed, wearing a bathrobe, her hair uncombed and tucked behind her ears, as she stumbled sleepily into the living room.

Stan sat on the sofa, the baby nestled in the Snugli.

"I can't believe I slept that long," she said, her gaze lingering on Kaitlyn. "How did you manage?"

"Just fine," he said. "No problem at all."

She put her hand to her chest and looked down at her breasts. "I hate to ask you," she said, "but next time you're at the store, could you look for some nursing pads? Even though I'm not nursing, I seem to be leaking a bit. I understand it's fairly common. . . ."

He felt his stomach flip-flop. Well, if he could buy Kotex and survive, he could do just about anything. "Sure," he said miserably, but then his eyes darted toward the apartment door.

Hannah followed his gaze to a white Jenny Lind–style crib with a bumper of pink clouds and a mobile of nursery rhyme characters.

136

"Stan, what did you do?" she gasped. With her hands to her mouth, she slowly walked over to it as if she half expected it to vanish into thin air. She lightly touched the sides, the top; she tapped the mobile and watched it dance, smoothed the sheets and mattress pad, fingered the blankets, all fresh and new and pretty, then whirled toward him. "It's gorgeous."

"Fit for a princess," Stan said. "It's from Angie. I'll wheel it into the bedroom, soon as I push the Bowflex out of the way." As he gave her Kaitlyn, her hands touched his arms, then her body moved close as she tucked the baby against her breasts. She looked up at him as if he were a knight in shining armor. He didn't remember anyone ever looking at him quite that way before.

He found it unnerving, coughed lightly, and the moment was broken. She turned toward the crib. "I never meant for you to go to so much trouble and expense. I don't know how to thank you. And Angie, too," she said, lightly touching the wood once more.

"It's my pleasure." He called as he rearranged the bedroom to fit the crib. Once all was settled, Hannah placed the baby in it and stepped back, teary-eyed.

"What's wrong?" he asked.

"Nothing. It's just that she looks so pretty there. It's so lovely. No one's ever been this kind to me." She gazed up at him. "Not ever, Stan."

"That's hard to believe," he said. "Did you . . . did you really grow up in foster homes?"

"Ah! You're wondering how many lies I've told you."

"Well . . ."

"That was no lie." His hand was resting on the top rail of the crib, and she placed hers gently atop it.

"Tell me about it," he said.

She leaned against him. "I went from one house to another, looking for someone to love me, and making sure I never found that person by being as obnoxious and as much a troublemaker as I could possibly be."

"You? That's hard to believe," Stan interrupted, his tone soft and soothing.

"Perhaps," she admitted. "It took me years to understand what I was doing, and I'm still not sure I do. Let's just say I was used to people sending me away because they didn't like me, and I didn't like them. But what if I found someone to love, and thought they loved me . . . and then they still sent me away? How could I cope? I was so afraid of that happening, of the rejection I'd feel, that I made sure it never did."

She went on to explain how, at age eighteen, the state stopped paying for her keep. Since her foster parents needed the income, she had to leave their home, her bed was no longer available to her. It never had been "hers," she realized. Nothing ever was.

She worked in Los Angeles a few years—first McDonald's, then a couple of waitressing jobs. Tired of it, getting nowhere, she moved to San Francisco and hooked up with some girls and guys who invited her to sleep on the floor of their flat in the Haight-Ashbury. The job situation, she quickly learned, was a lot worse than in L.A. She wasn't the only one bedding on the floor. Everyone who could contributed a little money toward the rent.

Things went on in that apartment she didn't like to think about, but she managed to stay out of everyone's way. It was a roof over her head, and that was all that mattered.

One day, Hannah was panhandling at Fisherman's Wharf when Gail Leer spotted her. Gail looked at her strangely, and Hannah later learned it was because she reminded Gail so much of her sister. Gail's husband owned the Athina, and she offered Hannah a job.

"It was surely nice of Gail to do all that for you," Stan said.

"She's a good person. I once asked her about it, and she said she and Eugene couldn't have children. If they had, they'd probably have a daughter my age, so I was taking the place of the child that never was. It was a strange thing for her to say, though, because I later learned they'd only been married about twelve years. I guess she was just trying to come up with an excuse for helping me."

Hannah dropped her hands from the crib and moved away from Stan. "I don't know what's come over me, jabbering about myself like this. I'm sorry. I don't mean to be such a bother."

"I'm glad you told me. Look, Kaitlyn's awake," he said. "Look at her smiling at us."

"She can't smile yet, Stan," Hannah said with a laugh as she picked up the baby and held her to her chest.

Unfortunately, as soon as she did that, all Stan

could think about was that her breasts might start to leak, right there in front of him, and the previously tender moment vanished.

"Time for dinner," he said, and stumbled quickly into the kitchen, hoping to clear his head. He never realized women were so . . . drippy.

He found a frozen macaroni and cheese container and plopped it into the microwave at the same time as he dropped some hot dogs into a pot to boil.

Meat, starch, and . . . vegetables! That's what was needed.

He grabbed the head of iceberg lettuce Angie insisted he buy, hacked it into fourths, placed two quarters on plates, and smothered them with Thousand Island dressing. *Chef Emeril, move over!*

He was dishing out the mac and cheese when the doorbell rang. It had to be Angie. He wasn't expecting anyone.

"Can you get that, Hannah?" he called.

"Sure."

He heard a female voice say, "I'm sorry, I thought this was where Stan Bonnette lives."

"It is," Hannah said. "Won't you come in?"

Just then, Stan stepped into the living room, a dinner plate in each hand. He saw Hannah in a robe, the baby in her arms, and Nona Farraday at the door.

Her eyes widened, then narrowed as she gawked at him. "I'm sorry," she said to Hannah. "I've got the *wrong* Stan Bonnette. Good-bye."

Dinners at four of the city's top restaurants were among the "big" prizes to be awarded each night at the public television auction, and it was Angie's job to read the pitch that would get donors to open their wallets wide.

Her voice quivered and her hands shook the first time she read the script aloud for the TV producer. By read number three, however, she was bored and calm. Her pitch would take place before, during, and after three hours of Julia Child reruns.

Before the show began, Angie went in search of the restaurant owners who would be part of the first night's auction.

Two of them she'd met before, but nevertheless, as she spotted each one, she walked up, held out her hand, and announced, "The name is Amalfi, Angie Amalfi." The first time she said it she felt like she was part of a Bond, James Bond movie, but she needed to be sure the owners distinctly heard her name, since she was hoping for a reaction such as, *Oh, my—we're holding your engagement party at our restaurant!*

It didn't happen. Not even when she added, "Have you met my mother, Serefina Amalfi? I believe she mentioned you to me."

They hadn't.

The evening didn't work out the way Angie had wished, but she had two more nights of this. She'd never had beginner's luck anyway, so why expect it now?

For her first appearance, she was given a cue and nervously made the pitch. By the end of the third hour, she was so far beyond being nervous she even ad-libbed and was ready to do more of it when she saw the director scowling at her.

She went back to the script.

When her job was over, she put in a call to Yellow Cab and asked for Peter Leong. He'd picked her up at her apartment to bring her to the studio and when she told him she'd be making the same round trip three nights in a row, he said to ask for him and he'd make sure she was safe.

KQED was located in a small building south of Market Street. Unfortunately, it wasn't in the central SoMa area that was being gentrified and revitalized, nor was it in the eastern area with the Pac Bell baseball stadium and other new office buildings. Instead, it was in the still-decrepit western sector. That was the reason she decided to take a cab instead of driving. The parking lot would be pretty lonely this time of night, and anyone could be lurking in it since public TV's security wasn't top-notch, nor needed to be. Besides that, it wasn't the type of area to leave a Mercedes CL-600, alarms and GPS notwithstanding.

She took the stairs from the studio to the lobby and huddled at the door to the main entrance, looking out the glass doors to the street for her taxi. Before long, she saw headlights. Peter got out of the cab and opened a back door. She hurried to it, glad to see him.

"Did you make a lot of money for public TV?" he asked as he drove.

The auction had gone surprisingly well. As they talked, she learned he'd been driving a cab for over twenty years, ever since his restaurant business bellied up. It had been a lunch spot in the Financial District, but there was so much competition, he couldn't make a go of it. Still, it gave them a lot to talk about. Angie had never wanted to open a restaurant. Too well did she know about the long hours, hard work, and struggle to make a profit. Only if one was very lucky and developed the kind of word-of-mouth that resulted in steady customers could a restaurant make money. If not, the waste of food was phenomenal.

"I don't want to make you nervous," Peter said suddenly, "but is there any reason a car might be following us?"

"What?" She turned and saw a car some distance behind them. "Not that I know of."

"I'm going to turn, just to see what he does," Peter said.

The car turned where they did. The residential streets were quiet this time of night. The coincidence of the only other car out there going in exactly the same direction was worrisome.

He made another left and watched from the rearview mirror. The other car made the left as well. Peter drove another couple of blocks and then made another left.

So did the car following.

"Sometimes taxis are robbed because these punks know we carry cash," Peter said. "Buckle up. I'm going to get rid of whoever it is."

"Go for it," Angie encouraged.

He stepped on the gas and they were off, first racing up the hills to Pacific Heights. From there he turned north onto Fillmore Street, one of the steepest in the city, and bounded downhill. At each intersection the street would level out, and then drop precipitously, causing the cab to become airborne a short while before landing with a thud on the pavement.

Angie wedged herself against the corner, clutching the top of the seat with one hand, the door with the other. Her teeth rattled, and it was all she could do to hold her mouth shut so she didn't bite her tongue.

Peter zigzagged through the Marina where the streets curved, mazelike, and some were only one block long.

Not until he was sure that the car following them was gone did he drive up to Russian Hill and Angie's apartment.

She thanked him, gave a big tip, and then tottered to the safety of her apartment building on shaky legs. The Disneyland attraction, Mr. Toad's Wild Ride, had nothing on Peter.

He drove around, block after block, pounding the dashboard and cursing. That rattletrap of a taxi somehow evaded him this time, but never again.

He pulled into a parking space and cut the engine, then stared up at the night sky, hoping the serenity of the full moon could calm him. There was still plenty of time, he told himself. No need to panic. He'd find her soon enough.

With that thought, he smiled. *Next time*, he told himself. *For sure, next time. . . .*

Chapter 14

"*Madonna mia!*" Serefina cried as Angie stepped out of the dressing room in a pale blue evening gown. The front dipped in a V almost to the waist, and the skirt was short. "Are you crazy, Angelina? There's nothing there!"

"It's fine, Mamma," Angie cried, looking down at herself. "Maybe a little short. And low."

"Exactly." Serefina folded her arms and glared at the offending dress. She was a short, stout woman with black hair pulled straight back into an elaborate bun, and wearing a rayon dress of white and navy diagonal stripes. As she marched around the boutique inspecting the clothes, the stripes pirouetted like a *dans macabre*.

Angie went back into the dressing room and switched to a different pale blue dress with a halter top and ruffles from knee to floor. Serefina's reaction was even more negative.

Next, Angie tried a pale blue dress with a lace bodice and bell skirt. It made her look like a schoolgirl. That one, Serefina liked. Angie didn't,

145

so she moved on to a pale blue bias-cut one-shoulder number that dropped to the floor in a straight skirt.

"Not bad, but why do you choose nothing but light blue?" Serefina asked, sitting now. "It's so drab on you. You look better with warm colors. You know that."

Angie had to admit it was true, but the more she thought about the purple cake, she feared the entire décor might be purple. A soft blue dress would look much better than the yellow Dior she loved.

Besides, her party was now only eight days away. Since she was having no luck finding out anything about it from anyone, she'd come up with this plan.

"Blue is a color that will go well with any décor," she said, then added pointedly, "I don't want to clash with the decorations or the cake, for example. Lots of them are in strong colors these days. Colors like, oh, for example, *purple*."

"Purple?" Serefina looked at her as if she'd grown two heads. "Who uses purple for engagement parties?"

"What? No purple?" Angie was both shocked and relieved. "What about . . . black doves?"

"Are they dead?" Serefina asked, horrified.

Angie's relief was so great she could have waltzed her mother around the boutique. "Well, maybe my yellow dress will be fine after all." She turned back to the dressing room. Serefina followed.

Back in the dressing room, Angie had to wonder: if Serefina wasn't behind the strange phone calls and dove delivery, who was? Her sisters didn't have that warped a sense of humor. No way would Connie or Stan do it. That left—Angie scowled—Nona Farraday!

It had all started after she met Nona at the Fairmont. That rat! That snake in the grass!

"Can we leave now?" Serefina asked. "I'm tired."

"We'll go." Angie started to change to her own clothes. Feelings of relief and revenge filled her, but she didn't want to think about that now. "By the way," she said, "Did Papà say anything to you about his meeting with Paavo last week?"

Serefina gasped. "He met with Paavo?"

Uh-oh. Angie gulped. "I saw them together at Moose's. Paavo won't say why."

Serefina's lips pursed. "Your father's been acting peculiar lately. Now I learn he's sneaking into the city without telling me! He's up to something and I'm going to find out what! You need to help me, Angelina."

Her mother's reaction, her expression, were strange. Angie felt suddenly uncomfortable. She didn't want to know about trouble between her parents. "It's probably nothing. Maybe they just decided to get along, like they said. For the sake of the party."

"Humph!" was Serefina's reply. Angie agreed.

She finished dressing and stood before Serefina in a red and black Donna Karan suit.

Suddenly tears sprang to Serefina's eyes.

"Mamma, what's wrong?" Angie asked, horrified. "Is it about Papà?"

"No. You!" Serefina fished a handkerchief from her black Coach bag.

"Me? What did I do?"

"I remembered when you were just a little girl in frilly dresses. Now you're a sophisticated woman, hawking stuff on television—"

"Hawking?"

"—and soon you'll be a bride." More tears flowed. "My little girl. Soon all my daughters will be married women, with families of their own. You won't need me or your Papà anymore."

Angie was near tears as well. Hands clasped, she moved toward her mother. "We'll always need you, Mamma. How often does Frannie come running back home when she gets mad at Seth?"

"I wouldn't wish a marriage like that on you and Paavo!" Serefina wiped her eyes, dropped the hankie back into her purse, and smoothed her hair. "Marriage does change a person, though. There's a reason it's called settling *down*."

"Mamma, it'll be all right." Angie tried to give her mother a hug.

"Don't be so mushy, Angelina! Of course it will be fine." She brushed her off and took out her compact to check her eye makeup. "Those were tears of joy. Now, before we leave, I saw an Hermès scarf I want to buy."

Angie wondered if she'd ever understand her mother. At least they enjoyed shopping together.

Paavo was beginning to understand Sal Amalfi a lot better, which was why he was certain he should drive by Elizabeth Schull's apartment building on her day off.

Sure enough, just like the other night, Sal's red

Lincoln was parked a few doors from it, as big and ugly as a neon sign flashing STALKER. If Elizabeth ever had any doubt that he was watching her, it had to be gone now.

Paavo parked and walked up to Sal's car, while Sal scowled at him through the window. The passenger door wasn't locked. He opened it and got in. "What do you think you're doing?" he asked.

Sal's eyes narrowed. "I know what I'm doing, but I don't know about you. I'm watching her! I want to follow her to see what she's up to. If she goes near Angelina or Serefina, I'll run her down."

Paavo decided he hadn't heard the threat, but more than ever, he was going to have to keep an eye on Sal. If Angie's father ended up in jail, she'd never forgive him. "Don't you think Schull will recognize your car?" he asked.

"Why should she? I never drive it to the stores. I hire a limo, or let Serefina drive. This car is special. Besides, it's comfortable for surveillance work. You can easily stretch out in it—at least, you can when no one's with you. Why don't you get out of here?"

In the car was a box of Krispy Kreme doughnuts, a thermos of coffee, and an empty Cran-Apple bottle with a screw top. Obviously, Sal had been reading up on how male private eyes do surveillance and had come well prepared.

"What would you do if she tried anything?" Paavo asked, working hard to keep calm and resist the urge to wrap his fingers around the man's scrawny neck and squeeze some sense into him. "You don't dare to confront her."

"I'd call you."

"Well, that's good, at least," Paavo said.

"Not that it would do any good," Sal muttered.

The garage door to Schull's apartment building opened and an old blue Ford Escort pulled out. "It's her!" Sal cried. He handed his coffee cup to Paavo and started the car.

The Escort put-putted down the street, sounding and looking like a lawn mower with a roof over it, and turned at the corner. Sal cranked the ignition and the Lincoln roared to life, but then he checked the rear- and sideview mirrors, pushed the lever into drive, wriggled it to be sure it engaged, put on his turn signal, and slowly eased the behemoth into the street.

Sal drove so slowly Paavo was sure if he got out and walked, he'd have reached the corner long before the car did. Once at the intersection, Sal stopped, slowly and carefully looked both ways, then turned.

At stop signs, Sal not only stopped, but even waited a beat before proceeding. Paavo was ready to shout, *This is California!* Nobody came to full stops here but out-of-state drivers.

Fortunately, Schull's driving wasn't any zippier. The whole thing was like watching a football replay with a slo-mo camera.

Schull turned into the Safeway parking lot. When Sal finally reached it, the Escort was empty.

Sal pulled into a space at some distance from the Escort, yet with easy eye contact, and then took back his coffee cup. Not a drop had spilled. He drove so slowly and steadily Paavo doubted any of it sloshed. Not even going around curves.

"You want a doughnut?" Sal asked.

Paavo's jaw was clamped so tightly it ached. "No, thanks."

They sat and waited, and after about twenty minutes, Schull came out pushing a cart. Driving slowly as ever, Sal followed her back to her house, where she entered the garage.

Sal parked back in the space he'd used earlier and looked at Paavo with disgust. "You do this kind of surveillance work often?" he asked.

"Sometimes," Paavo admitted.

"Your job is sure boring, isn't it?"

Earl White warmly greeted Angie at the Wings of an Angel Restaurant. "Long time no see, Miss Angie."

"Things have been a little . . . hectic," Angie said. After saying good-bye to her mother after their strange series of conversations at the boutique, she decided a glass of wine would be just what the doctor ordered. A glass of strong wine. Fortified, in fact.

He led her to her favorite seat. "I s'pose so, what wit' your engagement party an' all."

"My engagement party, yes." She shuddered. All that *wasn't* happening with it made her a little sick. At least she now could be certain that the cake and doves were nothing to worry about.

"What'll you have?" Earl asked.

"Port."

"No food?"

"I'm not hungry. Tell me, Earl, do you know

anything about the Athina Restaurant down at the wharf? It's just a little place. The owner's name is Eugene Leer."

"Can't say I know it, but I'll ask Vinnie and Butch. Why? You aren't t'inking of making dat your favorite restaurant, are you?"

"Of course not! There's something strange going on there, and I'd love to know what it is."

"Somet'ing strange? Hey, I'd love to know, too. I don't like strange. We gotta keep everyt'ing on da up and up."

Angie nodded and managed to keep a straight face. Earl, Butch, and Vinnie had met at San Quentin while they were all doing time for scams or burglaries. Considering their continuing interest in the shadier side of life despite promises to the contrary, Earl's talk about the "up and up" was more than a little hypocritical.

"Thanks, Earl. I appreciate it," Angie said.

She was halfway through her wine and calming down when her nerves made a U-turn. Nona Farraday stuck her engagement-party-meddling head in the door. "You're here!" she said, marching toward Angie's table. "I was driving down Columbus Avenue and saw your car parked outside. I have to talk to you."

"Speak of the devil. I was just thinking about you. Have a seat," Angie invited, eyes narrow. She supposed Nona had come by to learn how well she was holding up under the strain of a party in shambles. Wouldn't she be disappointed?

Earl came over with a menu, but Nona just wanted a glass of Riesling.

"Don't laugh," Nona said before Angie could get a word in, "but I want to ask about your neighbor."

That wasn't expected. "You mean Stan?"

"What's going on, Angie?" Nona asked peevishly. "*You* told me he was a good guy. I believed you! When he didn't call, I decided he was shy and kindly took the first step. I went to his apartment and it looks like he's got a wife and child! I don't like being played for a sucker. What's with the two-timing bastard?"

How could Nona sound so serious about Stan Bonnette? Maybe this was an act she was pulling to throw Angie off track. "I don't know," Angie said innocently. "Maybe he doesn't like black doves."

"Doves? What are you talking about?" Nona asked.

"Or strippers!" Angie practically spit the word at her.

"Who said she was a stripper?" Nona pressed her fingers to her temples. "I can't take it, Angie! I'm really sick of the men you throw at me. First that bossy Calderon, and now two-timing Stan. Don't you know anyone *decent*?"

Angie couldn't believe what she was hearing. "Are you trying to tell me you don't know about the black doves and purple cake?"

Nona gawked at her. "I'm out of here. The whole world has gone mad."

"Wait. Stan's no two-timer," Angie said, wondering why it was suddenly her job to defend Stan. "He met the woman at a restaurant, the Athina. She was pregnant, needed help, and turned to Stan."

"Help? Bone-crushingly desperate sounds more like it!" Nona sneered. "And what's this Athina business? Are you sure it's a restaurant? I've never heard of it, and I know all the restaurants in town. In my line of work, I have to, you know."

Angie hated it when Nona talked about her job. It was like rubbing salt in a wound. In fact, she was tired of being pushed around, used, lied to, and accused of having worthless friends. "You don't know the Athina?" Her eyes opened wide and shock reverberated in her voice. She might have been wrong about Nona and the engagement party, but she wasn't wrong about Nona in general. "I simply can't believe it!"

Nona's face hardened. "So, are you going to tell me or not?"

"It's the new in-place." Angie lowered her voice as if she were letting Nona in on a deep secret. "Shabby chic. It looks very prepossessing, frankly, but the singles crowd loves it. Which is why I don't go—being *engaged* and all." How she loved using her own brand of salt, so to speak. "But those who aren't attached hang out there. Especially Stan. He says the food is excellent. Apparently, he thinks the kitchen help is, too."

Nona blanched. "She's a *kitchen helper*? I thought she was a customer."

"No." Angie smoothed an eyebrow.

"He dumped me for a dishwasher?" Nona began hyperventilating.

"Finish your wine, Nona," Angie said. "Looks like you need it."

* * *

Melinda Stuart, legal secretary at Mills, Eddington and Farnsworth, stood staunchly over Paavo and Rebecca as they looked through the date books and other recent records of Sherlock Farnsworth III, Esquire. Every so often, a tear trickled out of the far corner of her eye and she wiped it away with a crumpled tissue.

From the records they saw, it was clear Farnsworth had kept up with a variety of aspects of the law, especially tenants' rights.

"Here's something different," Rebecca said after she opened a new file on his computer, "though I don't understand it."

Paavo stood over her shoulder, as did the secretary. "He never mentioned anything to me about that," she said.

It was a list of references to case law studies, and from what they could tell, all had a common theme: smuggling.

Chapter 15

Angie feared she'd have to drag Connie to get her to return to the Athina for dinner. She'd called Paavo at work, hoping he could join her before that evening's TV appearance, but she had no luck reaching him. That was happening a lot lately. When he was working, she didn't like to call his cell phone unless it was an emergency. She'd interrupted him in the middle of an important, delicately balanced interrogation one time too many and didn't want to hear any more lectures about it. Instead, she'd turned to her best friend.

She had to admit that the more she was learning about Hannah, the more curious she grew about her and the restaurant. Besides, the food was excellent. That was when inspiration struck. "You didn't try the baklava last time," Angie said, "but I'll tell you, it's to die for."

Connie decided the restaurant wasn't so bad after all. They discussed their strategy on the drive over. They didn't want to ask questions outright, since Hannah had been afraid of something or someone there and they didn't want anyone to think they knew more than they did. They also agreed not to say a word about Stan or the baby.

Instead, they'd find a friendly face and see what developed.

Rather than the familiar Tyler Marsh or Eugene Leer greeting them, however, the hostess was an older woman with short brown hair, attractively made up.

She showed them to a booth against the wall and soon a waitress they'd never seen before greeted them. Her hair was dyed black and her black-penciled brows were long and sweeping in a classic Greek look. She must be Eleni Pappas, Angie thought, the mother of Tyler's jealous girlfriend, Olympia.

After ordering stuffed artichokes and *pastitsio* for herself, and *moussaka* for Connie, Angie decided it was time to check out the place. She headed for the women's room. A short hall at the back of the restaurant led to it, but when she entered the hall, she opened the first door she came to. It was a closet filled with brooms, mops, and cleaning supplies. Quickly, she shut it.

The bathrooms were farther down the hall. Instead of going toward them, she hurried across the dining room and marched into the kitchen.

People always say not to enter a restaurant's kitchen if you ever want to enjoy a meal in it again. To a degree, that was right. She'd seen worse, but the smell of fish, more than the grease and the generally old pots and pans and appliances that were being used, was the most distasteful.

Michael Zeno turned and scowled at her, cap-

turing her with deep-set hazel eyes. She couldn't
move. "Ah, the little restaurant critic," he said.
"What do you want, to inspect the restaurant's
kitchen now?"

"No. I must have been daydreaming. I'm looking for the women's room. I guess I walked past it."

He strolled toward her, a large man, yet with a
strong, almost animal-like sexuality about him.
Her mouth went dry. "What are you looking for?
Or should I say *whom*? Hannah, perhaps?" His
lips tightened. "I saw her with your friend. Everyone did. She was a good, obedient girl until you
two came along. Now she's gone."

"I'm sorry. I had nothing to do with it."

"If you see her, tell her I want her back. Tell her
Michael will take care of her."

Angie's heart was thumping wildly as she hurried from the kitchen. After a quick trip to the
bathroom to maintain her cover story, as well as to
regain her composure, she returned to Connie.
"Nothing, except Michael Zeno may be on to us
and Hannah. He asked me where she is."

Connie's face went pasty white. "That's what I
was afraid of."

As they ate, another couple walked into the
restaurant. The man was tall and broad-
shouldered, with graying blond hair slicked
straight back off his forehead. The woman with
him was also blond and looked about twenty years
younger.

Eleni grabbed menus. "Welcome," she said,
"right this way." She started toward Angie and
Connie.

"We're not here to eat," the man bellowed. "My name is Lance Vandermeer. This is my wife. I demand to speak to Tyler Marsh."

"I'm sorry, he worked earlier today. He's already gone home," Eleni answered meekly.

The man glanced at the woman at his side, then to Eleni. "You have a young woman working here, I understand. May we see her? Hannah, I believe her name is."

Eleni paled. "She hasn't been here for a few days."

"A few days?" Vandermeer bellowed. "What do you mean? Where is she?"

"I don't know," Eleni answered, nervously backing away. "Let me ask the cook."

"Find out how I can locate her," Vandermeer snapped.

"Yes, sir."

Connie started to speak when Angie shushed her. She was leaning toward the couple, trying to listen, wishing she could move to a table even closer to them.

"She had the baby!" Mrs. Vandermeer said, elation clear in her voice. "I just know it. Lance, isn't it wonderful?"

"Quiet, Frieda." He spoke in low tones. "I don't like this. I don't like this at all."

Michael Zeno came out of the kitchen and eyed the couple, his expression harsh. "Who are you?" he asked fiercely. "What do you want with Hannah?"

Vandermeer glared back at him a moment, then spat out the word, "Nothing." He took his wife's arm and pulled her from the restaurant.

Angie sat and pondered what she'd just heard. Did anything here make sense? Increasingly nervous, she and Connie decided now wasn't the time to question anyone about Hannah or anything else. Their dinner half finished, they left as well.

"Wait!"

Angie turned at the sound and saw the hostess running toward them.

"What's going on with Hannah?" she asked.

"The missing waitress?" Angie asked innocently. Connie stood mute.

"Don't play dumb," the woman countered. "I saw her and your neighbor on the dock. I saw the way she looked at him. I don't know who else she would have gone to."

Angie looked heavenward. What did those two *do* on the dock, for pity's sake? "Who are you?" she demanded.

"Gail Leer. My husband owns Athina. I'm Hannah's friend. Her only friend." Gail looked over her shoulder back toward the restaurant. "Let's walk. Let's cross the street and head away from the wharf."

Angie and Connie followed as she led them down a block. "I'm worried about her," Gail said when they were out of sight of the restaurant. "Her baby is due and I know she doesn't have any money or relatives around. I want to help. I'd planned to tell her that, but before I could, she disappeared."

"She didn't know you wanted to help?" Angie asked.

Gail chewed her bottom lip. "I never put it in so

many words. I guess I thought she understood. Where is she?" She twisted her fingers with agitation. "I was sure she'd gone to your neighbor for help, especially since I saw him here several times. Something about her makes some men want to protect her, take care of her. And, in other cases, to use her." She shut her eyes as if trying to erase some ugly memory. "She's a sweet girl, an innocent, which is hard to believe in this day and age. Where is she?"

"If she's so sweet, innocent, and loved, why would she leave and not tell anyone?" Angie asked. "Especially in her condition. Was she afraid of something? Someone?"

Gail's gaze darted from side to side. "I . . . I don't know. I've asked myself what I could have done to help her."

"If you were a friend, why didn't she go to you for help?" Angie asked. "Me and my neighbor are strangers to her. I don't see a pregnant woman wanting a stranger to help her when she has friends, do you?"

"You think I'm lying about being her friend?" Gail shook her head woefully. "I'm not! I loved her like a daughter! Now, though . . . now she's gone and I don't know where. I've got to find her! She might be in danger."

"Danger from what?" Angie asked.

Gail paused, searching their faces. When she answered, her tone had become stiff and formal. "The baby's due anytime. Without help, it's a dangerous situation."

Angie caught Connie's eye. Even Connie realized Gail was lying.

"She can trust me," Gail pleaded. "You—both of you—can trust me. I wouldn't hurt her. I'd protect her. Please tell me what you know."

"Protect her from what?" Angie asked.

Gail shook her head again. "I don't know," she murmured. "You don't understand."

"Why do you think I know where she is?" Angie asked.

"Because I know Hannah!" With that, her frustration getting the better of her, she spun on her heel and headed back toward the restaurant.

Angie and Connie watched her a moment, then got into Angie's car.

"What are you going to do?" Connie asked. "Something awful is going on at that restaurant. I can feel it."

"That woman worries me," Angie said. "There's a lot she isn't telling us."

Chapter 16

Angie stood by the main entrance to KQED and waited for Peter to pick her up after another night of persuading people to bid for the dinners and pledge their support. He was late. Tonight's cooking extravaganza had been three hours of *Yan Can Cook*. She never wanted to see anyone julienne bamboo shoots again.

Tonight, none of the restaurateurs knew her or her mother. No, that was wrong. One of them remembered a rather negative review she'd once written about him for *Haute Cuisine*. Talk about embarrassing!

She was just about to call the cab company again when the taxi arrived. Someone other than Peter got out and headed for the building. He wore a baseball cap pulled low on his brow, his collar turned up, and dark glasses.

She stuck her head out the door. "Who are you looking for?"

"Angie Amalfi," he said.

"That's me." She didn't like the guy's looks, but

it was late and taxi drivers didn't necessarily dress for the cover of *GQ*. She got into the cab. "Where's Peter? The dispatcher said he was already on his way when I called."

"I think he broke down. I was told to come get you."

She guessed she should expect such things to happen.

The driver started up the cab. "Where to?" he asked.

"You aren't going to drive with those glasses on, are you?"

"The glare," he said.

"Glare? What glare? We're the only ones out here. It's after midnight."

"Where to?" he repeated.

"The corner of Green and Jones."

He nodded and started up.

Something made her uneasy. He put on the radio to KJAZ. John Coltrane played "Soul Eyes."

To her relief, he drove directly to her apartment building and parked. "That's where you live?" he asked.

"Yes."

"Big building. Are you up very high?"

"Yes." She handed him some money and he started to pull out some change.

"Doesn't it make you nervous being in earthquake country and all? Or with terrorists possibly targeting this city? You aren't on the top floor, are you?"

She was, but something made her not want to admit it. "I worry more about crossing the street in heavy traffic." She took out a couple of dollars for his tip and quickly hurried from the cab into her building. The building manager locked the front door this time of night. As soon as she got in, she locked the door behind her.

She hadn't realized how quickly she'd moved or that she'd been holding her breath.

Silly, she told herself. There was no reason to be so nervous around the cabdriver. So he wasn't Peter. So what?

"Angie," Paavo said softly. "Wake up."

She awoke with a start. The morning sun was just beginning to lighten the sky. Paavo stood over her bed. Slightly dazed, she sat up and looked around the bedroom, then at the clock. Seven fifteen. "Paavo? Am I still dreaming?"

He sat down beside her. "No, you're not."

She blinked and tried to shake the sleep from her. "Is something wrong?" As soon as she said the words, they worked like a jolt of adrenaline. Paavo would get first word if there'd been an accident—if something had happened to one of her relatives or friends. "What is it?"

"I just wanted to make sure you were all right," he said. She could see the worry etched on his face. Whatever had caused him to rush over to her apartment this way?

"I'm fine. Why?"

"I called, but then I remembered that you've been turning off the ringer on your phone so that the telemarketers and others don't wake you up. I tried your cell phone, but I guess it's off as well. So I came over. You didn't hear my knock."

"I got in late last night, then had to work two

crosswords and three jumbles before I could fall asleep. Why were you worried?"

"You've been riding with a Yellow Cab driver named Peter Leong, right?"

Her face fell. "Don't tell me something's happened to him? He's a good man."

"He was found this morning two blocks away from KQED-TV. He's alive, but in a coma. Someone bashed in the side of his head. Normally, they would have figured a passenger had robbed him, but the last passenger he dropped off was a little after eleven-thirty. He then spoke to the dispatcher and said he was going to get a cup of coffee and pick you up at twelve-fifteen. You were his last fare."

"Poor man! Is he going to be all right?" she asked.

"The doctors hope that once the swelling goes down, he'll be back to normal. They figure he was hit with a brick or something similar."

"How do you know about this?" she asked, confused. "You're in Homicide. Wait—you didn't even go to work yet, did you? It's too early."

"One of the cops at the scene is a friend. When he heard your name, he called me. We were worried about you. We didn't know if you were in the cab at the time."

Questions filled her.

"No money was taken from Leong's wallet," Paavo continued. "And we aren't sure why he went back to the area near the TV studio. What time did he drop you off at home?"

"Drop me off? He never picked me up. It was someone else," she said.

Paavo stared as if her words made no sense.

She continued to explain. "A taxi driver told me Peter's cab broke down. He said he was told to get me."

"No . . . not according to the dispatcher's records."

In the fog of her sleep, she hadn't put it all together until Paavo said that. If the dispatcher thought Peter was going to pick her up, she hadn't sent a replacement. "Are you suggesting that the man who . . . who drove me home . . . wasn't sent by the Yellow Cab Company? He wasn't a cabdriver?"

Paavo shook his head. "It doesn't make sense, does it?"

"My God! I'm taking a taxi to be *safe*! And now it seems they're even more dangerous than driving myself around!"

"What can you tell me about the person who took you home?" he asked abruptly. She expected that question, but not his next one. "Was it a man or a woman?"

"A man," she replied.

"Are you sure? Absolutely sure?"

He had someone in mind, she realized. "He had a beard—"

"A simple disguise—"

"Plus an Adam's apple and low voice. Why? Who do you think it was?"

"No one. I don't know," he said, lost in thought. "Can you describe him?"

She told him about the dark glasses and KJAZ on the radio, and then remembered how someone had followed her and Peter the night before.

She was suddenly very nervous, as was Paavo. She reached for him. He held her close, kissing and comforting her, but she could feel the tension this had caused him as well.

Neither could imagine what was going on. She had one night left of the KQED auction. That night, Paavo would be her chauffeur.

That morning, he was much more.

"If you're going to stay up all night," Angie's sister Frannie said irritably a few hours later, "you've got to sleep later in the morning. Having you visit and then watching you yawn the whole time I'm talking to you is not only disgusting, it's rude besides."

"I didn't stay up all night, but you'll have to admit that the news I woke up to was more than a little disturbing." All Frannie's talk about yawning made Angie feel the need for a nice long one, replete with a good stretch of the arms. She tried to suppress it.

Frannie looked even more put out as she handed Angie a second cup of coffee. She was just a few years older, but the two sisters couldn't have been more different. Frannie was taller, and since the birth of Seth, Jr., had worked so hard to lose the weight she'd gained that she was almost emaciated. Her hair was tightly permed and worn in ringlets that resembled dreadlocks. Floppy Birkenstocks and smocklike dresses were her clothes of choice. "I'm sure the phony cabdriver was just some kid wanting a joyride or doing some reality playacting. Maybe a gang initiation—"

"Oh, that's encouraging—"

"Who knows? Who cares?" Frannie said. "You're safe. It wasn't about you, no matter what you think."

"I wish I knew what to think," Angie murmured.

"He took you home, didn't he?" Frannie asked. When Angie nodded, she said, "All right, then. Forget it."

Angie would rather forget her sister. The only thing she could figure was that the guy who attacked Peter wanted to be a cabdriver and stole the cab, plus found information about Peter's next fare in the taxi, and that's why he picked her up. If he hadn't, the dispatcher would have known immediately that something had happened to Peter. Made sense, didn't it?

"I didn't really come here to visit—" She had to stop talking as the yawn overtook her.

Frannie scowled. "I know. You're here to find out what I know about your engagement party. Believe me, if I knew anything, I'd tell you. I don't see why you get a big, fancy engagement party. Mamma didn't do all that for mine."

"Your party was everything you said you wanted," Angie exclaimed. "How can you complain?"

"I thought it was, but now it seems lacking in imagination. I wish I'd listened to Mamma more, frankly. She had some good ideas. And my idea of a vegan party with a healthy tofu cake didn't go over nearly as well as I'd imagined."

"That anyone ate it at all was the surprise," Angie said as she sipped the coffee and tried to wake up. "But overall, I thought your party was fine except for when Papà found one of the caterers in the closet with Cousin Richie. They tried to say they were making sandwiches, and Cousin Pia said it was more like rolled pork. Remember that?" Angie began to chuckle, but her laughter quickly died. Could something like that happen at her party?

Frannie scowled. "You don't need to remind me! Anyway, since your party is supposed to be perfect, what kind do you want?"

"I'd like it to be like a fairy tale," Angie answered quickly.

Frannie chortled. "You're so fussy about everything, the only fairy tale that'd work for you would be one about little elves making everything exactly the way you want it. I don't know how Mamma puts up with you."

Angie fumed. "I'm not fussy in the least! In fact, I see myself as Cinderella. After all my toils, I've found my Prince Charming."

"Barf! Yech! Blaaaah!" Frannie screeched, to Angie's complete disgust. "Let's pray Mamma doesn't come up with anything so sappy! Maybe instead she'll remember the party you wanted when you were so madly in love with that boy in middle school. He was Japanese and you ran around the house with a kimono and chopsticks in your hair. At least you didn't go out in public that way. It was the funniest thing I'd ever seen!"

The horrible conversation Angie had had with

her mother about sushi came flowing back at her. No, it couldn't be!

Frannie howled with laughter. It had been a long time since Angie and her sister had a knock-down, drag-out fight—they'd had them all the time when they were growing up—but the old urge to pummel her sister was growing fast.

"I'd better get going," Angie said, standing. "Let's go find the car seat and other baby stuff you said I could borrow."

"We will, but first you've got to tell me all about Stan's girlfriend." Frannie refilled Angie's coffee. "Are you sure it isn't his kid?"

Since her sister was acting more civilized, Angie sat back down and filled Frannie in on all the facts as she knew them. She had to admit, they weren't much. "All I can say is that Stan seems really happy that Hannah and her baby are with him."

"Where's our baby, Lance?" Frieda Vandermeer asked. She stood at the window, looking at the noonday sun over the ocean from her Sea Cliff mansion. "They promised we'd have it by now."

"I'm sure we'll get him—or her—soon." He put his arms around his wife. He couldn't have children and felt like a monster for depriving Frieda of the one thing she wanted more than anything else. Maybe he wasn't a monster, just half a man. The part that should work was fine for sex. But nothing else. Nothing important, at least not to Frieda's way of thinking.

It was strange, loving one's wife this way. So many of the guys he knew had mistresses on the side, or at least flings, one after the other. Not Lance.

He'd never even thought about wandering. Not until Frieda decided, three years ago, that she wanted a child and threw away her pills.

When nothing happened after two years they saw some doctors. That was when he found out about his low sperm count.

Low, hell. It was practically nonexistent. He remembered the old joke where the redneck goes to a doctor and when he gets back home he struts around his wife, chest puffed out, and says "The doc tol' me I was the mos' impo'tent man he ever saw." The problem was that being the one who was so impo'tent wasn't half so funny.

Everything he'd ever wanted was either handed him on a silver platter or there for the taking. Okay, it had caused him problems now and then, but they didn't mean much. Winning Frieda had been the only thing he'd ever had to work hard at. And she was the one thing he was most afraid of losing. He didn't know if he could bear it.

Sometimes, though, his frustration was so bad he thought he should leave her. End the marriage. Find someone who appreciated him for what he was and not as the father of children they'd never have. But he loved her and couldn't go.

It was a cruel torture to them both.

If he left, the maddening part was that he knew how easy it would be for her to forget him, especially once she found a man who could give her what she wanted most.

Despite her disappointment, she swore she

loved him and wanted their marriage to last no matter what. As much as he tried to believed her, he also knew that dissatisfaction with her life grew every day.

He'd thought finding a baby broker had been a gift from the gods, but now it seemed he'd been wrong.

Already he'd paid a deposit of twenty thousand dollars for the kid. Maybe it was foolish on his part, but he'd do anything for Frieda. Money was nothing compared to their marriage and her happiness.

He was going to find out where their baby was. Now. Tonight. He'd already paid for it—girl or boy, they didn't care. No one played him for a sucker and got away with it.

He'd get his child. One way or the other.

He waited, silently watching, wondering when his search would be over.

The apartment building across the street was both tall and quite large. Too large. The kind where neighbors talked to each other and the night doorman would be on the alert. He'd rather not do anything that could cause him to be trapped in there.

Instead, he would wait until she was outside. Take her and run. Everything would be settled, and he could live his life again. No—he could live it better than ever.

A movement in the corner of his eye caught his attention. He stood in a doorway. Small, expensive one- and two-story homes lined the block. Someone was in the next doorway over.

How could that be? No others were watching the building for the same reason as he . . . were they?

No! That would be absurd. He was the only one interested in the place. His nerves were getting the better of him, that's all. Too much had happened already, and yet the most important task remained undone.

The Amalfi woman lived up there. . . .

He felt the stranger's eyes turn his way. He'd been noticed!

Nonchalantly, he turned his collar up, head down, and pulled his car keys from his pocket as if he'd only been hesitating in the doorway to find them. Then, his back to the watcher, he got into his Saturn.

As he drove away from the parking space he glanced in the rearview mirror . . . and nearly ran into a telephone pole.

Chapter 17

Angie was glad when her public TV stint ended. Tonight's three hours of reruns of two chubby British women slathering butter and cream over everything they ate made her a little woozy. Besides that, although two of the evening's four restaurateurs were old friends, not one of them knew of her party. Where in the world had Serefina chosen? It was making her crazy.

Paavo drove her to and from the station, but he didn't spend the night because he had to be in court early the next day to testify. From the time he picked her up, however, he'd acted strangely, and even searched her apartment as if he expected some bogeyman to jump out of the closet. He wouldn't tell her why.

He did tell her that they found Peter Leong's cab parked near a BART station. Whoever took it apparently wore gloves, because the fingerprint tests yielded nothing. So far, they'd reached a dead end. Angie wondered if Paavo was concerned about the fake taxi driver as he checked through her apartment. He said no, but he was obviously worried about something.

When they returned later that evening, he made another sweep through all the rooms. As he left, he told her to lock the door and not open it to any stranger, man or woman, because there'd been some burglaries in the area.

If that had happened, she was sure she'd have heard. As much as she pressed, he wouldn't give her any more information. She put the deadbolt on the door.

Angie finished her last crossword, solved the anagram—NEVER SAY DIE—and was about to shut her bedside lamp when she heard a knock.

She froze, then quietly tiptoed to the door and looked through the peephole.

Stan! And he hadn't given his usual "shave-and-a-haircut" knock, which meant something was desperately wrong. She pulled open the door. He looked like he hadn't slept in days. His clothes were spotted and unironed—he usually used a dry cleaners for everything, even his casual shirts—and he had Kaitlyn in the Snugli around his neck.

"It's Hannah," he said, his eyes hollow. "She went for a walk this afternoon and never came back. I don't know what to do. I'm sick with worry."

Angie couldn't remember ever before hearing Stan talk about being worried about another person, and he usually only got sick from eating too much of other people's cooking. "Okay. Don't panic," she said, on the verge of panicking herself. "I'll be right over."

She was already troubled by Paavo's search of her apartment and the attack on her cabdriver, and now this. They couldn't be connected, could they?

Quickly she dressed, and when she left, she locked the door behind her even though she was only going across the hall. She hated feeling so paranoid.

In Stan's once-meticulous apartment, with the stacks of folded diapers, half-eaten TV dinner trays, unread newspapers, and pieces of the stroller Angie had bought all over the floor, it took a while to find the phone. Once they did, they called hospitals and Central Station, the police precinct for their area. When Hannah wasn't found, they also called the neighboring Northern, Southern and Mission stations.

Stan suggested they use both Hannah Dzanic and Hannah Jones in their inquiries, but nothing turned up under either name.

"Do you think we should try to locate the people at the Athina?" Angie asked, ticking names off on her fingers. "There are the Leers, Tyler Marsh, Michael Zeno, Eleni Pappas, and her crazy daughter Olympia. Maybe she's with one of them."

"I don't think we should let them know she was here or that she's missing," Stan said. "She didn't want them to know she had the baby. I think she was afraid of them—all of them, not just Tyler. Now I'm wondering if she didn't have good reason."

Angie shuddered. "A couple was looking for her when I was at the Athina. The husband was kind of creepy. Their name was . . . Vandermeer? Yes, that's it. Did she ever mention them?"

He shook his head. "Never."

"What about a girlfriend or a relative?"

He quickly told her Hannah's foster home background. "The only person she ever mentioned liking was some homeless guy, Shelly Farms. She also has a social worker—Dianne Randle, I think her name is. Hannah hoped for welfare money to help her get back on her feet. She said she'd never return to the Athina."

"Shelly Farms was murdered," Angie said, her eyes suddenly big and round. "Paavo's working on the case and they haven't found the killer yet."

Stan's stricken expression matched Angie's. "I read about it in the newspaper. So *that's* why his name sounded familiar when she said it. My God—there couldn't be a connection, could there? I mean, she said Shelly Farms was a friend, but nothing more." He turned so pale Angie was afraid he'd pass out.

"Shelly Farms hung out at Fisherman's Wharf," Angie said. "And died not too far from the Athina, according to the papers."

"The problem, whatever it is, is centered at that restaurant," Stan said. "Can you watch Kaitlyn while I borrow your car? Maybe Hannah's there."

"You aren't going to go knocking on the door of a place that might be dangerous, are you?" Angie asked, horrified.

"Of course not. If there's lights and activity, I'll call the police and have them knock."

Angie had ridden with Stan once. There was a reason he didn't have a car—his driving veered between near-stuporous paranoia and doubling for Evel Knievel. And the thought of watching Kaitlyn had her recoiling. Her ears still rang from holding the baby while Stan fixed her a bottle.

"I'll go with you. Two can search better than one."

"You'd do that?" he asked.

"Oh, yes." Angie bundled the baby in warm blankets and a knit bonnet. While Stan put together her diaper bag and bottles, Angie told him about the strange things that had happened to her on the cab rides. They decided there was no way those occurrences were related to Hannah's disappearance. Yet she couldn't help but wonder if it wasn't wishful thinking.

A little after two A.M., Angie turned onto Jefferson Street. She found parking directly across from the narrow side road that led to the Athina, giving them a clear view of the restaurant and the wharf beyond. She'd never found a parking space so close to it before. Now she knew: Want to park near a restaurant on Fisherman's Wharf? Get there before dawn.

The night was chilly. She approached the restaurant. About three steps behind her, trying to keep up, was Stan with Kaitlyn content in the Snugli against his stomach and a huge diaper bag filled with formula, changing paraphernalia, extra clothes, and blankets over his shoulder and hanging down his back.

All the restaurant's lights were out.

Angie stopped, but Stan continued up to the front door and knocked loudly.

"What are you doing?" she cried in a distraught whisper. "You said you wouldn't do that!"

"I said I wouldn't do it if the lights were on, but they aren't," he whispered back. "Maybe Hannah's hiding in there."

"Hiding! What if someone else answers? You're crazy!"

"I'll say you left your wallet somewhere and I'm helping you search for it."

"At three A.M.? With a baby?" She was beside herself.

"You couldn't sleep."

She shivered in the cold night air. "Well, at least that part's true."

When no one answered, he and Angie tried to get inside. The doors and windows were locked tight. Stan tried sliding a credit card like they do in movies, but all he got was a bent American Express.

They returned to Angie's car and waited.

One feeding and two diaper changes later, they saw a boat approach. They left the car and crept toward the wharf, staying close to the buildings. As soon as they had a clear view of the docks, they ducked behind a pile of wood that looked like it'd been lying there since some building was demolished around the time of the big earthquake—the one in 1906, not 1989. Stan brought the diaper bag with him, and as soon as Kaitlyn began to squawk, took out a bottle and stuck it in her mouth. Angie had to admit he'd turned into quite a good little nurse.

From their vantage point, they could see the boat slow down to almost nothing, carried by currents. The engine revved as it was thrown into reverse and then slowly backed toward the dock closest to the Athina. A man stood on the stern and looped a rope over a mooring as they passed it. The boat glided gently back to the ladder that led up to the wharf.

"Maybe it's their daily catch of fish," Stan suggested.

"Isn't this the time of day most fishermen go *out* to fish?" Angie asked.

"I'm the wrong person to ask, Angie."

Angie and Stan watched, expecting to see someone come out with some fish.

Instead, a tall man with curly black hair climbed up the ladder from the boat to the wharf, carrying a strange object.

"Isn't he the cook?" Angie asked.

"That's right—Michael Zeno." Stan squinted, trying to see if anyone else was approaching. "Hannah told me a little about him. Him and one of the waitresses, an older woman named Eleni, are the only things Greek about the place. He was the original owner, but nearly went bankrupt. Eugene Leer bought him out, and kept him on as the cook. I saw him watching Hannah once when I was in the restaurant. The way he looked at her, I think he's in love with her himself."

"He seems a little old for her; in his forties, I'd say. But he is a good-looking man."

"He is?" Stan did a double-take. "I'll never understand women."

How many times had Angie heard that before?

"What in the world is he carrying?" Stan asked.

"It looks like a baby cradle." Angie rubbed her eyes. "Could he be getting it for Kaitlyn? Could Hannah be with him after all?"

"She went to Zeno, then." Stan sounded completely dejected. "She's gone to him."

"Wait!" Angie pointed. Eugene Leer also got off the boat, following Zeno with a similar cradle-type case. "Maybe they aren't cradles at all, but something else."

"What else?" Stan asked.

"Fish carriers?" she suggested.

"I think you know less about fishing than I do."

They waited for nearly an hour. Kaitlyn was again sleeping peacefully, curled against Stan's chest. His neck and shoulders ached from her weight.

Angie ached as well, from crouching low behind the woodpile. Sore, she finally sat on the ground. Her clothes were as ruined as her night's sleep. She shifted, unsuccessfully trying to get comfortable, when she saw a wharf rat looking at her out of one beady black eye. She froze, too scared to even say a word to Stan. Its body was fat, gray, and swollen, its teeth enormous, but the worst was its long, hairless tail.

"Ouch, my leg is stiff," Stan whispered. He started to shift, moving his hand toward the beam where the rat lurked.

"No!" Angie cried, pushing him back.

Stan's arms went around Kaitlyn as he and Angie fell in one direction, while the rat ran in the other.

Stan and Angie clutched each other, expecting Leer and Zeno to swoop down on them at any second.

They didn't.

"You go home," Stan said after a while as he flipped his cell phone to vibrate mode, then took off the Snugli and Kaitlyn and handed them to Angie. "Call me if Hannah comes back. I'm going to stay here and watch."

"Are you sure?" she asked, more than glad to leave. The baby immediately began to fuss.

"I'm sure." He helped her hoist the diaper bag onto her shoulder.

As Angie tottered down the side street to the rat-free safety of her car, carrying the now-crying baby and all her baggage, she realized that for the first time in her life she actually felt sorry for Stan and what he was going through. Would wonders never cease?

Chapter 18

With the baby screaming in the car seat, Angie drove straight to her sister Bianca's house. Bianca was the best person she knew with babies. She handed over Kaitlyn, then went home and collapsed in bed.

The first thing she did when she awoke was phone Paavo. "Are you going to be at your desk for a while?" she asked.

"Yes, why?" he asked.

"I've got a long story to tell."

Although he didn't actually say it, she could hear the *uh-oh* in his voice.

An hour later, she sat at the side of his desk and relayed the story of Hannah's disappearance. She decided it would be best to leave out the part about her and Stan spying on the Athina. It hadn't amounted to anything, and Paavo tended to get testy when she did something he considered potentially dangerous. His attention grew even stronger when she mentioned that Hannah knew Shelly Farms.

"Let's see what I can find out about Hannah

Dzanic." He scanned the arrest and accident records for the past two days to see if a Dzanic, Jones, or anyone matching Hannah's description had been picked up. No one had.

He ran a check against DMV records and found only one Hannah Dzanic in the state. Age twenty-three, brown hair and eyes, five-foot-eight, 120 pounds. Her address was 481 Broadway. "Looks like she was living near the strip clubs," he said, copying down the address.

"Hopefully, she's gone back there for some reason." Angie stood, purse in hand. "Let's go find out."

"That's police work, Angie," Paavo said. "What we find there might be pretty ugly."

Her gaze remained steady. "And your point is?"

Without Angie to talk to, Stan soon decided to sit on the ground . . . then to rest his head back against the wall . . . then to shut his eyes a moment.

He felt the shoulder of his jacket being lifted and woke with a start.

Michael Zeno was pulling him to his feet. "What are you doing back there?"

"Doing? Uh . . . ?"

Zeno grabbed his lapels and pulled Stan nose to nose. "You're spying on us, aren't you?"

"I'm not a spy. I never spy. I was waiting for the restaurant to open. It's a little early, and I guess I fell asleep." Stan was so scared his teeth chattered.

Zeno let him go. "It's Hannah, isn't it? You're looking for her."

"Who?" Stan asked.

"Don't lie. You keep away from her." Zeno

breathed down on Stan. "If I catch you around her again, I'll kill you."

He turned and strode into the restaurant.

Stan sank back against the wall. He knew he couldn't go anywhere until his heart stopped pounding and his knees stopped shaking.

The section of Broadway Street that separated North Beach from Chinatown had a number of run down apartments and rooms over the topless nightclubs that had flourished in the sixties and seventies—places like the Condor, where Carol Doda was the first topless dancer to achieve fame through massive amounts of silicone. The last rumors Paavo had heard about her had the liquid that created her 44-DDs traveling to strange and mysterious places. Today, the clubs were still there, and sleazier than ever.

Paavo escorted Angie past a barker promising "girls like you've never seen them" to get to the main door of Hannah's apartment building.

"No wonder she didn't want to bring her baby here," Angie said. Paavo had been thinking the same thing.

"Don't say a word," he cautioned. "They'll think you're a detective, too"—he looked down at her: petite, not a hair out of place, and dressed in designer clothes—"sort of. Stay back and let me do the talking. All the talking."

"Okay." She looked so wide-eyed and thrilled to be there that he had a sudden ghastly vision of her turning in an application for the police academy.

The main door to the apartments was unlocked.

When they entered, the first thing that hit them was the stench—a mixture of urine, rancid oil, and cooking smells of cheap mutton and fish stew.

They walked up two flights to Apartment 15.

Paavo knocked on the door several times. When no one answered, he began to knock on other doors nearby. Finally, an elderly man peered into the corridor.

Paavo showed his badge as he introduced himself. "I'm looking for Hannah Dzanic. Have you seen her recently?"

"Hannah, you say?" The old man shouted. He wore a stained undershirt and pants that nearly fell off his butt, and smelled like cheap whiskey. "You're looking for Hannah?"

"That's right. Have you seen her?"

"Me? No." He shook so badly he could hardly talk. "Can't say as I have."

"Is there a manager in the building?" Paavo shouted.

"Apartment One. You got any money you can spare?" He held out a thin, quivering palm.

Paavo gave him five bucks. A boozer in as bad shape as this old fellow could die from DTs if he was cut off from alcohol altogether.

"Thanks, mister."

Paavo put his hand on Angie's back and walked closer to her than he ever would if she were another detective. He wondered what he was thinking, bringing her to a place filled with this wreckage of humanity.

He had her stand to the side as he knocked on the manager's door. A middle-aged blonde an-

swered, gave him the once-over, and leaned se-
ductively against the door. Her light cotton
bathrobe was tightly cinched at the waist, and the
front gaped open. "And what can I do for you?"
she asked, her voice sultry.

Angie peeked around Paavo, clearly curious to
see what was attached to a voice like that. The
woman didn't seem to notice her.

"Inspector Smith, SFPD. I'm looking for Hannah Dzanic." He showed his badge. "Are you the
manager here?"

The woman's name was Martha Brass. Paavo
asked her basic identifying questions for his records, then continued. "No one answered Dzanic's
door when I knocked. Apparently she hasn't
shown up for work for a few days."

"Did you try the hospital?" Brass asked. Her
eye caught Angie's, and her hand went to her
neckline, closing the gap a little. "She was due
anytime. Maybe she's there?"

"We've checked. When did you last see her?"

"I can't remember. She worked at some dive
down the wharf. That's all I know."

"Did she come home most nights after work?"

"I don't run a Sunday school here, mister," she
said with an aptly brassy laugh. "But I'll say that
when she first moved in, she was hardly around.
Once she got herself knocked up, she was here
most nights. I've seen that before, let me tell you."

"Did she talk much about the baby's father?" he
asked.

"She never talked to me, period—other than to
pay the rent and complain about the noise when
the people next door got in an argument. Kind of

stuck up, though I don't see why. She had nothing going for her that I could see."

"Any idea where we could find her other friends?"

Angie made a "Mmph" sound. He ignored her.

"She didn't have any other friends that I could tell," Brass said. "Maybe she had the kid and took off. She seemed pretty unhappy most of the time."

Angie tugged at his sleeve. She looked ready to explode. He couldn't take it. "Okay," he told her.

"Did she talk to anyone else in the building?" Angie asked. "She must have been friends with one of the neighbors. Didn't anyone notice she hadn't been home for a few days?"

Brass looked at Paavo. "Is she for real?" Then to Angie. "Miss, this ain't the kind of place where the neighbors hold Tupperware parties, if you get my drift. They probably don't know she's missing, and they sure as hell don't care."

"Oh." Angie shrank back into the woodwork.

"I'd like to make sure she isn't in her apartment," Paavo said. "Maybe she's sick in there. Or worse."

Brass's eyes went round and bulging. "Good God! Let me get my keys."

They followed Brass up the stairs. Angie half expected her to dislocate her hips the way she swung them as she walked, her hands stuffed in her pockets in a way that made the robe cling to her huge, obviously silicone-enhanced breasts. Angie couldn't help but wonder if she hadn't once worked in one of the places below them. Or if she still did. With that body, most of the patrons probably didn't care that her face looked like Father Time.

Martha unlocked the door to Hannah's apartment and stood back, letting Paavo enter first, Angie next.

The apartment was bare except for what probably came with it—a double bed with no headboard, a bureau, sofa, table, and two chairs.

Even seeing the bareness of the place, Angie was still troubled that Hannah had made no provisions for her baby. No baby clothes or furniture, not even diapers or receiving blankets. It wasn't natural. No matter how poor, women had a nesting instinct when pregnant and found a way to provide no matter what it took.

This made no sense at all to her.

"Here's her hairbrush," Martha said, lifting it from the dresser top. "Do you want it? You can pick up DNA from hair, and this has lots of hair in it. I saw that on *CSI*."

"Thanks," Paavo said, his expression strained. "We'll keep it in mind. Hopefully, we won't need it." He handed her a card. "Here's my phone number. If Hannah returns, or you see or hear anything at all about her, give me a call. Anything at all," he repeated.

"I will," she said, reading the card. "Paavo. That's an odd name. What kind of name is it?"

"Odd? I didn't know that," he said, then gave Angie a time-to-get-out-of-here nod.

She saw it but was so busy studying the apartment it didn't register. How could a person live in a place like this? she wondered. It was so sad, so depressing. She'd want to at least put some flowers in it. Or bright curtains. Anything to take away the dinginess, not to mention the stuffy, moldy smell that permeated the room. She wondered if they'd let her open a window.

Paavo nodded at her again.

She nodded back. On the dresser she saw a card for "Dianne Randle, Department of Social Services, City and County of San Francisco." Angie vaguely remembered Stan saying something about Hannah going to county welfare.

If so, would it give Hannah enough money to get her out of this apartment? Maybe Hannah had gone to this Randle for help. Or to find a place to hide, perhaps?

Angie had to believe Hannah would come back—and that Stan could do something to help her. One solution would be for him to marry Hannah and take care of her child. That wasn't such a far-fetched idea. Hannah looked at him with something akin to hero worship, and he was clearly in love with her. In fact, the more Angie thought about it, Hannah would be perfect for Stan.

She'd make him settle down and develop a sense of responsibility. Not only would such a marriage benefit Hannah and Kaitlyn, but Stan as well.

On the other hand, Angie remembered what happened not so long ago when she tried to help Connie with her love life. She shuddered at the memory. Maybe it would be best to stay out of Stan's romantic affairs.

But on yet another hand—had she just come up with three hands?—someone had to do something about Hannah and Kaitlyn. If not Stan, then who?

Speaking of hands, she suddenly felt Paavo's grip her arm. Her feet scarcely touched the ground as he led her out the door.

"Did I miss something?" she asked.

Chapter 19

Paavo and Rebecca reconnoitered in Homicide to talk about Sherlock Farnsworth. Rebecca told him about the goose egg her investigation had become, and he told her about the missing Hannah Dzanic.

Rebecca went back through her notes and read aloud the parts about Farnsworth's concerns about a pregnant woman.

Much as he hated to, Paavo phoned Stan, waking him from a deep sleep, and asked for everything Hannah had ever said about Farnsworth, a.k.a. Shelly Farms.

"All I remember was that he helped her with things like getting her and the baby on welfare, and that she was worried because she hadn't seen him for a few days."

Paavo and Rebecca nodded. "Let's go," Paavo said.

The Athina was nothing like the type of restaurant Angie usually frequented. Paavo was astonished by it.

They interviewed Eugene and Gail Leer, Tyler

Marsh and the cook, Michael Zeno. No one could
tell them anything about Hannah's whereabouts
or Shelly Farms. "I know nothing!" was everyone's favorite line. Tyler wouldn't even admit to
being the baby's father, but fell back on the old
line that he was one of several men Hannah had
been seeing. From the way Angie had described
Hannah, as well as what he'd gleaned from Hannah's landlady, that wasn't very likely.

It was also clear the Athina people were nervous about something, and having two cops in the
restaurant made it worse. They'd be watched.

At the same time, Angie sat in the living room of
the beautiful Marin County home of her second
sister, Caterina. It was in Tiburon and had a mag-
nificent view of the city across the bay.

"Cat" as Caterina currently preferred to be
called, handed her a caramel macchiato latte.
She'd just bought herself a nine-hundred-dollar
espresso machine and was trying out all her favorite coffee shop recipes.

"I don't know what to do," Angie said, eying
the tall drink topped with whipped cream. "My
party's next weekend and everybody's acting so
strangely it's driving me crazy. Paavo and Papà
are pretending to be friends—you know that's a
disaster waiting to happen. Mamma burst into
tears, Frannie's jealous, Connie keeps to herself,
and Stan has forgotten about food and is lovesick
over a woman with a baby who's run out and left
him with the kid. Is the world coming to an
end?"

"Well, I'm sure your party, at least, is under control," Cat said. "You're probably seeing preparty stress in Mamma, Papà, and Paavo. And it's about time Stan thought about something besides his stomach. Things will work out."

"Has Mamma said anything to you about the party?"

"Not a word."

Angie couldn't believe it. Serefina was one of the great talkers of the world. Keeping all this bottled up inside had to be a horrible strain. "Not even where it'll be held? Surely you know."

"I don't." Cat's eyes sparkled. "But even if I did, I wouldn't tell you."

How many times had Angie heard *that* already?

"What does Paavo think about all this?" Cat asked.

"He's more appalled than anything," Angie admitted. "I thought he was okay with it, but he acts strangely whenever I bring up Papà. I wish those two would settle their differences. Did Papà treat all of your fiancés this way?"

"You've always been his favorite," Cat said. "He's more protective of you than the rest of us."

"I don't think so!" Angie cried.

"It's natural. You're the baby. You don't know how much they missed you when you spent that year at the Sorbonne. They cried over every one of your letters, and read them over and over until the paper wore out."

"I didn't know that," Angie admitted.

"It's not something they would have told you. Relax about your party! You're so much like

Mamma, you want to stick your fingers into everything! They want your party to be as lovely and memorable as you do, and it will be. Don't worry."

Angie was dumbfounded. "*I'm* like Mamma?"

Feeling somewhat better after the heart-to-heart with her sister, not to mention the caramel macchiato, Angie set off for a place she'd never been to before: a welfare office.

The waiting room was packed with women and squalling children, and many of the mothers looked like they were children themselves. Most of the youngsters appeared well fed and happy. Some of the mothers were exceedingly well fed, but none seemed happy.

Several glowered at her, and she realized this was not the place to wear an Escada pantsuit with a Gucci bag and shoes. Her handbag alone probably cost close to what these women had to live on for a month. She tucked the offending bag under her arm but then realized they probably thought she was protecting it from them. At that point, she wasn't sure what to do with it.

The line to the front desk was long. It wasn't as if she were there to apply for anything, so she stood off to the side until she caught the eye of an employee in the back. The woman looked stunned to see Angie waving at her and approached.

Angie met her at the end of the front counter. "I need to talk to Dianne Randle," Angie said.

The clerk's head bobbed up and down several times, taking in Angie from head to toe. "Is she your worker?"

"My what?"

"Your social worker. Does she handle your case?"

Angie glanced down at her clothes. She might have to rethink her casual attire. "I have to speak to her about one of her cases. Hannah Dzanic is missing. It's . . . it's a police matter." She half cowered, expecting the wrath of Paavo to swoop down on her for hinting she might have anything to do with the police. She hadn't actually said *she* was with the police, of course, and the woman hadn't asked. Instead, she'd hurried into the back room.

Less than five uncomfortable minutes passed before the woman reappeared and asked Angie to follow her.

Dianne Randle handed the teenage girl sitting at her desk some forms and sent her away, then stood and invited Angie over. The social worker was in her fifties and matronly, with wiry salt-and-pepper hair capping her head. She wore a polyester gray suit, the jacket and skirt looking like one box atop the other. Every so often the jacket would shift and Angie could see a plain white shell under it. A gray and white scarf at the neckline looked more awkward than stylish.

The two shook hands. Randle had one of those enthusiastic I'm-here-to-help-you grips that left Angie's knuckles aching.

"What is this about?" Randle asked as they sat. "Edith told me Hannah is missing."

"That's right." Angie intended to tell Randle everything. "I was wondering if you've heard from her."

Randle's piercing blue eyes studied Angie. "What's your interest in her?"

"I met her and liked her, then she disappeared. I'm afraid something may have happened to her. For one thing, she was genuinely fearful of the baby's father, although she never said why. I was wondering if she came to you for help, or if you have any idea of others she might have gone to."

Randle looked confused, then her jaw tightened. "Edith said . . . didn't you say you're with the police?"

"Me? No. The police are looking into this, but they have no leads, either."

"Where's the baby?" Randle asked.

Angie shifted. "The baby?"

"You said Hannah's missing, but you didn't mention the baby. Where is she?"

Suddenly Angie realized her mistake. If she told this woman that a man who was practically a stranger to Hannah was caring for her child, she'd have Child Protective Services descend on him and take Kaitlyn away. Once Hannah returned—and Angie had to believe she would—she could be charged with child abandonment and ruled an unfit mother. "I'm sorry," Angie said nervously. "Hannah took the child with her."

The way Randle's eyes bored into her, it was all she could do not to drop to her knees and beg forgiveness for lying. She was sure Randle was quite successful at keeping her charges well in line.

"I don't believe I can help you, Miss Amalfi." Randle's firm tone offered no compromise.

Angie stood. It had been a mistake to come here. Randle walked her to the door. The black

Ferragamo pumps she wore surprised Angie. She might not have any taste in suits, but her feet were happy.

With that admittedly strange thought, Angie left.

Chapter 20

The two sat on a bench in the middle of the Stonestown Mall holding newspapers in front of their faces as Elizabeth Schull walked by on the way into a party goods store, Paavo scowling, Sal curious.

When Paavo learned Sal was casing his own store to see what Schull was up to during her lunch break, he decided he'd better get over there, much as he didn't want to.

Schull went first to the food mart section for a cobb salad to go, and now this. They'd simply moved from bench to bench, nose in newspaper the entire time, watching her.

"It's good you have a badge," Sal said as he eyed the party goods store. "You show it to the store owner, and he'll tell us what she bought in there. Then we'll know if it's anything we need to worry about."

"He doesn't have to tell us if he doesn't want to," Paavo pointed out. "There are rules against such things."

"He'll want to," Sal said. "Or else."

Yeah, right, Paavo thought. As if it were that easy.

"Is this like police work?" Sal asked behind the newspaper.

"We rarely do anything like this," Paavo said, wondering about the man's obsession with his job. He shifted the paper to the side, his gaze on the storefront.

"Ever kill anybody?" was Sal's next question.

"Yes." After a moment, Paavo added, "It was terrible."

"I know that Angie saved your life around the time you first met," Sal sat quietly. "I was worried about her, what she had to do, but she was level-headed."

"It was clearly self-defense as well."

"I know. Still . . ." He sighed. "Do you know how much Serefina and I worry about her? She's impulsive. Doesn't always think things through."

"She's also smart and clever," Paavo insisted.

"She always has been. She used to follow me around all the time, more than any of the other girls ever did. I'm not sure why, but for whatever reason, I'm closer to her than the others. Maybe because I spent so much time working when the older girls were growing up, I didn't see them as much. But as my business started to make money, I was able to hire more help and that meant I had time to go to her ballet recitals and listen to her sing in school plays."

Sal chuckled, more to himself than anything. "She was so awful in ballet it was funny. She looked pretty, but when she tried to leap, well, it was more like 'the galumph of the sugar plum fairies.' For school plays, she always got big singing roles because she has a loud voice. It's too bad that she doesn't sing in any key—more like between the cracks."

"I've heard her sing," Paavo said with a smile. "She won't even talk about her ballet lessons."

"How did you two meet?" Sal asked.

"When she put a bomb in her dishwasher. I was sent to investigate." He remembered thinking Angie was a crazy woman—who "drowns" a mail bomb?—except that her bizarre action saved her apartment and her life. And completely changed his.

Sal shook his head. "We were worried then, too."

"So was I."

"You're the man she loves, but I'm her father. You must understand what it's like for me," Sal said. "For any father. For your own father, perhaps."

Paavo glanced at him. "I never knew my father."

"Yes, that's right," Sal murmured, silent a long moment. "Angie told me." He added, "I'm sorry."

Elizabeth walked out with a big cardboard box. Sal and Paavo shifted the newspapers up in front of their faces as she passed by. Paavo prayed she wasn't observant enough to notice that the same two men were reading the exact same newspaper sections wherever she went in the mall.

She left the building and got into her car, Paavo and Sal in hot pursuit.

Actually, it was more like lukewarm pursuit. They followed at a crawl. She drove straight home and into the garage.

"Who does she think she is?" Sal bellowed. "I have to race like Mario Andretti to keep up with her!"

Paavo held his tongue.

"Thank you so much for looking after the baby," Stan said to Bianca as he wrapped Kaitlyn back in the Snugli.

"My pleasure," Bianca replied, rubbing her ears. "I can't get over how she stopped crying as soon as you picked her up. She cried most of the time she was here."

"I don't understand it, either," Stan said, looking dismayed. "Believe me, I wish I did."

"I take it you didn't find the mother yet?" Bianca asked with a glance toward Angie.

"No," Angie answered. "Paavo's helping, but he says we're going to have to wait for some kind of a break. In the meantime, I have no idea what to do."

Bianca's eyes were sad as she gazed at Kaitlyn. "She's a beautiful little girl. I hope her mother is found. I'd hate to think of her going from foster home to foster home."

As Angie gathered the baby bottles, formula, diapers, and such, she could imagine doing this for her own child, hers and Paavo's. Bianca followed. "Don't ever leave that baby with me again," she whispered so Stan wouldn't hear. "She cried all day."

"I was afraid of that," Angie admitted.

"I've never seen anything like it." Bianca just shook her head. "So tell me, how's the engagement party search going? I talked to Frannie and Caterina. They couldn't stop laughing!"

"It's not funny!" Angie cried. "They wouldn't laugh at all if it was their party."

"No, that's for sure. Listen, don't think it'd necessarily be better if it was in your hands. I'll never forget how I wanted everything green—even the cake. Heaven only knows why. I thought it was my favorite color, my 'identity.' Wrong! The party looked like an Irish wake. Mamma had tried to talk me out of it, to her credit, but I wouldn't listen. To this day, I get hives when I see too much green. Then Maria," she said, referring to Angie's third sister, who was on tour with her husband Dominic and his jazz band, "refused to have an engagement party at all, saying they weren't cool. Mamma disagreed, but couldn't get Maria to change her mind. She's regretted it ever since."

"Coolness has its price, I guess," Angie said.

"What I'm trying to say to you," Bianca continued, "is that you never know what will happen, no matter how much you plan—or don't. That goes for marriages, too. So relax, and enjoy the ride. It's a wild one."

"It's breaking and entering!" Paavo shouted.

Soon after arriving home, Schull left again, presumably to return to work. Paavo expected Sal to follow, but he didn't. Instead, he took a large set of keys from his glove compartment and got out of the car.

"Keep your voice down!" Sal said as he walked toward Schull's apartment building. "It's not breaking and entering because I'm her landlord.

I've got a key, see?" He lifted it. "I'm going to find out what was in the big box she bought. I want to know what she's hiding in there."

"You can't break into her apartment!" Paavo said firmly. "I'm sorry, but that's just going too far. I won't allow it. Tenants have rights."

"I walk into my tenants' apartments all the time." Sal waved his hand dismissively. "Before they move in, I tell them I do that to check on or repair any the equipment that comes with the apartment—the heat, gas, electricity, what have you. That's what I'm doing now. Checking to make sure the heat supply is adequate. It's been cold lately. Haven't you noticed?"

Sal took out his key and entered the building. Paavo followed him up to the apartment.

"What if she walks in while we're here?" Paavo asked.

"She's at work. Relax or leave. You're making me nervous. I didn't know cops were such nervous Nellies."

"Only the ones who are breaking and entering," Paavo said under his breath.

The first thing he noticed was that the apartment was sterile to a fault, looking as if no one lived there. The few pieces of furniture were lined up against the walls. Nothing was out of place, and tabletops and even the hardwood floors appeared so clean, waxed, and shiny they all but squeaked.

"She is a good tenant, as you can see," Sal said.

"Did she live in the apartment before she came to work for you?" Paavo asked. He quickly surveyed the room for any of the spy equipment that was available off the Internet. They looked like radios, smoke detectors, and the like, but contained hidden cameras and videotape. In his experience, paranoid and troubled people like Schull often used them.

"She did, then she was downsized from her job at a bank when there was a merger and said she'd have to move if she couldn't find work. She had shoe experience, so I offered her a job as a clerk, and that was that. She did well, and now, thanks to rent control, she gets this beautiful apartment for a song." Sal frowned. "That's the downside. But if she ever does move, I won't have to do a thing to the place other than touch up the paint on the walls."

Sal gasped, hand to his chest.

Paavo froze. "Your heart?"

"No. I forgot to lock my car! What if someone steals it?"

Not many car thieves have such a sense of humor, Paavo thought, trying to calm himself after the fright Sal gave him. He headed for the door. "You're right to worry. Let's go."

"On second thought, this is a safe neighborhood." Sal started to open drawers. "It should be fine for a little while. Let's see what we can find."

We? Paavo watched anxiously. What if she came back? How would he explain his presence, even if she believed Sal? If she went to his boss, he'd be in so much trouble, he'd be busted back to patrol. Midnight shift.

That'd make his father-in-law-to-be feel even more warm fuzzies about him. He hadn't spotted any surveillance equipment, and so he slipped the chain lock in place. At least with it, if Schull decided to come back they'd hear the chain rattle and have time to duck out the back way.

As Sal went through the living room and kitchen, Paavo methodically made sure everything was put back the way it had been so it would appear as undisturbed as possible. If they were going to do this, they should at least do it right.

As Sal went through a kitchen drawer filled with recipes and coupons, Paavo said, "You know, most people who hide things put them in their bedroom. Especially in their underwear drawer."

Sal tossed aside the papers. "Is that so? Makes sense. Let's go."

Before following, Paavo quickly put the materials back the way they'd been.

The bedroom was even starker than the living room. It had one twin-sized bed, a chair, and a narrow single dresser. The bed was covered with a white sheet, white pillowcase, and white blanket folded at the foot. Nothing more. It felt eerie.

Sal was rummaging through the underwear drawer when Paavo turned to the closet. "You seem to know a lot about this kind of thing," Sal said.

"Cops and criminals learn to think like each other."

"So, you'd make a good criminal," Sal mused.

A moment passed before Paavo answered. "You could say that."

Very few clothes were hanging, and they were all either white or black. She had three pairs of black shoes with various-sized heels. In the back of the closet, he found the party goods box.

"She's not a good advertisement for my shoes," Sal said sadly. With Paavo's find, he left the oversized bras and enormous cotton briefs in a jumble.

"Or anything else," Paavo murmured, glancing at the drawer and not relishing the thought that he'd be the one to make it neat again.

"She always looks nice, though. And always matches," Sal added.

The box was so light that Paavo was afraid it was empty. Inside, under reams of tissue paper, he found a wedding cake topper of a man and a woman standing under a bower of flowers.

This one had obviously been customized according to Schull's directions. The man wore a tuxedo. He was thin; his hair was gray and he had a little gray mustache. The woman was a bit heavier, very busty, with blond hair pulled back into what could easily be a French twist. She wore a full-length formal gown. The strangest part, though—the part that caused a chill down Paavo's spine—was that the wedding dress was black.

Chapter 21

Paavo was shown to Dianne Randle's desk at Social Services. She stood, frowning. "Are you really with the police this time?"

"Excuse me?" he said, stating his name as he showed his badge.

"Okay, at least you sound legit," Randle said. "Have a seat. This is about Hannah Dzanic missing, I take it."

"You know about that?"

"Some woman came here quizzing me about her. I somehow got the impression she was with the police. She was a pretty little thing, brown eyes, red highlights in her hair. Great clothes."

Paavo blanched. "Yes, well, I think you can ignore her inquiries. I'd like to ask a few questions about Shelly Farms. It seems he was concerned about Miss Dzanic. Did he ever talk to you about her?"

"Not specifically," Randle said. "I've worked with Shelly in the past—it's so sad about him— and I usually got the referrals he sent over, just like

I took on Hannah. Why? Do you think she could have had something to do with his murder? Is that why she's missing?"

"Why did Farms send Hannah here to see you?" Paavo asked.

Randle shrugged. "Same old thing. She got pregnant and her boyfriend didn't want to get married. That place she worked paid her so little it's criminal. I set her up for aid. Nothing else."

"What about Marsh? Why was she afraid of him? Did she tell you or Shelly?"

Randle shook her head. "She never said anything specific to me. I thought she just got upset about the way he disappointed her. Maybe she said more to Shelly, but as I told you, I never talked to him about her."

Paavo soon left. He didn't find out much from Randle, other than that Angie was going around pretending to be someone she wasn't. He phoned to discuss this with her, but as soon as she heard his voice, she burst into tears.

"What is it?" he asked, worried. "It's not Hannah, is it?" When her sobs grew louder, he added, "Or Stan? The baby?"

She sniffled and snuffled and finally cried, "It's our party."

Relieved, though he'd never tell her that, he tried to calm her. "Don't cry, Angel. It's nothing we can't fix, I'm sure. Take a deep breath and tell me what happened."

"I was out with Connie and when I got home, I walked into my apartment and there on the coffee table were a man and a woman—"

"*What?*" he yelled.

"Not real! A wedding cake topper. Only . . . only the bride wore black! Do you know what a bad sign that is? Do you know how horrible that is? What an ugly, terrible omen? I can't stand it! Somebody hates me; hates us. I don't know what to do, Paavo!"

"I'll be right there."

"No . . . you're busy. I'll be all right. I feel better just hearing your voice. Besides, I've got to go see how Stan is doing. He's upset about Hannah."

"Keep the figurine. I want to see it."

"I smashed it up, then shoved it down the garbage disposal. I'm sorry; I just wasn't thinking, just upset. This was supposed to be such a happy time for me—for us—and it's all going to hell!"

"For me, Angie, it *is* the happiest time of my life," he said gently. "An ugly figurine isn't enough to ruin it. I love you."

"Oh, Paavo . . ." Her voice caught and she excused herself a moment. He could hear her blowing her nose. "Your words make me feel foolish for crying over something so trivial—and make me want to cry more because you're so understanding. I love you, too, more than you'll ever know."

As soon as Paavo hung up he called Sal. "Where can we meet that Serefina won't see us? We've got to do something. Schull has just gone too far."

"How did she get into Angie's apartment?" Paavo demanded, still furious about how badly Schull upset the woman he planned to marry. "Does she have a key to it?"

"Of course not!" Sal looked squeamish. "Of

course, I have keys to all my tenant's places, as I told you. Angie's I keep on my key chain."

"Could Schull have gotten hold of it?"

Sal shrugged. "I guess, a time or two, I may have left my keys lying about on a desk or table while at the store. In fact"—his eyes widened—"I remember one time, I couldn't find them, and she found them for me. She could have taken them, made some copies. She could have my house key as well!"

Paavo was in the library of the Amalfi home, one of the many mansions in Hillsborough. It looked like a Mediterranean villa. Serefina was out for the evening.

Paavo handed Sal the note he'd found taped to Angie's apartment door the night he went to pick her up and take her to KQED. Encased in a plastic sleeve, it was in Schull's handwriting and threatened a 'big surprise' at the engagement party.

"So now the threat's in writing." Sal rubbed his hands together. "You can arrest her."

"Not for a threat."

"I'll kill her!" Sal exploded.

"Don't even joke about it!" Paavo warned.

"Who's joking?"

Paavo drew in his breath. He talked again about the need to tell Angie and Serefina what was going on. With each step, Schull seemed to have grown bolder. If she was going inside Angie's apartment, who knew what she might try next?

"And if Serefina learns about it," Sal said warily, "who knows what might happen to Schull?"

Paavo's brows crossed. "Serefina wouldn't hurt her."

"No." Sal shut his eyes a moment as if debating just how much he should tell Paavo. Finally, he said, "She wouldn't, but she's got lots of relatives—brothers, uncles, cousins—who don't like to see her unhappy. And this would make her *very* unhappy."

Paavo had heard about some of Serefina's colorful relatives from Angie. They weren't exactly criminals; they simply knew how to get things done. How to get . . . anything done. And woe betide anyone who stood in their way, or who threatened a loved one like Serefina or Angie.

Paavo had once had some dealings with Angie's Cousin Richie, who was bad enough—and he was on Sal's side of the family.

"I see," Paavo said.

"Good."

"It's up to us, then," he added.

"That's what I been trying to tell you!"

Paavo's mouth tightened. "We've got to come up with something fast. I won't put up with her making Angie cry again."

"Well, that's a change," Sal said bitterly.

"What's that supposed to mean?" Paavo asked.

"You know what I mean."

"Look," Paavo said, finally and completely exasperated, "I don't care if you don't like me, but just what is it that you object to so much?"

"Did I ever say I objected?"

"You didn't have to." Paavo grimaced. "You show it with every word you say, every gesture. You're just going to have to get used to me, Sal, because I'm not going away."

"Look at it this way," Sal said, eying him fiercely. "If you were me, would you want your daughter to marry you?"

"I'll be good to her."

"If you don't break her heart," Sal shouted. "You know about cops' marriages. Between divorce, getting killed in the line of duty, and trouble with alcohol, the future isn't pretty. My Angelina is a happy, sunny person. She's special and always has been. I don't want you to be the cause of her changing!"

Paavo's brows knitted. So that was it. "Troubled marriages are found everywhere in today's society," he said. "And I don't drink, so you don't have to worry about that. Most of those divorces are between people who married young, which I'm not, and I've learned from my job that death can strike anyone, anytime."

"But your job is more dangerous than most, for cryin' out loud! Why can't you be a shoe salesman, like me? Don't you worry about it? Not only for yourself, but what it would do to her."

"I worry about it every day," Paavo said quietly. He peered at Sal a moment, and then decided to tell a story. "I once knew a woman who was a health fanatic. She never ate fat, avoided red meat, desserts, cigarettes, and alcohol. She left the city because there was too much crime here, and went to a small, safe town. She exercised every day, and would never travel by airplane, go out late at night, or go anywhere or do anything that might put her in the slightest danger."

Sal nodded.

"One day, she was jogging down a safe street in the quiet town, waving to neighbors who knew her and watched out for her, having come up with a careful route with little traffic so she didn't even have to worry about errant drivers. As she passed under an oak tree, a limb—at the very moment she was under it—broke off, fell, and landed directly on the top of her head, killing her instantly."

Sal frowned.

"Shit happens to lots of people," Paavo said. "And I've known many retired cops who've died in their beds from old age."

Sal harrumphed.

"Believe me when I say I understand exactly how you feel," Paavo added. "I felt that way, too, at first. Even though I fell head over heels for your daughter, I didn't think we were right for each other and tried to stay away. It didn't work. It couldn't. Now I can't imagine trying to live without her in my life. She makes me feel alive, brings light where there wasn't any before. I can't really explain it. . . ."

"You're doing all right," Sal said morosely, rubbing his chin. "So, you tried to get rid of her?"

"Ask her," Paavo said. "I tried—but I'll admit I'm glad I failed."

"She's a lot like her mother, you know," Sal said.

"I know." Paavo tried his best to say that with no inflection.

"I'll think about it," Sal said, his mouth forming a slight pout. "For now let's talk about Schull."

The two put their heads together and eventually came up with a plan which involved making it clear to Schull, who Sal was sure was watching him, that Serefina would be out of the house, and Sal would be in it alone.

Paavo stood. "I'll get going. Good plan."

"I agree." Sal stuck out his hand to Paavo and they shook. "The women will never know."

"Never know what?"

The two jumped at the sound of Serefina's voice, dropped their hands, and stepped away from each other.

"What are you doing home?" Sal asked.

Serefina studied them suspiciously. "*Dio!* Such a night! The woman whose house we were at had this terrible cold, coughing and sneezing over everything. We couldn't eat anything she served. I felt such hunger I had to leave early. So . . . what's going on? Is Angie here?"

"No." Paavo wracked his brain. "We were just talking about her. About the engagement party."

Serefina looked surprised. "Oh . . . ?"

"Gifts, you know."

Her eyebrows lifted. "Gifts?"

Both men looked a little sick as they stiffly linked arms. "Why not?" Sal said. "We're *compagni*. We want everything to be beautiful for our Angelina."

"That's right," Paavo said, grimacing. It was bad enough he had to lie to Angie, now he even had to lie to Serefina.

Serefina scrutinized the sickly angelic expressions the two men wore. "*Bene!* It's about time. So, maybe you two can help me." She walked to the desk and pulled out a picture of an enormous cake with white icing and silver roses. "I picked out this, but her dress is yellow, and then I saw this." She showed them a second photo, of a similar cake but in multiple hues of yellow. "What do you think? Will Angie like this one or that one?"

Paavo and Sal walked closer to the display.

"I don't know," Sal said.

"Me neither," Paavo replied. "But probably the yellow." He couldn't help but wince as he said it. This was another thing he was going to have to keep from Angie.

Chapter 22

"Aren't you tired of this yet? Tell me where she is and you'll be out of here. I'm tired of your lies, Hannah. You lie about everything, even the sex of our child. *Where is she?*"

Hannah watched the man she once loved more than life itself pace back and forth in the dark, musty cellar. And now she knew he could easily kill her.

The basement reeked of fish. It had to be near Fisherman's Wharf, but exactly where, she had no idea. The wharf was covered with small, dilapidated buildings that no one used ever since the tourist trade became more profitable than fish canning.

She sat on the concrete floor, her wrists and ankles tied with duct tape, but he'd left her mouth uncovered so that she could answer his questions. Her only answer was a simple but quiet, "No."

Tyler's eyes were filled with hate and rage. He rubbed his fist, and she wondered if next he was going to hit her. "There's no reason for you to be so stubborn," he ranted. "You can't keep her. You can't even take care of yourself, let alone a baby. I know it, and so do you."

"I can and I will," she said, her voice still strong even though she was hungry and exhausted by the ordeal. "What's wrong with you? How can you do this to me?"

"I'm trying to help the baby. *Our baby*," he said.

"If you think reminding me will make me feel any better about you, you're wrong! It only makes me despise you that much more!" He raised his fist and she flinched, eyes shut, waiting for the blow.

"You're making me crazy, Hannah!" he yelled, lowering his arm. "The Vandermeers are good people, a warm, loving couple. They're filthy rich. They have a huge house. They can give a child everything she could ever want, plus lots of love. They're already talking as if they love her. They wait to name her Morgan. Classy name, isn't it?"

"Morgan? It sounds like a horse," Hannah said bitterly.

"Think of the child." He got down on his knees in front of her. "They want her, and the possibility of getting a healthy white baby from this country means a lot to them."

"So much they'd pay big bucks for her. That's what you said, Ty," she cried. "I still can't believe you want to sell our daughter."

"Vandermeer has already put up a huge deposit. We can't risk his anger."

"What will he do?" she asked, disgusted. "Go to the police?"

"Be reasonable," he pleaded. "You were willing

to give her away to an adoption agency. Why not make some money while we're at it?"

"An adoption agency would screen the parents. They have rules. But none of it matters. I told you I changed my mind. I'm keeping her."

"You can't change it, Hannah. It's too late."

"Leave me alone!" she screamed.

"I'll leave you, all right," he said, but couldn't resist one last shot. "If you loved your child, you'd want her to go to the Vandermeers. They can give her more than you. That's what being a loving mother is all about. You know it, too. You know I'm right."

Hannah couldn't stop the tears from rolling down her cheeks. A part of her agreed with everything he said, damn him! Why did she listen to him? Why did she let his words curl into her heart and confuse her? "I can't give her up, damn you. She's my baby! She's my life!"

"Stop blubbering and listen to me!" He grabbed her shoulders. "I want that baby. You thought you could hide her from me. You lied and lied, 'Yes, Ty, whatever you say, Ty,' then as soon as you got the chance, you ran off with some rich dude, making everyone think I can't keep my end of a deal. You aren't going to leave me holding the bag, Hannah. It's not going to happen."

Her body went rigid. "What do you mean, *everyone*? Who else knows about this?"

He let go of her. "You're such a fool, Hannah. Such a naïve, romantic, unobservant little fool."

Nona Farraday walked inside the Athina and almost turned right around again. It wasn't the kind of place she reviewed, and it certainly wasn't the hot spot Angie had said it was. The best thing she could say was it appeared to be clean.

A blond-haired waiter came out of the kitchen and greeted her. She felt his eyes take her in, and when he smiled appreciatively, she decided to give the place a chance.

She ordered *taramosalata* canapés to start, chickpea soup, beet salad, *moussaka*, veal in lemon-wine sauce, and *smyra* meatballs. Normally, she went to restaurants with friends and sampled their dishes so she didn't seem quite so piggish, but she couldn't ask anyone to a place of this low caliber. That meant she'd have to try several dishes and desserts herself, odd though it might seem. Not that she cared what the help here thought, anyway.

She'd already determined she wouldn't like the food. It was Stan's favorite restaurant, and obviously his taste was bad. In everything.

The food, to her dismay, was surprisingly good. She was basking in desserts—fried *loukoumades* with honey, custard-filled *svingi*, and an almond *kataife* roll, when a dark, magnetic individual presented her with Greek coffee and a glass of ouzo over ice. She gawked and decided she might develop quite an appetite for baklava—something she'd never known a Greek restaurant to run out of.

"I'm Michael Zeno, the cook," he said, his voice deep. "I had to see the woman who orders so much food, only to send most of it back to the kitchen."

She shifted nervously. "I wasn't sure what I'd

like—and I was in the mood for variety. Is there a problem? I'm paying for it."

"Did you like it?" He seemed to be glowering at her. Was it so bad not to clean one's plate here?

"It was . . . quite good, actually," she replied.

"Why are you here?" he asked bluntly.

She put down her fork. "Now that I've finished, I can tell you. I'm a critic for *Haute Cuisine*."

He eyed her harshly. "Sure. All of a sudden this place is crawling with food critics. Where were all of you when I needed you?" He walked away.

She was puzzled and gulped down the ouzo. Time to leave.

To her surprise, the blond waiter came by not with the check, but with a whole bottle of ouzo. He sat down across from her, poured himself a glass, then refilled hers, the ice in her glass turning the ouzo milky white. "Don't let Zeno bother you. He's a gruff sort."

"It's not a way to win customers." She was still smarting.

"I heard you're a restaurant reviewer," he said with a smile. "Is it true?"

She eyed him and the liqueur. Both looked scrumptious. "Yes."

"Since you're my last customer," he continued, "I thought you might have some questions about the restaurant before you leave. Anything I can help you with?" He held out his glass to her. "*Yasas!*"

She clinked her glass to his. "*Yasas!* This is strong stuff." She took a sip, then put down the glass. "I don't think I should have any more."

"Think of it as flavored wine, that's all," he said. "Don't worry. I'll see that you get home safely."

She liked the sound of that. "I thought ouzo was like vodka."

He sniffed his glass. "Notice the subtle anise aroma. What vodka has that?"

She sniffed her glass. "It does smell good, doesn't it?" She drank some, then a lot more as Tyler regaled her with stories about the restaurant from the days when Michael Zeno first opened it, how fresh fish was brought from the boats out on the dock into the restaurant, and how people would line up to eat here. Mostly, they were people who worked in the area, and they knew the Athina's food was fresh, cheap, and plentiful. In time, as more tourists came, more restaurants sprang up, the blue-collar workers got pushed out, and the Athina was simply too small and rough to appeal to the newcomers. Zeno sold the place to Leer.

"Why did Leer buy an unprofitable restaurant?" Nona asked.

"Needed a tax write-off, I guess." With that, he poured them both another glass.

Tyler was interesting, charming, humorous, and knew how to flirt, even when telling stories about the past. He brought her more thick Greek coffee, plus tasty sesame cookies, a thin slice of walnut torte, and, as if in answer to her secret desire, baklava.

Nona felt warm, contented, light-headed, and was having trouble focusing when Tyler changed topics. "I know another restaurant reviewer," he said, "Angie Amalfi. I suspect you know her and her neighbor—Stan, I believe his name is."

"I'm no friend of Stan's," she said. Her jaw

didn't seem to quite work, and her words sounded a little slurred. "He's nothing to me. And not half so cute as you are." Had she really said that? The ouzo was a lot stronger than she had thought.

Tyler laughed. "You're too kind, and too charming. Actually, I don't see you with Stan. You've got too much class for him."

"I know," she said with a moan and a sigh.

"Did you two date long?"

"Of course not!"

"But I'll bet he took you to his apartment, tried to put a move on you."

She shook her head, frowning at the memory of going to Stan's place. It'd been humiliating. "Not really."

"I can't imagine. What's wrong with him? He must have taste in his feet."

"Maybe." A melancholy moroseness struck her. "Or another girlfriend."

Tyler nodded. "Even worse! How could he, when he knows you?" He took her hand in both of his and lightly stroked her fingers. She felt a tingle down to her toes. "Is his apartment really right next door to Angie's?"

"Across the hall."

"I wonder what others on their floor must think, with all the running back and forth they must do."

"They're the only two on it."

"Really?" He lifted her hand to his mouth and nibbled on her knuckles. She was sure she was seeing stars. "Which floor is it?"

"The top floor—twelve. The building is older—

it was tall when it was built, but now twelve floors is nothing, even on the top of Russian Hill."

He lowered her hand to the table. "The twelfth! Nice. I suppose Angie has the apartment with a view of the bay."

"Her place has a beautiful view, but so does mine. It's very"—she kicked off her shoe and rubbed her toes against his leg—"very comfortable."

"Well," Tyler said, jumping to his feet. "I think I should call you a cab to go back to it. You don't want to drive in your condition."

"A cab?" She looked around. *What happened?*

"Let's walk down to Jefferson Street. There's always one coming by looking for tourists."

"But . . ."

He helped her to her feet and held her jacket as she first stepped back into her shoe. When they reached Jefferson, a cab was just driving by. Tyler hailed it and put Nona inside.

She hardly knew what had happened when she found herself alone, once again. Here she thought Tyler was interested, sexy, and willing . . . yet she'd gotten the bum's rush!

What's wrong with the men in this town?

Hannah worked the duct tape on her hands, trying to stretch it, to loosen it, to get it to *move*, somehow, with no luck. She was exhausted. Her legs and arms had gone numb from the way they'd been tied, a numbness she knew would turn into deep shooting pains if she couldn't stretch or otherwise help her circulation.

Hours had passed since Tyler was last there. At

least when he was with her, she could hope to talk him into letting her go. Hope that she'd get out of here and not be abandoned. Where was he?

Her biggest worry was that he'd find the baby. She didn't understand how he'd figured out that Stan was the one she'd gone to. Stan was a just a customer. If every customer she'd ever talked to was tracked down, it would have taken months to find Kaitlyn. What went wrong?

Perhaps she gave something away in how she'd talked with Stan. Was that it? Had she been too obvious in her interest in the man, or had Stan been too obvious in his interest in her? She remembered the way Stan's sweet brown eyes had settled on her with so much warmth, and how she'd felt the color rise in her face because of it.

What was Stan doing now? What was he thinking about her being gone so long? Did he still have Kaitlyn, or had he sent her off to Social Services because her mother had abandoned her? Somehow, she didn't think Stan would do that. He'd wait. He'd give her time to come back for the baby. He knew she wouldn't abandon Kaitlyn.

She prayed he knew it, at any rate, and that he'd wait for her to return.

Her throat was parched and her stomach ached from emptiness. Was that part of Tyler's plan? To wear her down with hunger?

He'd pour her water from a glass jug when he came in, nothing more. After that, he'd badger her with talk.

He almost made her believe she should give her baby up. But when she thought about losing Kaitlyn, she couldn't bear it.

He'd called her selfish.

Was it so selfish to want to raise one's own child?

The cellar was dark and empty. She'd seen how empty it was when he came in with his flashlight and lit the battery lantern. When he was gone, it was darker than night.

She remembered the words from Louis Armstrong's "What a Wonderful World." Something about the bright, blessed day, and the dark, sacred night.

She'd never see the dark as sacred again. It was evil. The evil of death.

It reached out for her. Would she ever see her child again?

She could feel herself growing weaker. It had been bad at first when the hunger pangs struck, but they were gone now, replaced by a dull, constant ache.

Where was he? What if he never came back? No one would know she was here. She'd die of thirst, a slow awful death. She licked her lips. They were starting to crack.

The water bottle was kept on a shelf.

A glass bottle. . . .

It gave her an idea. If it worked, she'd be free. But if it didn't . . . She wouldn't think of that now.

She scooted along the wall to a corner, then twisted herself around and rocked back and forth until she was able to get up onto her knees. Using the walls to brace herself, trying time and again, she managed to maintain her balance and lift herself up to a standing position.

She pressed close to the wall so she wouldn't

fall and moved by sliding her feet, first toes, then heels, toward where the jug sat.

When she reached it, she felt the jug with her nose, then used her head to shove it off the shelf. It fell to the cement floor with a crash. Glass shattered around her.

Carefully, she lowered herself to the floor once again and felt in the rubble for a large piece of glass. The entire bottom of the jug had stayed intact. It was exactly what she needed.

She braced it against the wall and lowered the duct tape onto a sharp edge, then slid the tape slowly back and forth over the glass until the tape broke in two.

After tearing the tape from her wrists, she grabbed the glass and used it to cut through the tape at her ankles. Blood streamed from her hands, lots of blood, but it didn't matter. Freedom was near.

Sense and feeling pushed aside the overpowering despair and numbness she'd felt, but still it took several moments for her to be able to walk.

She stumbled toward the door, knowing it would be locked. The good news was that it was just a normal interior door. Nothing especially thick or strong.

She kicked it. It didn't budge. Fury filled her as she thought of how he'd tried to kill her, as she thought of never seeing her baby again, and she kicked harder, again and again.

A panel on the bottom half of the door cracked. She aimed her foot at the crack and struck until it split wide.

She worked at it, kicking, grabbing it with her hands, rocking the wood back and forth until she made an opening, then tearing at it more until the opening became large enough that she could squeeze her body through it.

It was amazing, she realized when she calmed down enough to think about it, that no one had heard her breaking the door. No one came to investigate the pounding and crying, for only after it was over had she realized she'd been screaming with fury.

The need to move slower struck. Freedom was so close, so precious, that she didn't want to do anything in haste that might jeopardize it.

After she felt her way to the stairs, then up them, a door at the top caused her heart to sink. It might be locked and far more solid than the one she'd just fought through.

It opened.

The main floor of the building had windows that were cloudy with dirt and grime. Only a little light shone into them. It must have been nighttime, she surmised, and the lights were street lamps.

The building appeared to be filled with old machine parts. She found a door and opened it just a crack, then peeked out. The street was dark and empty. She slipped into the night, staying close to the building as she went, until suddenly it felt safe to run.

At the corner stood a street sign: Battery and Filbert. She was near the Embarcadero, near the waterfront, but more importantly, she was less than two miles from Stan's apartment. She could make it.

Up ahead was Broadway Street. It'd take her around Telegraph Hill, and from there she could quickly climb to the top of Russian Hill and Kaitlyn. Tears filled her eyes as she went, staying close to the buildings, not wanting anyone, not any of the night people, to delay her.

But then she stopped. The question that had bothered her the entire time she was tied up struck. How had Ty found her? She had just rounded the corner from Stan's apartment building when she was grabbed. A rag was placed over her mouth—it must have had chloroform or something similar because she was soon out cold.

When she awoke, she was being pulled from the car. She was too woozy to understand where she was or what was happening.

Had Stan given her away? Was he involved in this? Or was it Angie? Ty had talked about her. Angie led him to her, he'd said. Had it been a mistake on her part? Or did she do it on purpose?

No! Angie was a good person, like Stan.

Wasn't she?

And if it was Angie, why would she tell him the building address, but not Stan's apartment number? Thank goodness it was a twelve-story building, or Tyler might have gone door to door looking for the child.

Confusion filled her. She'd trusted foolishly once, given a man her heart, lowered all the defenses she'd built up over a lifetime to let him get close to her. Dianne Randle had questioned her judgment about men. Maybe she should question her judgment about women as well.

Nothing made sense! She couldn't think, and felt only fear and complete exhaustion. If she rushed to see Kaitlyn and was wrong, she might never see her daughter again.

She stood on the sidewalk in front of Angie and Stan's apartment building. She ached to go inside, but she also had to think this through. Who could she trust? What should she do to assure that she and Kaitlyn would never again be in danger?

Tyler was the biggest threat to her and her daughter. The one thing she wanted more than anything else in the world was to see Kaitlyn's father dead. Unbidden, the thought came to her—find him and kill him.

Olympia Pappas tried to concentrate on her job, but the letters and numbers blurred before her eyes.

She couldn't stomach it any longer. Not his lies, his deceit. He'd loved her once, but it was over. She had to face it and get on with her life. But the thought of a black, loveless, desolate future brought angry tears to her eyes.

Why couldn't he see that she was the best one for him? Why didn't he understand that she loved him enough for both of them?

She tried to concentrate on matching the case number on the paper she held with the number written on the folder, but it wasn't working. All she could see was Tyler.

She could make him happy if he'd only give her

a chance instead of wasting his time on other women. She'd seen how they'd go alone to the restaurant and then throw themselves at him. That skinny blonde whore did it tonight. It made her want to throw up!

Did he think she hadn't seen? That she hadn't known?

How dare he treat her like this! Take her love and toss it aside as if it were nothing—as if she were nothing.

She stuffed handfuls of papers into folders, her hands flying, her mind paying no attention to what she was doing.

She'd show him. She'd make him sorry he ever, ever dared to treat her that way. He'd be hers or he'd be no one's. She'd rather see him dead.

Chapter 23

A crowd gathered on the sidewalk outside a small Stockton Street building that housed four small apartments. Homicide Inspector Rebecca Mayfield scanned the faces as she entered the one downstairs, right. Her partner hadn't arrived yet, which was hardly a surprise. She should be used to it by now; still, it irked her.

A male Caucasian lay sprawled face down on the living room floor, the area around him thick with blood.

The policeman who found the body stepped up to Rebecca. "Officer Dandridge, Inspector. We received a 911 call from this apartment and came by to investigate. The landlady let us in when our knocks received no answer. We found the victim. In his hand is his cell phone—one of those that pressing one number calls 911. That's how he reached us." His gaze shifted to the bloodied corpse. "Not that it helped."

Rebecca snapped on her rubber gloves and lifted the body so she could see the victim's face.

When she did so, she started. She knew the man; she'd spoken with him in connection with Sherlock Farnsworth's death. It was Tyler Marsh.

He'd been stabbed several times in the heart and stomach. It appeared that whoever did it had been very, very angry.

The last thing Paavo expected when he knocked on Angie's door was to have it opened by Stan Bonnette wearing nothing but an undershirt and BVDs.

Stan looked sleepy, but jerked quickly awake at Paavo's scowl. "Uh . . ."

"Making yourself at home, aren't you, Bonnet? Where's Angie?"

Stan hurried to put on his pants as Paavo entered the apartment. "It's Bonnette," he said automatically. "I was here talking about Hannah, then Kaitlyn fell asleep, then Angie, and I didn't want to disturb them . . . and Angie's couch is more comfortable than mine, which I can hardly find anymore . . ." He stopped talking.

The baby was in the stroller, dozing contentedly.

Angie stepped out of the bedroom, rubbing her eyes. "I thought I heard voices." Suddenly, looking at Paavo, at Stan, at the early hour, all the color drained from her face. "Has something happened?"

Stan saw her reaction and the possible reason for it struck him as well. He dropped onto the sofa, his knees weak. "Hannah?" he murmured.

"It's not Hannah," Paavo said. "We haven't found her yet." Both Angie and Stan sighed with relief.

"This is so much like the morning you came by

to tell me about Peter Leong," Angie said. "I had the feeling something bad had happened."

"It's not exactly the same," Paavo said with a grimace in Stan's direction. "But something bad did happen. Does the name Tyler Marsh sound familiar?"

"Yes," Angie said. "He works at the Athina."

"When did you last see him?"

"Hmm, several days ago, at least," Angie answered.

"Me, too," Stan added.

"Why?" She looked from Stan to Paavo.

"He was murdered last night."

Angie glanced again at Stan. "Murdered? My God!" Her eyes saddened. He wasn't a good man, that she'd learned, but no one deserved that fate. "He was so young, so full of life. I'm sorry he's dead."

Stan's eyes were like an owl's. "Do you know who did it?" he asked, his voice quavering.

"He was found in his apartment. It apparently happened around midnight. We'll know more later. Right now I'd like you both to tell me everything you know about Tyler Marsh and the other people at the restaurant."

Rebecca talked to Marsh's neighbors and wrote down names for follow-ups later. No one admitted to hearing or seeing anything out of the ordinary other than the fact that Marsh's next-door neighbor heard his front door slam a couple of times late at night. Its latch wouldn't catch unless pulled hard.

As soon as the Athina opened that morning, Re-

becca headed there with Paavo. She'd only
worked on a case with him once before and took a
moment to brush her hair and freshen her
makeup. She had to admit she never felt quite so
nervous or upbeat when she rode in the SFPD-
issued Ford beside her usual partner.

At the Athina, they spoke first with Eugene Leer.
He believed the killer was Hannah Dzanic. Her
disappearance showed how unbalanced she was;
she killed Tyler because he wouldn't marry her.

Rebecca asked if Leer knew of any other enemies Tyler might have had. He didn't.

Michael Zeno was sure Olympia Pappas had
killed Marsh. They'd dated before Hannah entered the picture, and Olympia never got over
him. She was hot-tempered and insanely jealous.
When Hannah left, she tried to get Tyler back, but
he wasn't interested.

Eleni Pappas thought Michael Zeno killed him
out of jealousy and Tyler's treatment of Hannah,
while Gail Leer believed he was simply the victim
of a botched robbery attempt.

Interestingly, Paavo noted, no one seemed partic-
ularly upset or troubled by their co-worker's death.

Earl and Vinnie sat at Angie's table at Wings of an
Angel. Butch would have joined them as well, but
they had a couple of customers who wanted
lunch, so he had to stay in the kitchen and cook.

Angie told them about the Athina waiter's
death, and was eager to hear what they'd learned
about the place.

"Everyone says there's something not kosher
about it." Vinnie poured chianti for them.

"We don't t'ink you should go dere no more, Miss Angie," Earl added. "An' dat was before we hoid about da waiter being offed."

"For one thing," Vinnie said, "the restaurant don't do the kind of business to make enough money to keep up a waterfront restaurant with a pier, not even a dump like that one is. You're talking big bucks to buy or rent it." He lifted his glass. "*Salute*."

The others joined the toast. "So where does the money come from?" Angie asked after taking a small sip. Wine in the early afternoon wasn't a favorite of hers.

"That's the thing. It's got to be something illegal," Vinnie suggested. "Dope, maybe, but not likely. The big boys who deal dope don't like little two-bit players like Gene Leer taking a cut. I don't think that's it."

"What, then?"

"Who knows?" Vinnie swirled his wine glass. "Back to the murder, word on the street is some woman killed the waiter when he wouldn't marry her. Everyone says she was a stalker. She'd follow him to work, home, everywhere he went, keeping an eye on him and any other woman he paid any attention to."

Angie found that interesting. "Do they mention a name—like Olympia or Hannah?"

"I didn't hear no names, but some broad—'scuse me, Miss Angie, I meant some dame—is missing and people say she's the one who came back and offed him."

"I see." She was surprised others thought Hannah was a killer. To Angie, she seemed too nice. Of course, wasn't that what everyone always said about killers? *She was such a nice woman.* "Do they have any proof?" she asked.

"Not that I heard," Vinnie said. As more customers entered, he and Earl went into action.

Angie drank the wine, lost in thought about the way she'd helped Hannah leave the hospital, and how she'd driven her around in her car. Could Hannah be a killer? It was odd how she went missing. Paavo had gotten Missing Persons involved, but still there was no trace of her. And now Tyler's murder . . .

Angie finished her glass. Why did she get involved with people with such complicated lives when all she wanted to do was enjoy her engagement party?

Just as she was about to leave, Nona Farraday charged into the restaurant. She looked like hell with bags under her eyes, her skin a sickly sallow color, and her hair flat and lank. "I thought I'd find you here! Never again, Angie. Never again!"

"What?"

All heads swiveled toward Nona as she stood over Angie. "You sent me on a wild goose chase to talk to a man who plies me with liquor for no good reason, and then I find out the Casanova is a murder victim! You can just keep your sick male friends to yourself. I'm giving up on men altogether!"

With that, Nona turned on her heel and marched out the door. The other customers buzzed over her words.

Angie had no idea what the crazy woman was talking about, but she grabbed her purse, threw money on the table, and left. She needed to get home to warn Stan about Hannah. And maybe Nona, while she was at it.

Before rushing home, Angie realized she knew one person who could answer a lot of her questions. One person who also wanted answers. She phoned Gail Leer, and they agreed to meet at Ghirardelli Square for coffee.

Gail was standing by the door waiting as Angie entered the ice-cream and coffee shop. They ordered lattes, then found themselves a table.

As soon as they were seated, Angie opened her small handbag and pretended to switch off the cell phone so they could talk undisturbed. Instead, she switched on the new mini-tape recorder she'd bought on the way over. She wasn't a Homicide inspector's fiancée for nothing. The purchase, she was sure, would get plenty of use.

She then propped her purse on the table against the wall, halfway between herself and Gail.

"So tell me," she asked after the waitress brought their coffee, "what do you think is going on? Hannah is missing. Tyler is dead."

"I don't know," Gail clasped her hands, elbows on the table. "It's such a worry. I assumed Hannah was safe and staying with your friend Stan, but you said I was wrong about that. And now Tyler. I don't know who could have killed him."

"What about a jealous girlfriend?" Angie asked.

"Olympia?" Gail shook her head. "She's got a terrible temper, but I don't see her as a murderer."

"What about Michael Zeno?" Angie asked.

"I hope not," Gail murmured. She stirred the latte, lost in thought. "From the moment he looked at Hannah, though, when I first hired her, he was like a lovesick puppy. She saw him more as a father figure or older brother—a friend, nothing more."

"Tell me about Hannah and Tyler," Angie said.

Gail told her how Hannah had been interested in Tyler from the moment he first started working at the restaurant. A couple of times before that she'd gone out with Michael Zeno, but he was too old, and far too serious. Michael loved her—it was obvious to everyone—but Hannah wasn't interested in him. He got mad when she broke it off. He told everyone that someday he was going to be rich, "Rich as Eugene Leer," was how he put it, and then Hannah would be sorry she didn't love him.

Hannah didn't care, though, because Tyler was working side by side with her, all charm and sparkling handsomeness. For months she'd pined for him while he dated Olympia Pappas. Then, one day, he asked her out.

She was in love, and soon she was pregnant as well. She clung to the dream that when he learned about the baby he would propose or do something, anything, to show he cared for her, the mother of his child. But he didn't, and life continued as it had been.

"When did the two break up?" Angie asked.

"I guess it was right before she disappeared. She was unhappy, but we all thought they were still seeing each other. When Tyler said she was gone, we were shocked."

"What did they fight about?"

"The baby. Apparently they had an agreement to put it up for adoption. But then Hannah started having thoughts about keeping it. That was the last thing Tyler wanted."

"Why did Hannah feel she and the baby had to hide from Tyler? It sounds like more than a simple disagreement."

Gail's brows lifted. "You make it sound as if she already had the child."

Angie stirred her latte while thinking, and then decided to try the truth. "She did. A little girl."

Gail's jaw dropped. "She had the baby."

"So?"

"Maybe Tyler . . ." Gail's eyes met Angie's and she stopped talking. "Nothing. I don't know." She stood and picked up her purse. "I've got to go."

Without another word, she left the shop.

When Paavo returned to Homicide, he learned that Rebecca had gotten a search warrant for the Athina and Lieutenant Hollins had ordered her partner to accompany her. After that, she planned to question Olympia Pappas. He had to admit to being curious about the woman himself.

Paavo agreed with Rebecca's search of the Athina. He didn't like anything he was learning about the Athina Restaurant, the Leers, Michael Zeno, Tyler Marsh, or even Hannah. The place obviously wasn't making enough to keep its doors open as a restaurant, so why was it still open? It was clear that everyone there was uneasy talking to the police.

He picked up his notepad and a pencil and jotted down key facts. Shelly Farms was found murdered not too far from the Athina. He was known for giving help to the poor, and one of the last people he was known to be concerned about was a single woman about to have a baby. Hannah worked at the Athina, single, pregnant. She ran away to have her baby and then disappeared. Tyler Marsh worked at the Athina, was the baby's father, and now he was dead.

How did it all tie together? It had to. A series of unrelated murders and kidnappings in one spot made no sense.

Paavo was so deep in thought, the pencil eraser pressed to his bottom lip, he didn't hear Angie come in until she plopped down in the chair at the side of his desk, pulled out the tape of her coffee with Gail Leer, and played it for him.

"What do you think?" she asked with a smile when it ended.

He glared at her. "What do you think you're doing? That woman could be involved in something dangerous! You could be taking your life in your hands!"

"Calm down," Angie said. "I'm fine. What's interesting is that she's lying. You notice how, as soon as she learned the baby had been born, her whole demeanor changed?"

Paavo stared at the tape recorder. He had to admit it was interesting. "All right," he said through gritted teeth. "You did this, but promise me you'll stop now. No more going to the Athina. No questioning these people. Is that clear?"

She frowned. He was making it very difficult for her to help him. "If you insist," she said finally. "But just let me say that I've been giving my conversation with Gail a lot of thought—too much, considering that our party is in only four days!

COURTING DISASTER 243

Still, I keep going back to Hannah's apartment and how she made no preparation at all for the baby. It's unnatural—unless she never expected to bring the baby home."

Paavo had to agree. He jotted a new word on his list: adoption. "It goes along with what Gail said— that she'd agreed to give it up for adoption."

She told him about the Vandermeers' visit to the Athina, how upset they were to learn Hannah had been gone several days and no one had contacted them. "What if Hannah and Tyler were planning to let the Vandermeers adopt their baby? She might have changed her mind, and that's why she called Stan. To hide from the Vandermeers as well as from Tyler. Maybe he met the Vandermeers at the Athina, learned they wanted to adopt, and made a deal."

Paavo tapped the eraser against his desktop. "You may be right. Stan was perfect. She saw him as someone Tyler couldn't track down. Except that he did. That must be why she ran. Or he snatched her, wanting to convince her to give up the baby."

"But how did he find her?" Angie asked. "Stan has an unlisted phone number, he's not listed on Google or anything. I can't even remember him ever introducing himself to anyone at the Athina."

"But you probably gave your name, right? Maybe you even told them about your job on KQED." At her nod, he continued. "That's it then. That's why you were followed, why the ruse with the taxi. Someone—Marsh?—wanted to know where you and Stan lived so he could get to Hannah."

It made sense, Angie agreed. "Hannah went for a walk alone, and if he'd been watching the apartment, he could have grabbed her, taken her to his apartment. She could have gotten free and killed him," Angie cried. "Good God, I hope not."

"It hangs together, but it's also pretty far-fetched," Paavo said. "Not many people want to give up their babies, or have potential parents show up out of the blue. Unless . . ." He stopped, staring at his list as something niggled in his memory.

"Unless . . ." Angie's eyes widened. "What if all this isn't as much out of the blue as we think?"

She told him about her and Stan seeing the owner and the cook carrying what looked like cradles from the boat to the restaurant. "We assumed they must be some strange kind of fish crate, but what if they really were baby cradles?"

"Shelly Farms had been looking at case law about smuggling," he remembered, then shuddered at the thought. "Let's hope these people aren't involved in baby smuggling, Angie."

She nodded as the ugliness of it struck her.

"What was the name of the people who asked about Hannah? Vandermeer, was it? Do you have a first name?"

"Hers was Frieda, which is odd enough, but I remember thinking his was even weirder. Like an old-time movie star. Rock? Tab? Lance? Yes—that's it. Lance Vandermeer."

Paavo keyed "Lance Vandermeer" into California's criminal database. Several clicks and the man's rap sheet appeared—two assaults and a "misappropriation of funds" charge, which was dropped or it would have meant his "third strike"—and a lifetime in jail.

Angie stared at it, stunned. The only thing she could say was, "Wow."

Surprise, then delight filled Stan's face as he opened the door. "Hannah! Thank God! Are you all right?" He took a step forward as if to hug her, but something in her eyes stopped him, and he stepped aside to allow her to enter.

She eyed him and then the room. It was a mess, and so was he. It had been bad enough when she was there to share the burden of taking care of a baby and trying to keep up an apartment and clothes, and diapers, formula, food for him since he had no time to go out, and somehow try to find time to sleep, but now, doing all that alone, he was ready to drop.

Cautiously, she walked inside. She'd spent the past few hours at a homeless shelter where she ate, cleaned up, and had her hands bandaged. "Where's Kaitlyn?"

"In her crib, asleep." He stared her as if she'd just dropped out of the sky. "She's fine. What happened to you? I was so worried."

Now it was her turn to back away. "Were you?"

"Sit down." He gestured toward the sofa. "You're acting strangely."

She remained standing and rigid. "I want Kaitlyn."

"You want to take her and leave?" Stan was shocked.

"That's right."

"Hannah, what's wrong? Tell me what happened."

She pulled out a knife and shakily pointed it at his heart. "I'm leaving and taking my baby with me." Then she burst into tears.

Chapter 24

Angie was frantic. All her time, it seemed, was being taken up helping Stan care for the baby and trying to keep him calm about Hannah. And now that Tyler had been killed and Rebecca Mayfield suspected Hannah, things were worse than ever. Stan was a basket case, wondering if he should contact somebody in authority about Kaitlyn. With Angie's engagement party startlingly near, desperate times called for desperate measures.

She went to the one person she knew she could count on at such a time: Connie Rogers.

"You want me to do *what*?" Connie cried when Angie arrived at her apartment that evening. "No way!"

Connie lived just a few blocks from her shop in an old comfortable building that, fortunately, allowed dogs, since she'd recently acquired one. Lily was curled up on the sofa, her head on Connie's lap, eying Angie with sadness and grave disappointment in her big brown eyes.

Angie usually brought her a gourmet doggie

biscuit. Today, though, she'd forgotten. She felt guiltier than a war criminal.

"It's not really breaking and entering," Angie said, trying not to look at Lily. "I've got a key." She remembered her father using that same line many times.

"It's still sneaking into a house uninvited and going through someone's personal papers—even if it is your own mother!"

"I'm begging you, Connie," Angie said. "I need someone to watch from the windows in case they come home. That's all."

"This is ridiculous."

Angie heaved a sigh of relief. She knew she was winning. When Connie ran out of rational arguments, she turned to the ridiculous factor. As if Angie cared!

Fifteen minutes later, Connie relented and the two were off, Angie at the wheel.

She parked near the back of an empty lot over two blocks from her parents' home. There was so little street parking in this neighborhood her Mercedes would stand out like a beacon anywhere else—not to mention her license plate: GR8COOK.

She and Connie had to stop and pick stickers out of their shoes and pantyhose after they trooped through the weed-covered lot to the sidewalk. Once there, they hid behind a rhododendron and waited until they saw a Rolls-Royce pass—Serefina at the wheel and Sal clutching the dashboard. Tonight's ballet was one Serefina had been especially interested in seeing. Sal looked upon it as penance.

"Let's go," Angie said, and the two hurried to her parents' home. She unlocked the door and disarmed the alarm. Fortunately, her parents hadn't changed the code in years.

Once inside, she headed for the study and Serefina's desk. "Here are her to-do lists," Angie called excitedly as Connie went through a stack of papers she'd found on a low wooden cabinet.

"Good," Connie said, "because there isn't much here but a lot of old historical papers."

"Historical? Since when is Serefina interested in history? Is it Italian?"

"No. San Francisco seafaring, as a matter of fact."

"Weird. Must be another of her crazy volunteer groups. Hmm, here's a receipt from Juliette's. It's a boutique that Serefina loves—they carry a lot of plus sizes, but don't mark them that way. Very clever marketing. Serefina is convinced she's a ten, and has no idea why she doesn't fit in that size at other stores."

"I think I should start shopping there," Connie said.

"You pay a price for that deception," Angie said. "You'd have to sell a lot of teacups, believe me."

"In that case, I'll keep going to sales at Macy's and cutting off the size labels."

"Ah, thank God!" Angie held up another receipt. "She isn't buying my cake from Diamond Pastry. Looks like she's going to Victoria's. Great! Their Italian rum cake is my favorite. I hope that's what she's ordered. To think I once actually worried about a purple cake. How silly was that?"

"Purple cake? Or do you mean purple cow? Wasn't there some kind of nursery rhyme about one? You should start boning up on them, since the way Stan is acting, I think Hannah and Kaitlyn will be next door for quite a long time."

"You may be right, I—"

Angie stopped talking. She heard a noise.

"My God," she whispered. "They're back! You were supposed to be watching!"

"I can't do everything!" Connie wailed, papers in hand. "Anyway, it's not as if your parents will call the cops on you."

"No, I'll just hurt my mother's feelings so much she won't talk to me and my engagement party will be ruined!" Angie wrung her hands. "We've got to hide."

"Hide?" Connie looked around.

"Come on." They darted down the hall. In the kitchen, they'd almost reached the back door when they heard a key in the lock. Angie did an about-face and ran into Connie. "They're coming in the back way!" she cried, pushing Connie into the hall.

"But we heard them . . ." Connie pointed toward the front of the house.

They stood in the hall. Connie was right, hadn't they just heard someone in the living room? "This way." Angie pulled her into the dining room. There was a swinging door between the dining room and the kitchen.

Angie slowly pushed it open, hoping the kitchen was empty. The door suddenly stopped moving. Odd. She was trying to figure out what had happened to it when the door began opening on its own, and toward her.

She and Connie backpedaled, eyes glued to the self-propelled door.

Suddenly it opened all the way and a strange blond woman dressed in black walked into the dining room.

Angie and the stranger gaped at each other. The blonde jumped back into the kitchen.

Connie ran in the other direction.

Angie stood there, not knowing what was going on when the kitchen door swung open again.

Angie grabbed a candlestick to protect herself, but this time Connie stuck her head into the dining room. "Come on. Let's get out of here!"

"Isn't the woman in the kitchen?" Angie asked, confused.

"You mean the maid?"

"She's not the maid! I've never seen her before in my life," Angie cried. "What was she doing in my parents' home?"

"Maybe she's a friend. They're home, right?"

Angie blanched. "Right. And they might find us! Hurry!"

The two darted out the back door and crouched down behind a vine-covered pergola while Angie caught her breath. Come to think of it, it was odd that she hadn't heard her mother talking. Serefina talked nonstop when she was in the house, even when alone.

"Something's very wrong here," Angie said, worried.

"You're right. Let's go home," Connie suggested.

"I mean something's *really* wrong."

"What can you do?" Connie asked. "No, don't answer that!"

They slowly crept away from the house. "Okay, first things first," Angie said, bending forward so her head wouldn't show above the shrubbery. She grabbed Connie's shoulder and pulled her down as well. "You put the papers you were holding back on top of the cabinet, didn't you?"

Connie, bent over, said, "Well . . ."

"Are you telling me you didn't put the papers back where you got them?" Angie's tone had climbed so high she was lucky the neighbor's dog didn't bark.

"You said to hurry!" Connie cried, now irritated as well as uncomfortable.

"I said I didn't want to be caught!" It was hair-clutching time. "Now she'll know we were looking at her stuff."

"Maybe she'll think someone else did it." Connie tried to sound reasonable. "Like the blonde. Let's go. My back hurts!"

"We can't go! We've got to go inside and put the papers where they belong."

"I want to leave," Connie wailed. "I know this is your parents' home, but I don't like this."

"You're such a moan artist!" Angie was beside herself.

"Moan artist! Well, excuse me for living! I'm dragged here to help you and don't complain one little bit, and you—"

"Stop!" Angie clutched Connie's arm as they stooped behind some hibiscus bushes. "I saw someone moving back in those bushes."

"How can you see anything? We're facing the ground!"

"I wonder if my mother is out here sneaking around for some reason, and that's why we didn't hear her in the house."

"Why would she be hiding in her own garden?" Connie sounded as if Angie had taken leave of her senses.

"I don't know, except that she's got to be furious with my father. She was already upset with him about something, and I know she was looking forward to this ballet. Now, if he made her come home, and some strange woman's lurking around the house . . ."

"Wouldn't she just go alone?" Connie asked. "It wouldn't be the first time, from what you've said. And if I end up hunchbacked because of this, I'm never going to forgive you!"

"Go alone? While my father returns home to meet some woman? Is that what you're suggesting?" Angie asked hotly as she began to sneak from bush to tree, making her way toward the side of the house where she'd seen the movement.

"I'm not suggesting anything. I meant I want to straighten up."

"No!" When they got closer, Angie saw the blonde again, pointing a telephoto lens camera at the house and taking pictures. Angie looked toward the window. The interior lights were on, and she could see right into the library at her father.

Outraged, Angie snuck closer to the woman, and once near, reared up and sprang from the bushes. "What the hell do you think you're doing?" she cried, and yanked the camera away.

"How dare you!" the woman shrieked, and

pulled on the camera's straps, which she hadn't let go of. She nearly yanked Angie off her feet, but Angie hung on tight.

"What are you doing, taking pictures of my father?" she yelled. "Who are you?"

"Mind your own business, you spoiled brat!" The woman raised her hand and swung. Angie raised her arm in time to protect her face from the slap.

Her arm hurt from the blow. It hurt badly, in fact. She couldn't believe anyone would do such a thing to her, especially not this Peeping Tomasina. Fury rose, the world went red, and she launched herself at the woman, knocking her flat on her back.

The woman grabbed Angie's hair, and Angie grabbed hers, both shrieking and kicking. They started rolling in the dirt.

Connie screamed, hopped about, and tried to get close enough to pull the woman off Angie, but whenever she'd get close, she had to jump out of the way or risk being kicked, gouged, or slapped herself. In desperation she ran toward the house. "Mr. Amalfi! Sal! Help!"

From around the side came not Sal, but Paavo. He stared at Connie with surprise and horror.

"It's Angie," she cried, and pointed toward the part of the garden where no people were seen, only puffs of dirt rising above the bushes.

Paavo ran toward the yelps and squawks. Not far behind him was Salvatore.

Paavo lifted Angie up by the waist and swung her away from Elizabeth Schull. Schull looked at him, then got up and started to run. He set Angie on her feet and took off after Schull, catching up with her after only a few steps.

Angie was fuming and started after Paavo when her father grabbed her arm. "Don't," he said.

"What's going on?" she cried. "She was in the house! When she saw me she left, and now she's taking pictures."

He shrugged. "Must be a burglar casing the place. Paavo will take care of her." He picked up the woman's camera. "This is probably evidence of what she's been up to."

Angie noticed that Paavo had kept going.

"Where's he taking her?"

"Jail, I suppose," Sal said.

"I'm going to go see."

Sal's grip tightened. "No, you're not. Come inside. Let's get you cleaned up."

"But—"

"You don't want Paavo to see his bride-to-be looking like a female mud wrestler, do you?"

They turned toward the house. "You're lucky you don't have a black eye or something," Connie said, walking beside Angie. "You two were really going at it."

Visions of appearing at her party in her beautiful dress, her hair perfect and her eye multiple shades of blue, black, green, and purple, made Angie shudder. "Don't even talk about such a thing," she said, furious to discover a broken fingernail.

Paavo came back alone after Angie had washed her face and hands and brushed the twigs, leaves, and weeds from her hair and clothes. She and Connie were sitting in the Italian provincial living room with Sal, sipping brandy and sodas.

"That was fast," Angie said to Paavo. She stood as he entered. "Don't tell me you let her go?"

He held her shoulders, checking her face and making sure she was all right before giving her a quick kiss and hug. Sal's black eyes bored into his back the whole time. "A patrol car arrived. They've got her. I wanted to be sure you're okay."

"I can hold my own," Angie announced, chin up, her arms around his waist.

"That, I already knew," Paavo said with a smile, starting to draw her close again when he heard Sal's voice.

"Here's film from her camera." Sal held the roll out for Paavo.

"Thanks." He put it in his pocket.

"All right, you two." Angie's pointed gaze went from one man to the other. "What's going on? Where's Mamma?"

"Your mother went to the ballet," Sal said, then met Paavo's eye as he said, "I felt sick and had her turn around and drop me off back home. Then Paavo showed up looking for you."

Paavo nodded to Sal before facing Angie. "That's right. I have the evening off."

"But I didn't tell you I was coming here," Angie said.

"I must have just guessed it," he answered.

She turned to her father. "Who was the woman? It wasn't just chance that she was lurking around."

Sal was all wide-eyed innocence. "No? Seems like chance to me. I have no idea why any woman would want to do that. Or maybe it's that I'm still such a handsome old coot. Did she say anything to you about why she was out there, Paavo?"

He faced Angie. "She refused to say a word to me just now," he answered honestly.

Just then, Serefina appeared in the doorway. "*Che fai?*" she cried. "There were cops outside my house and your Stonestown manager was sitting in a patrol car crying. As I watched, they drove off. I'm tired of you keeping me in the dark about whatever's going on, Salvatore. You tell me right now why you've been acting so strangely." She shook her finger at Paavo. "And don't think I'm letting you off the hook. I want to find out what's going on from you, too. But first, it's Sal's turn."

"It's nothing, Serefina. *Niente.*"

"Sal," Paavo said sternly, then nothing more.

Sal's gaze darted from Paavo, to Angie, Connie, and then Serefina. "It's the truth!" he cried.

"You know you're the worst liar in *tutto il mondo*!" Serefina screeched. "Now tell me what this is about, or I'll go find Elizabeth and ask her! This doesn't have anything to do with the fact that she's got her eye on you, does it?"

"What?" Sal gaped.

"She's got her eye on you," Serefina repeated. "That's it, isn't it? Don't tell me she did something stupid! I know she's a little bit"—she tapped her temple—"*pazzo*, but I didn't think she'd cause trouble. Is that it? Is that why Paavo is here?"

Sal just stared at his wife. Angie gawked at both of them and only from the corner of her eye did she see Connie give her a high sign before sneaking off to Serefina's study to put the papers back where they should be. Angie was glad somebody around here had a little sense left.

"You knew she had a crush on Sal?" Paavo asked.

"Of course." Serefina chuckled. "She looked at him as if he could walk on water. I wanted to tell her she should try living with the man, then she'd change her tune." She gazed curiously at Sal. "You didn't think I noticed? What, am I blind? So, who'll tell me what happened here?"

Sal glanced at Paavo as if for help.

"Angie's engagement apparently pushed Schull over the edge," Paavo said. "She had trouble at her own engagement party years ago, and it unbalanced her. I can't help but suspect she was unbalanced before and that's why her fiancé abruptly cut off the wedding. In any case, watching you, Angie, and Sal, she probably felt jealous and lonely, and exhibited it by making threats. She'll most likely be spending some time at Langley Porter again."

"Why didn't you tell me about this, Salvatore?" Serefina looked at him crossly. "Or Angelina. If she was making threats, didn't you think we should know?"

"Well, you know your relatives. . . ."

"My relatives! Are you crazy? How can you keep these things from me! I should have made you tell. *Madonna mia!* Such a *stupido* I married!"

"Does this mean . . ."—Angie looked from Paavo to her father—"that the whole time you two were going around saying you were trying to be friends, trying to get to know each other better, you were just pretending? That it was all a ploy so you could catch this horrible woman?"

"Horrible?" Sal said indignantly. "I don't know if that's the way to characterize her. Her taste in men is good."

Angie put her hands on her hips. "So, you've been playacting!"

"No, we're friends," Sal said, grabbing Paavo's arm. "Tell her."

"Uh . . ."

Angie glared at Paavo. "Don't you dare lie to me, Paavo Smith!"

"I won't lie, Angie," he said. "Sal and I have reached an understanding. We never really talked before, but now we have. It's made a difference, one that will be for the better . . . in time. Wouldn't you say that, Sal?" Paavo asked.

Sal just stared at him a long moment, then finally he nodded. "Yeah. It made a difference." He faced Angie. "Not a whole hell of a lot, I'll admit, but it's better."

"I'll never understand either of you," Angie said, wrapping an arm around Paavo, "but I love you both, so it's okay."

He held her close and smiled down at her, as she did up at him.

Sal gave Serefina a forlorn shrug. She laughed heartily. "*Ti amo*, Salvatore," Serefina said. "Even if you are an old fool."

Chapter 25

 The next day in Homicide, Paavo told Rebecca Mayfield about Angie's conversation with Gail Leer and shared her speculation.

It was clear to Rebecca that Tyler must have known the murderer because there was no sign of a break-in or struggle. She doubted it was a robbery-gone-bad since nothing was stolen. Hannah was her prime suspect—and now her prime suspect in Shelly Farm's murder as well.

Hannah had to be the pregnant woman he'd talked about. What if he'd learned of Hannah and Tyler's plan to sell the baby and tried to stop it? She might have killed him and eventually decided to kill Tyler as well for being the cause of so much death and misery. Until Rebecca could meet and question Hannah, anything seemed possible to her.

Rebecca relayed to Paavo all she'd learned about Marsh's background. He'd been born and raised in Oakland. At seventeen, he was arrested for stealing from a 7-Eleven and hit with a misdemeanor. Shortly after that, he moved across the bay to San Francisco and stayed clear of the law for nearly twelve years. He began working at the Athina about two years earlier.

The weekly entries to his bank account showed how little he earned at his job. But other monthly deposits brought him over a hundred thousand dollars for the year. Where that money came from was anybody's guess. They couldn't find any reason for Tyler having that kind of income.

People said he was filled with charm. They also indicated that under that charm was a cold heart.

By late morning the results of fingerprint analysis came in. There were two hits at Tyler's apartment: Hannah Dzanic, whose prints were on file because she'd been raised as a ward of the court, and Olympia Pappas. What was interesting about Ms. Pappas was the reason her fingerprints were on file: she worked in records at the SFPD's Central Station.

What Paavo found even more interesting, though, was the report on the murder weapon. He and Rebecca had been surprised to find it at the scene. Most killers tried to hide their weapons unless they were so shocked and disoriented by what they'd done that they couldn't think past the need to run. Given the report's findings, that was a distinct possibility here.

Only one set of prints was on it. As soon as he read the report, he left the office and headed for Angie's apartment building.

Paavo knocked on Angie's door, but she wasn't home. He turned toward Stan's and gave a loud, this-is-the-police-open-up-now kind of knock.

Stan peeked into the hallway. "You want to see *me*?" he asked, his surprise evident.

"That's right. I want to talk to you about Hannah Dzanic."

Stan darted into the hallway and nervously shut the door behind him. "The baby's asleep. I don't know that I can help you."

"Any word about Hannah's whereabouts?" Paavo's demeanor was stern and formal.

Beads of perspiration broke out on Stan's forehead and he looked pleadingly toward Angie's door. "Uh . . . I tried to find her, but I had no luck."

"If you hear from her," Paavo said, eying him closely, "contact me as soon as possible."

"How was Marsh killed?" Stan asked suddenly.

Paavo paused a moment, but Stan deserved to know. "He was stabbed through the heart."

Stan turned so pale Paavo was ready to catch him if he fainted. "That's horrible."

Paavo continued. "We've got a match on the only set of fingerprints found on the murder weapon. It was a fillet knife from a set at the Athina—very sharp, very strong. Finding Hannah Dzanic isn't a matter of choice anymore. The fingerprints are hers."

Stan stared at him, shocked and speechless.

"If you see her, keep away and call me," Paavo repeated. "Don't let her in your apartment and don't let her near Angie. She could be dangerous."

"But . . ."

"Yes?"

"She's not a killer, Inspector," Stan protested weakly.

"That's what they all say, Stan." Paavo turned and headed for the elevator.

"Stan Bonnette is hiding something," Paavo said when he stopped at Rebecca Mayfield's desk back in Homicide. "I can't tell if it's because he knows something or that he's shook up over Hannah's possible involvement in Marsh's death."

"Possible? It's more than possible, Paavo. And from what I've seen, just being around you makes him so nervous he looks guilty," Rebecca said with a fond smile.

"Hey, look at you two," Yosh bellowed from his desk. "It's like watching a tango. I'm starting to feel like the odd man out here. Should I worry about losing my partner, Paav?"

"Maybe Angie needs to worry more than you do," Calderon called from the coffeepot, where he was getting his twentieth refill. "I heard they worked on the Marsh case all night." He waggled his eyebrows.

"Cool it," Paavo warned.

Rebecca stood, glaring hard at Calderon. "One more comment like that, and you're dead meat!"

He threw up his hands. "Just a joke! Relax. We know you better than that. Hell, we don't call you the Iron Maiden for nothing."

"*What?*" She put her hands on her hips.

Calderon slinked back to his desk, head down. "I thought we were friends," he muttered.

"Jackass," she tossed back at him.

"Ignore them, Rebecca," Paavo said. "What've you got?"

Still smarting, she handed him a piece of paper, then sat. "It's a warrant for Dzanic's arrest."

"Aren't you being hasty?" Paavo pulled up a chair and read the warrant. "I don't want to rule out others until we're certain of her guilt."

"We *are* certain," Rebecca stated. "We've got her fingerprints on the murder weapon."

"True. But it was a knife from the place she worked as a kitchen helper."

"So? That only incriminates her more."

"What if someone wanted to set her up? She was the one who cleaned the kitchen. She'd wash the knives and put them away. Until used again, they'd only have her fingerprints. Anyone who worked there, who spent much time there, would know that."

"Possible," Rebecca admitted. "But a long shot. Also, you can't ignore the connection with Shelly Farms. The two deaths have to be linked somehow. Hannah knew both men, and I don't buy coincidence. You taught me that. Besides, the only other person with prints in Tyler's apartment was Olympia Pappas, and her alibi is rock-solid. She was at work at Central Station."

"Central isn't all that far from Marsh's building," Paavo mused. "When was her lunch break?"

She flipped pages in a binder until she came to the one she wanted. "Here we go. Olympia Pappas. Work at nine P.M., lunch with two girlfriends one in the morning, back on duty one-thirty, out at five-thirty." She stopped reading. "Marsh was killed, best we can figure, between midnight and one A.M."

"You think she's innocent?"

"Yes." Rebecca frowned. "She seemed like a nice woman, and not heartbroken and jealous the way her mother and others were saying. She said she'd gotten over Tyler months ago."

"Interesting," Paavo said. That didn't jibe with the way Angie had described her, and Angie was one of the best readers of people he'd ever known.

Rebecca picked up her shoulder bag. "I'm out of here. I'm going to try to reach some of the neighbors who weren't home last time I went by. Want to come along? Maybe someone's seen something we've missed—like Hannah Dzanic lurking around Tyler's apartment."

"Good idea," he said, turning back to the paperwork. *Hannah Dzanic lurking around Tyler's apartment . . .* Where had he heard that, or something like it, before? Was it something Angie told him?

He didn't notice Rebecca roll her eyes in exasperation before she headed toward the door, but he did see her sock Calderon in the arm to show all was forgiven.

Calderon winced. Her weight training was obviously paying off.

Angie was troubled by her suspicion of Hannah and Tyler wanting to sell their baby to the Vandermeers. If the Vandermeers were interested in adopting, why wouldn't they simply go to an adoption agency?

Paavo suspected that Vandermeer couldn't adopt because he was a violent felon, but he wasn't sure.

Angie knew someone who could help—Dianne Randle. Surely a social worker would know the answer, and if not, she could make a few phone calls and get the answer in minutes rather than Angie running off on a wild goose chase. She didn't have time to waste. With only two days before the day of the big event, the hope that somehow, some way, she'd find out about her party still glimmered. Dimly, true, but she hadn't yet given up. This party had to be the most exasperating experience of her life—and all caused by her own mother!

She ignored the glares and scowls of the women waiting in the welfare line as she asked an assistant for a couple of minutes with Miss Randle concerning Hannah Dzanic's possible involvement in a murder case.

The assistant's eyes bulged as she hurried back to the offices.

Less than five minutes later, she returned. "I'm sorry," she said. "Dianne has no information for you. She said she can only talk to the police due to privacy concerns. In the meantime, if you'd like to make an appointment, she has an opening in three weeks."

"If I *what*?" Had she heard right? It sounded like a typical bureaucratic runaround. What was wrong with these people?

"I'm sorry," the assistant said.

"Thank you, that helps," Angie said, hoping to win the girl over. The clerk nodded sympathetically. "Actually, all I wanted to do," Angie continued, "was to ask about adoptions. I wanted to find out if a couple named Vandermeer tried to get one."

"Vandermeer? Oh, man, you don't mean Lance

Vandermeer, do you?" The assistant's expressive eyes were saucerlike again.

"A big, blond, Teutonic-looking guy," Angie said. "You know him?"

"I know who he is. He came here once." The girl grew a little breathless from the memory.

Angie leaned closer. "Did he? He's kind of scary, isn't he? I heard he's been in prison."

"That's right," the assistant whispered. "Now, I didn't say this, hear? But when he was told it would be hard, maybe impossible, for him to adopt because of his record, he blew up and swore the charges were false. He had us so scared we had to call a guard to escort him out! I hope he never gets his hands on a child. I don't like or trust him one bit."

Angie thanked her and as soon as she was clear of the office, she smiled broadly. *Privacy laws, hah!*

Angie knocked on Stan's door when she got back to her apartment. He was wearing Kaitlyn on the Snugli. The front of his hair was plastered to his forehead. She couldn't figure out what was wrong with it until she realized it was covered with baby formula.

"I think Hannah killed Tyler!" she cried.

He shut his door and hustled her into her own apartment. "You, too?" The words were a *cri du coeur*. "Paavo was here earlier. He said the same thing. She had no reason to do it!"

"But she did. The two of them planned to sell the baby. Hannah changed her mind and killed him."

Stan stood still as if in shock. "They wanted to sell Kaitlyn? Impossible! Not Hannah."

"It's true." Angie grabbed the sleeve of his sweatshirt, giving it a little shake as she spoke. "Not only that. Remember those things that looked like cradles that Leer and Zeno were carrying? I think they *were* cradles! I think they smuggle babies into the city on the boat and then sell them. Hannah must have been a part of it but then changed her mind and decided to keep her own child. That's why she was so scared and ran away. Big money is involved. If she ever does try to come back, we've got to call Paavo immediately."

"I can't do it," Stan said, breaking free and walking toward the sofa. He sat, covering his face.

Angie put her hands on her hips. "What's going on, Stan?"

He dropped his hands. "Hannah's back. She's in my apartment. She's sleeping and Kaitlyn was fussing and that's why . . ." He glanced down at the baby, stuck like a barnacle against him. He told Angie about Hannah's capture, and how she had a knife and was scared and crying, desperate to take the baby and run. "She'd never sell her."

"If all that's true, why didn't Hannah go straight to the police to report Marsh?"

"I'm not sure . . . maybe she didn't want to send someone she once loved to jail."

"Oh, please!" Angie sneered. "You know what the police will think. They'll think she didn't go to them because she was involved, a part of the smuggling ring. And she killed him."

"That's impossible. You should see her. She's weaker than ever, and mentally as well as physically exhausted. There's no way she could have killed Tyler. She can scarcely think—she just leaned on me and I had to tell her to eat, tell her to go to bed. It was unbelievable."

"Did you also tell her Tyler was found murdered?" Angie asked.

"No. I didn't want to upset her more than she already is."

Angie didn't like the way he answered. "She may be weak now, but how do you know she didn't kill him in the passion of the moment, so to speak?"

Stan looked scared. "I believe her. Anyway, if even *you* think she might be guilty, what good would it do her to go to the police? She wouldn't stand a chance." He rubbed his forehead. "I've got to prove she's innocent. You need to help me, Angie. Somehow, we'll do it."

"I can't work against Paavo!" she cried.

"You won't be. You'll be helping him find the true murderer."

Stan was right. "Everything revolves around the Athina," she said. "There's a murderer out there . . . and possibly a smuggling operation. We've got to find out what's going on."

"Hell, no! I'm not going back!" Stan said. "They know too much about me. They'll kill me. I think Michael Zeno is the one who killed Tyler because he was jealous of him and Hannah, and he feels the same about me!"

"I'm not saying go into the restaurant. I'm saying we've got to hide somewhere after hours and watch it."

"What if we don't hide good enough? We're talking about someone who's already *killed*, Angie.

What if he finds us?" He shuddered, and in a whimper said, "There's got to be another way."

"There isn't. I don't want to be in danger any more than you do," she said firmly. "Besides, I promised Paavo we wouldn't go near the restaurant. Instead, we'll use binoculars and hide far away. If we're going to do this, though, you need to decide right now. As soon as we know for sure that Rebecca Mayfield has a warrant for Hannah's arrest, we either tell where Hannah is, or we're harboring a fugitive. I don't want to spend my engagement in jail."

"Do I have a choice?" Stan asked in a tiny voice.

"No."

The more Paavo thought about Olympia Pappas, the more curious he became. Unless Angie had badly misread the woman, which wasn't likely, she'd lied to Rebecca about her feelings for Tyler. The lie made sense, considering the situation, but it was troubling enough to make him want to check her out further.

He called John Erickson, Central Station's captain, and a guy he'd worked with on several cases over the years. He explained his interest in Pappas. "I'd like to know, as closely as possible, what her duties were between midnight and one A.M., May first," he said.

Erickson phoned back about ten minutes later. "She'd worked in files, alone, basically taking stacks of forms and reports and filing them in the proper folder, or making up folders if it was a new case. That time of night, no one had supervised her, or even paid attention to how much, or how little, work she'd gotten done."

"You've been a big help, John. Thanks," Paavo said. "Is she on duty tonight?"

"Let me see. . . . No, she's off. She'll be here tomorrow, though, swing shift. Three to midnight. Is Olympia a suspect?" Erickson asked.

"Not yet. I'll have to talk to her, though."

"She's a good woman," Erickson said. "A little messed up about the dead guy, but I can't see her killing him."

That seemed to be how everyone felt, Paavo thought. "Let's hope you're right, for her sake."

At three A.M., Angie drove to Fisherman's Wharf and easily parked. She was getting to like these hours.

Stan brought Kaitlyn, afraid to leave her home with a weak and sleeping Hannah. Not to mention that the woman had possibly murdered the baby's father. Stan didn't think she had, but if he was wrong, he didn't want to take the chance with Kaitlyn—and Angie had promised they wouldn't get too close. It should be safe, and if it wasn't, he wouldn't endanger the baby by taking part. That was that.

Near the Athina, the Hyde Street Pier had several schooners set up as living museums on the water. They headed out onto the pier, binoculars in hand. The eerie night fog gave the ships a ghostly quality.

Stan fastened the Snugli, hefted the diaper bag onto his shoulder, and he and Angie set off into the mist. Soon, he grabbed Angie's hand. "This looks like a scene in a creepy pirate movie," he said.

"Yo, ho, ho," she whispered, then chuckled nervously. "Let's go a little farther out onto the pier. I can't quite see the restaurant."

"But we can see the dock, and no boat is there. Let's stay here. It's safer . . . for the baby."

"Come on!" She pulled him and he stumbled a few steps farther out in the open. "If we want to spy on smugglers, we've got to find a good vantage point. This isn't it."

"No!" He pulled back, and she was jerked toward him.

"You're being silly!" She tugged again.

"You're being nuts!" He dug in his heels. Kaitlyn began to cry, and he put the heavy diaper bag on the ground and unzipped it, looking for a bottle to quiet her.

Suddenly a bright flashlight coming from the direction of the Athina aimed directly at them. The two froze. They couldn't tell who or what held it.

"Run!" Angie cried. "They might have a gun!" She turned and raced out of the light, away from the ships, the wharf, and whatever else threatened. Stan grabbed the open diaper bag in one hand, the other holding the baby close. As he awkwardly ran, diapers tumbled out, got caught in the breeze, and flitted around the dock like so many miniature ghosts.

On the sidewalk, they saw some men running their way.

Angie froze.

Stan somehow got the strap of the diaper bag over his head, around his neck and shoulder, and with his now-free hand, he grabbed Angie and pulled her along toward her car, running like a galumphing pack animal as fast as he could, and crying, "*Oh no, oh no, oh no!*" the entire way.

Angie doubted it was chivalry, though. She had the car keys in her pocket.

Chapter 26

Paavo had just reached his desk with his morning cup of coffee when two men in gray suits approached. They looked so different from "normal" people, the word FED could have been stamped on their foreheads. He stood.

"Paavo Smith?" a fifty-something man with short-clipped gray hair asked.

"Yes."

"I'm Agent Doone. This is Agent Thompson, FBI." Thompson was a younger man, blond and brash with a tough-guy stance that made Paavo want to smirk. They showed their badges. "We'd like to talk to you and Inspector Mayfield," Doone said.

"Mayfield's in court this morning," Paavo explained. "She should be back around noon."

"You'll have to do, then. Seems we're right behind you in this investigation," Doone said.

Experience told Paavo that FBI involvement in anything he was doing meant bad news. "Which investigation is that?"

Thompson bristled and answered for Doone. "Sherlock Farnsworth, a.k.a. Shelly Farms." He spat out the name as if Paavo were an idiot for not knowing.

Paavo sucked in his breath. "What's your interest?"

"Nothing that is of concern to you or Mayfield," Doone replied. "In fact, the more you two find out about the case, the more trouble that might cause us."

"Farnsworth was killed in our jurisdiction," Paavo said. "We need to find out who did it."

"You need to stay away from the Athina," Thompson added, his voice raised.

"No way," Paavo said.

Doone looked around the bureau. Only the secretary and Bo Benson were there. Benson looked ready to intercede if necessary. "Where can we talk in private?" Doone asked.

Paavo led the agents to Homicide's interrogation room, a plain, windowless room with only a wooden table in the center and two metal chairs on either side.

"Okay," Doone growled. "We'll fill you in on what's going on. It's probably better than to have any more slipups like last night's."

"Last night?" Paavo asked.

Doone ignored that question, and instead told him about what the Feds called the "baby train." It involved a team of smugglers. When they found a woman who was pregnant and didn't want the child, they told her abortion and state-sanctioned adoption weren't the only alternatives, that the child could be given life, a good home with well-to-do parents who wanted it enough to pay big bucks, *and* the mother would be amply compensated for her troubles as well— usually to the tune of $20,000 to $25,000 cash. For many women, that represented a year's salary or more.

If the mother agreed, as she neared delivery time she'd be moved to a small apartment somewhere in Los Angeles, away from family and friends so no one could come along and talk her out of what she'd agreed to. After giving birth, she'd return to the apartment or a nice hotel to recuperate for a week or two. The baby would be put on a fishing boat that was set up like a traveling nursery and brought to the city. Such a boat was easy to hide in Fisherman's Wharf and easier to use to transport several babies at once than was a car or bus.

The soon-to-be parents would stay in San Francisco awaiting the child's arrival. Once the baby was in hand, they'd pay the rest of the money— often a total of around $75,000.

The day before he died, Farnsworth had tipped off the FBI that the Athina was central to this scheme. Since then, they'd been trying to get two things: proof of involvement of the people at the Athina, and to find out who the true honcho was that oversaw the whole operation. They'd finally gotten the okay from on high to set up surveillance of the restaurant, when a young couple with a baby wandered onto the scene and disrupted everything.

Paavo listened to Doone's story with interest.

From what he'd seen, the Athina owners might be a lot more involved than the FBI thought. Look at their treatment of Hannah. He wondered why she hadn't been sent away to Los Angeles, and if it had anything to do with Tyler being the father.

"You have no proof?" Paavo asked.

"Farnsworth was working on getting some. We're sure that's why he's dead. We think that may be why your other case—Tyler Marsh—is dead as well. He was on our list of people to watch. Farnsworth was very interested in the man for some reason."

Suddenly the interrogation room door opened and Angie and Stan peeked in. "Oops! I'm sorry," Angie said to Paavo. "When I heard you weren't doing an interrogation, I thought it meant you were alone. I've got to talk to you soon as you're free." She backed from the room, pulling the door shut.

Thompson's eyes widened with shock. "Freeze!" he yelled, and jumped to his feet as his hand slipped under his jacket to his shoulder holster. Paavo put a hand on the man's arm, stopping him.

"Me?" Angie asked, her head swiveling from the crazy man to Paavo. Stan, who was peeking into the room with the baby still glued to his stomach, clutched Angie's arm.

"What are you doing?" Paavo's tone was loud, firm, and furious. "That's my fiancée."

"What?" Thompson and Doone both gasped.

"Angie Amalfi," Paavo said, as she let the door swing wide open, "meet Agents Thompson and Doone. And"—he did a double-take as he looked at Stan, unshaven, hair in need of a trim and un-moussed, wearing wrinkled clothes with baby spit-up on his shoulder, and a small bonneted baby in some kind of sling against his chest—"this is her neighbor, Stan Bonnette."

"They're the two who wrecked our operation last night," Thompson yelled. "We should arrest them for obstructing justice!"

Angie and Stan huddled in the doorway while the baby made gurgling noises.

"They're the couple with a kid?" Paavo asked, shocked.

"Well . . . uh . . ." Thompson now looked confused, and glanced at Doone for help.

The way the older man was glaring at her, Angie half expected a low-hanging ceiling light and rubber hoses to appear, but as she thought about it, she grew irritated. "It was the FBI crawling all over that pier?" she asked, disentangling herself from her supposed partner in crime. "Chasing us and scaring us half to death?"

Thompson waggled his thumb toward Stan, and in a falsetto said, "*Oh no, oh no, oh no.*" Then he laughed. The others ignored him except for Stan, who flushed rosy red.

"We set up surveillance and wondered why you were watching us," Doone said. "We thought you might be connected with the restaurant until we saw the way you ran. Still, you were so loud we had to pick up stakes for another day."

"You're the ones who scared us with that light beam. We would have been quiet if you hadn't done that," Angie insisted.

Thompson puffed out his chest. "You two civilians screwed up everything. A boat is due in soon. Now we aren't ready."

Angie glanced at Stan, then noticed Paavo glowering at her.

"I've warned you the place is dangerous, Angie," Paavo said. "You and Stan will stay far away from it if I have to lock you both in City Jail until this is over. Is that clear?"

"We were just trying to help!" Angie said. "Nobody there cares about us."

"Tyler Marsh did," Paavo said. "When Peter Leong woke up—he'll be all right, by the way—he ID'd Tyler as the man who attacked him."

"I see," Angie said with a gulp, suddenly not nearly so sure of herself. "Let's go, Stan." The two marched out the door without a backward glance, Angie with her head held high. She knew when it was time to keep her mouth shut.

When Stan entered his apartment, Hannah was seated on the sofa by the window, the sun streaming in on her, showering her in golden light.

At the sound of the door, she faced him, her eyes sad and red, as if she'd been crying. "I decided to look at the newspaper today while you went for a walk with Kaitlyn. Why didn't you tell me?"

He detached Kaitlyn and handed her the baby, who only squawked a short while before settling down as her mother gave her a bottle.

He knew Hannah was talking about Tyler. Had he purposefully saved those old *Chronicles* so she would spot them? It was a coward's way out, but he didn't think he could bear to tell her and then see her face reflect her grief over the scumbag. Or worse, her guilt.

He sat in the easy chair near her and clasped his hands. "You should know," he began softly, "the police suspect you did it."

"Me?" Her brown eyes searched his face as if looking for a sign that he was joking, all the while knowing he wouldn't joke about this. Finally, she dropped her gaze. "I'll admit," she whispered, "there were times I would have liked to kill him, but I didn't. I couldn't."

"I know." He tried to run his fingers through his hair, but it was caked with baby formula. He dropped his hand to his lap in disgust. "You've got to tell me what's going on. Where were you when Tyler was killed?"

Her face stricken, she stood and grabbed a diaper to change the baby. "You believe I killed Tyler?"

"Why not?" His tone was harsh. "When have you ever opened up to me enough that I should believe or understand anything about you?"

In silence, she took care of Kaitlyn and then laid her in her crib. Stan looked down at the baby. "Angie said you and Tyler planned to sell her."

Hannah froze. "It's not true!"

"Isn't it?" Stan asked.

She walked to the sofa and he followed. She sat, and then slowly began to talk about the day Tyler informed her of a loving, wealthy couple supposedly too old to adopt through the agencies. He explained that they would set up the child with trust funds and every possible need should something happen to them. Their child would be well looked after the rest of its life.

At first, willing to do anything in hopes Tyler would love her again, she'd agreed.

Stan sat beside her. "How did Shelly Farms come into the picture?"

"He helped me be firm with Tyler," she said, "and advised me to run, to go far away from the restaurant. But he wouldn't say why."

She put off leaving—afraid to stay but even more scared of being alone. It was her job, and Gail Leer was more than a boss, was someone she looked up to and respected. And she still clung to the foolish hope that Tyler would change his mind, just as she'd changed hers.

Then Shelly disappeared, and she met Stan.

In Stan, she saw a way out. She could have her baby, hide from Tyler, and, when strong enough, leave the city. She never counted on two things— that she'd fall in love with him and not want to leave, or that Tyler would find her.

It was only when Tyler held her as prisoner, however, that she learned why he'd been so desperate to let the Vandermeers have the baby— they were paying him money. He was selling his own child.

"You saved me," she said, pressing close to Stan. "You're my hero. I don't know what I would have done without you. Please don't hate me for my stupid mistakes. Please." She tilted her face toward his, her mouth upturned and inviting, her eyes filled with love and something akin to reverence.

He swallowed hard, then wrapped his arms

around her and lowered her head to his shoulder, offering comfort but nothing more.

What, he thought, *have I gotten myself into?* Being a hero wasn't all it was cracked up to be.

Chapter 27

Paavo phoned Olympia and asked her to come to the Homicide bureau at the Hall of Justice. She didn't ask why, which he appreciated. As one who worked with cops, she should be smarter than that.

When she walked in, though, she wasn't nearly so docile. Or so smart. She was an attractive woman, the sort a man immediately noticed, with her wild mass of dark hair, large breasts, heavily made-up eyes, red lips, and a personality that matched her appearance.

"I already talked to Inspector Mayfield," she said as Paavo led her into the interrogation room. "I thought we covered everything."

"There's a bit more," he said. "You worked in files on the night Tyler was killed. Who saw you there?"

"What are you talking about? I was at work! Everyone saw me! I told Mayfield. Check with the others." She reached for cigarettes in her purse, then threw them down in disgust, knowing without asking about the workplace no-smoking policy. She was emotionally on edge, and Paavo could make good use of that.

"You were in the files area alone," he told her. "It's easy to leave it unseen by going through the back door near the women's room."

Her eyes flashed. "Sounds like you've been there."

He nodded.

"It might be easy to sneak out," she said, "but I didn't."

"You saw Tyler that evening at the Athina," he prodded, then stood. "It wasn't the first time you'd taken off work to see what he was up to."

Her gaze lifted, following him. "You're crazy!"

"Am I? Why would he have told people you did it, if it was all fantasy? Why else would your mother have said she was afraid you'd be fired because of Tyler?"

"You talked to my mother? She never would have said that!"

He placed his palms on the table. "She also said you loved him."

"Nonsense!"

"Why would Eleni lie about it?"

"Go to hell!" she yelled.

"Tyler is dead, Olympia. And now you deny you loved him? Was it so meaningless?" She stared at the marks and blemishes on the table-top, not answering. His voice gentled. "You loved him. Everyone knows it. Why do you deny it now?"

"God! All right!" Her eyes grew teary and she covered them a moment before saying, "I cared about him, okay? Maybe I did love him. But I wouldn't hurt him."

"You followed him that night, though, didn't you?"

She shut her eyes a long moment. *She's going to confess*, Paavo thought, surprisingly sorry at the thought. It was a shame that scum like Tyler Marsh should cause this vivacious woman to spend the rest of her life in prison.

"All right," she said, grabbing her cigarettes, removing one from the pack, and holding it even though she couldn't smoke. "I'll tell you what happened. I looked in the restaurant before going to work and saw him with an attractive blonde. She was alone, and clearly enjoying his attention. I was sure he was going to take her to his apartment. I hated the thought—another conquest for him. I thought when he and Hannah split he'd come back to me. He did, but not like before. He didn't love me. There were always other women—"

"So what did you do?" Paavo asked, wanting to bring her back on track. He didn't need her tales of a jilted lover.

She tapped the unfiltered end of the cigarette against the pack. "I snuck out from work and went to his place to see if my suspicion was right. I sat in my car, watching. The lights were on in his apartment. I saw movement. I was sure it was the blonde. I was deciding if I wanted to go in there and break up his little tryst when a man left Tyler's, got into a car, and drove away. Relieved, I went back to work. That was all."

"Did you?" Paavo asked. "I should think you'd

have gone into Tyler's apartment. That was why you were there. You wanted to see him. Confront him."

"No! I only wanted to know what he was up to. And I had to get back to work. My files shift was nearly over. I've been warned, you see."

He nodded, studying her. "Didn't it occur to you that you might have seen his murderer? That you should have come to the police with this information?"

She shook her head. "The man I saw wasn't running or acting guilty. In fact, he looked familiar—one of Tyler's friends from the Athina, I figured. He didn't look like a killer. The one who killed him, I'm sure, was Hannah. Everybody thinks so."

"And Hannah Dzanic does look like a killer to you?" he asked.

"Absolutely!"

"I see." He sat on the edge of the desk near her. "You work around cops, Olympia. With the timing of Tyler's murder, and the man you saw, surely you had to consider—"

"Maybe I did, Inspector," she blurted out as she hurled the cigarette hard into the wastebasket. "Maybe I also thought . . . No, I shouldn't say. You'll think me too heartless."

"What?"

She began to gasp for breath as she forced out the words. "That if he was killed by a friend, it meant he did someone else dirt just like he did me. And . . . and I was glad he was killed!" The words were no sooner out of her mouth than she began to sob.

Paavo went out to the secretary for a box of Kleenex and water, gave her moment to herself, then brought them into the interrogation room.

"You said the man looked familiar. Any idea who he might be?"

She wiped her eyes and shook her head.

"Did you get his license plate number?"

Same response.

"What did he look like?"

She swallowed hard a couple of times, then sipped some water, trying to compose herself. "He was tall," she began. "Taller than Tyler, I'm sure, and his hair seemed either blond or gray—it was hard to tell in the streetlight. His face was pale, and very stern."

"Age?"

"I'm not sure. He didn't dress like a young man. He wore an overcoat. It appeared black in the darkness, but I'm not sure it was. He had a bulky middle-aged sort of look—a bit of a stomach, you know?"

"What was the make of car?"

"That I remember well because I thought Tyler's friends had either moved up in the world, or he was a drug dealer. It was one of those big BMWs, not the kind you usually see."

"Was he wearing gloves?"

Olympia turned sharply, her gaze questioning. "Gloves? I'm not sure. The night was cold, foggy."

"If there was blood on him, could you have seen it?"

She shook her head. "The street lamps were too far, and his clothes too dark."

Paavo nodded. That was as he'd expected. Still . . .

"Money, middle-aged, blond . . ." he murmured. He'd seen someone not long ago who fit that description. "I'm going to show you some mug shots, Miss Pappas. I'd like you to see if you can identify the man."

"As I said, it was dark, Inspector."

"Do your best."

He brought her a pile of mug shots of middle-aged blond men. She picked one out immediately.

"This is him! I can't believe it." She pointed to a photo of Lance Vandermeer. "Who is he?"

"You're fairly certain?" Paavo asked.

"As certain as I can be considering that it was night and some distance away."

"Do you think you might be confusing the man you saw that night with someone else from the Athina?"

She studied the photo. "No. I *have* seen him before with Tyler, though—maybe the Athina, maybe elsewhere. I can't remember. You see, I've followed— Hell, never mind. But I'm sure this is the man with Tyler the night he died."

Paavo stood. "You've been a big help, Miss Pappas. Thank you for your cooperation. We'll be calling you soon."

"Inspector Smith," she said after shaking his hand to leave, "Tyler Marsh was a good man. A little greedy and he did a few things wrong, but his heart was good. I could have turned him around. I know it." Tears glistened. "That's why I never gave up on him. Why I still love him."

Paavo showed her to the door and made a call to Rebecca Mayfield. Time for them to pay a visit to Lance Vandermeer.

"Angie, what am I going to do?" Stan asked when she opened her door. He looked worse than ever. The bags under his eyes had turned into steamer trunks. The baby was still adhered to him.

"It's Hannah, isn't it?" Angie asked, opening the door wide so he could enter her apartment.

"That's right. I don't know what to do about her." He headed straight to Angie's refrigerator.

She followed. "I'm sure she'll come to love you the way you do her," Angie counseled. "Just give her time."

He gaped at her, a plate of leftover lasagna in his hand. "What are you talking about?"

"Don't play coy. You, Hannah, and the baby are so cute together," she said, beaming at him. "You're completely devoted to them both. I can tell these things. Now, you simply have to decide when's a good time to make this a permanent arrangement."

"No!" He shouted.

She was taken aback. "Why not? You're in love."

"This is not love!" He heated the food in the microwave.

Angie put a place mat and utensils on the kitchen table for him. "What's that supposed to mean? You're happy, aren't you?"

"Happy? Oh, sure. Look at me, don't I look happy?" He gazed woefully down at himself. So did Angie.

Stan was a man who'd used "product" in his hair even before it became fashionable for men. Now his hair was dry and unruly, and Angie had to admit she'd never seen him before with splotches of grease and gunk on his clothes. Even his casual clothes had always been tailored and neat, with a marked preference for just-from-the-dry-cleaners button-down shirts and knit pullovers. Lately, however, all he wore were T-shirts.

She couldn't help but frown. "Well, actually . . ."

To her horror, he burst into tears. "I knew it!" he wailed. "I'm a mess. A complete mess!"

"Don't be silly." The microwave beeped and even after Angie put the lasagna in front of him, his tears continued. "It's not that bad," she hurried to add. "I mean, for the sake of the baby—"

"Everything's for the sake of the baby!" he cried, bawling harder. Angie ran to the counter and pulled out a wad of Kleenex. She'd never seen Stan so upset before. He took it, but instead of using it, he just held it in his hands. "She's a beautiful baby, a great kid, in fact, and she has the good taste to really like me and wants to be with me all the time. But my clothes perpetually smell like a baby, Angie! I don't have time to do anything but take care of her. She's taken over my entire life! If I had a girlfriend who was half so demanding, I'd ditch her so fast she'd spin like a top from turbulence as I ran out the door!"

"Stan, calm down," Angie said.

"Calm? You're telling me to be calm? How can I be calm? I don't have time to even get a haircut, let alone take my clothes to the dry cleaner. For the first time, ever, I've had to use my washing machine and dryer. Up to now, they'd been plant stands. Hannah was the one who showed me how to work them!"

"Good for her." Angie folded her arms.

He scowled at her with disgust. "How can one baby take up so much time? Do you know how starved I am for adult conversation? Even when Hannah's awake, which isn't often, we talk about Kaitlyn!"

Angie poured them both some iced tea and sat across from him. "I'm sure it's not that bad."

"Bad? I'll tell you what's bad. It's being Mr. Nice Guy who lets a stranger and her baby take over his apartment, his kitchen, even his bathroom! Do you know what it's like to find a woman's underwear in my bathroom? I'm sleeping on the sofa, and most nights it's so covered with stuff from the baby I can hardly find it to go to bed. And she's always apologizing for being there, for being trouble. Do you know how annoying it is to be around someone who's constantly grateful? And when I ask her what she wants to eat, she says she doesn't know, that it's up to me. I have to make all these decisions about food, when all I really want to do is to come over here and see what you've got left over."

He took a big bite of lasagna and seemed ready to cry again, this time from pure ecstasy.

"She's trying to be a good guest, that's all," Angie patiently explained. "And to not interfere with things you want. How can it bother you?"

He ate another big bite, then swallowed. "How can it? Good question. That's what I tell myself. I shouldn't care. I should put up with it. All of it. The constant smell of slightly soured milk in my apartment. Trying to decide if I prefer to use Pampers and have them sit in plastic bags fermenting until I gather them together and dispose of them, or use cloth diapers that have to be shaken out in the toilet then lay rotting in a pail until a sour-faced delivery man picks them up. And I thought my job was crummy! *What do I care about diapers, anyway?* Nothing! I've found out more about diapers than I've ever wanted to know." He began to sob even harder. "Just thinking about them makes me sick!"

"Stan, control yourself!" Angie said, growing increasingly worried.

"I don't want to control myself! I have controlled myself, over and over for days, watching my nice life turned completely upside down! Did you know I tried making her omelets, for God's sake, just to get her to eat more than a few little nibbles? The woman wasn't well nourished to begin with, and then having the baby, and soon after going through all that with Tyler, she needs bed rest, almost constant bed rest, and lots of good food. But I don't want to cook. I don't know how to cook. I hate to cook! And I especially don't want to cook smelly eggs! The apartment reeks of them for hours, along with all the baby smells. Do you know babies do nothing but sleep, eat, cry, and dirty their diapers? That's it."

"Stop already!" she pleaded. "I had no idea."

He grabbed another wad of Kleenex and blew his nose. "Angie, what am I going to do? I want my nice life back! Hell, I want my bed back!"

Chapter 28

The day of her engagement party Angie was in a tizzy. Apparently the U.S. Postal Service had done its job and delivered the directions to the party on time, but not even Connie would tell her its location, only chuckling and saying it was someplace "special." Special? What in the world did that mean? Angie was more worried than ever.

She planned to pay Connie a visit. Stan had probably received a special delivery letter, but she didn't even want to try to get any information out of him.

He was a babbling mass of confusion. Last evening after his breakdown, they'd come up with a plan. This afternoon, he was going to call Hannah's social worker for the name of a trustworthy babysitter and then he and Hannah were going out for lunch. There, he'd tell her that he liked her, but that was it, and that she'd have to find her own place to live. He'd go with her to Homicide to talk to Rebecca Mayfield. She could probably get pro bono help from Shelly Farms's law firm since they'd been friends. Stan would do what he could to help her, but the bottom line was she needed to move out.

Angie could only hope it'd work.

In late morning, Paavo stopped by. One look at his face and she could see he was still angry with her. "Please tell me you haven't done anything else since *ruining an FBI operation and putting yourself in danger.*" Normally, Paavo never yelled. Today was an exception. "There's a murderer out there, Angie. What the hell were you and Stan thinking?"

She guessed this wasn't the time to tell him how she wanted to be helpful in his business the way Serefina had been with Sal's. "I'm sorry," she said, and that diffused him more than any argument could have.

In no time she placed a fluffy cheese and Italian sausage omelet in front of him, then sat down and watched his mood relax. "I was worried about you," he said, by way of apology.

"I know. You're so cute when you do that." At his stunned expression, she continued, "So, what did the FBI have to say? I can't believe that they're involved. It makes me think I might have been right about the baby smuggling."

He nodded, and between bites filled her in. "The FBI estimates there was a shipment every week or two. Usually two or three babies a shipment, at fifty to a hundred thousand per, no taxes. That's at least five million a year."

"It's scary to think there are that many women willing to sell their children."

"Or unwilling. Who knows what goes on when

these people need money or have customers? Hannah wasn't exactly willing."

"You're right." As she cleaned up the kitchen and they moved into the living room, she told him Hannah's story of being a foster child and deciding to keep her baby. She pretended it was something Stan had learned a while ago, since she'd promised Stan she wouldn't reveal Hannah's whereabouts to Paavo, but would give Hannah a chance to turn herself in for questioning.

Paavo stood by the window as Angie talked, looking out at San Francisco Bay. To his surprise, he found himself moved by Hannah's struggles to keep her child.

Like Hannah, he hadn't been raised by his parents. He was lucky that Aulis Kokkonen took care of him and managed to keep him out of the view of the Child Protective Services. Angie once said to him that no one simply raises someone else's kids. Aulis did, and for that, Paavo would be forever grateful. Hannah didn't have an Aulis Kokkonen in her life.

He wondered if Hannah felt, as he often did in the darkness of night when he was alone, that the reason her parents gave her up was because she was unlovable and that no one, ever, would be able to truly love her. He understood it was something many foster and adopted children felt—despite themselves.

He often wondered, in those same black hours, if one day Angie would wake up and realize she didn't truly love him, that she only "thought" she had, and now was going to dump him the way he "deserved." As much as he knew better intellectually, he couldn't control what his heart told him. And his heart had learned to think that way at a very young age.

In her search for love, Hannah had turned to Tyler, letting her emotions overrule her judgment until her maternal sense took over and made her run away.

She ran to Bonnette, again hoping for love. From what Angie had implied about the relationship, Hannah had made another mistake. At least this time it wasn't a dangerous one.

"If Hannah's innocent," he said, "we'll find a way to help her."

"You don't think she killed Tyler after all?"

"I don't, and even Rebecca is wavering now. We've got another suspect—Lance Vandermeer. Olympia Pappas saw him with Tyler shortly before Tyler's death. The problem is Vandermeer claims he was home with his wife, that the witness may have seen him with Tyler at the Athina and is confused, and there's still the problem of only Hannah's fingerprints being on the murder weapon."

Angie was intrigued. "But you think he's a possibility?"

"I think he did it. The problem is that we don't have enough evidence to refute his alibi and get a search warrant."

"Why would Vandermeer want to kill Tyler?" Angie asked.

"Good question. We know he wanted to sell

Vandermeer his baby, but then Hannah refused to part with her," Paavo said. "Why that would lead to Tyler's death is a problem."

"We also know," Angie said, standing as she got more and more into this, "that Vandermeer had a violent temper. If he killed the baby's father and set up the baby's mother to go to prison for it, that would leave the child without a guardian and he could take her!"

"Only if he went through a private party," Paavo added, "like the people at the Athina—because we know Social Services wouldn't let him have her. But if Hannah were arrested, wouldn't she give Kaitlyn to Stan to care for?"

Angie shook her head. "I don't think Stan would do it." She rubbed her forehead and paced. "Think! There's got to be a reason."

"Let's look at this logically," Paavo said, leaning against an antique chest. "The Athina is involved in smuggling babies. Shelly Farms finds out. He tells Hannah to get away. He also wants to talk to Tyler—maybe about Hannah—then turns up dead. If Tyler killed him, it may have been because Tyler saw their meeting as an opportunity to get rid of danger to the whole smuggling operation. After all, not only was Shelly a threat to the sale of Kaitlyn, but a threat to Tyler's source of income. A whole lot of income."

Angie nodded. "So, the other smugglers may have known Tyler was a killer—and that means he could have become a liability to them, a hunted man. Or, the smugglers might have felt they couldn't trust him for some reason. Or, maybe he demanded too much of a payoff for his crime . . . and that's how Vandermeer got involved!"

"It is?" Paavo asked.

"Exactly," Angie continued. "One of the people at the restaurant could have easily convinced Vandermeer that Tyler was scamming him, would take his money and not give him the baby. Whoever did that gave Vandermeer a knife from the kitchen with Hannah's fingerprints and told him to use it on Tyler!"

Paavo stared at her. "You've got a devious mind, Angie." Then he grinned. "And you may be right."

"Not only that," she said proudly, "but I know who killed him."

"You do?"

She smiled, and after a dramatic pause, announced, "Gail Leer! She's behind all of it—and she killed Tyler in a fit of rage when she learned what he'd done to Hannah."

Just then her phone rang. She answered. It was Gail Leer.

Gail stood at the bar of the Buena Vista, a popular tavern overlooking Aquatic Park. An Irish coffee was in front of her as she waited for Angie. It wasn't Angie who approached, though. It was Paavo.

The BV had two exits, one near each end of the bar. As soon as she saw him, she headed for the exit opposite. The crowd of people made it hard for her to get through quickly, and before she escaped, Paavo grabbed her arm.

"We've got to talk," he said.

"Where's Angie?"

"She's not coming."

"You have no reason to hold me." She tried and failed to pull free. "I'm leaving."

"You told Angie the FBI is on to you, that you needed to talk to Hannah. I'm here to listen," Paavo said.

She studied his eyes a long moment, as if trying to decide whether she could trust him or not. "I'd hoped Angie would bring me to Hannah, or at least relay a message to her. Tell her I didn't know about Tyler's plans. If I had, I would have stopped him. Tell her I wasn't a part of any of it, that . . . that I was hoping to help her raise her baby."

Her words surprised him and he let her go. Oddly, at that same moment, the pieces of the case began to fall together. "If not you, who was Tyler working with?"

A long moment passed. "My husband. I wasn't a partner in what he was doing, Inspector Smith, you've got to believe that! I knew about it, and in that I know I'm complicit. But I never actually did anything."

"Who else did he work with?"

She looked stunned by the question. "Well . . . Michael Zeno."

"And?" Paavo asked.

She rubbed her head. "I don't know. I once heard a name—Nadine Nadler. But I don't know who she is. I'm not even sure if she's involved."

He thought about that a moment, then asked, "Did you ever tell Hannah you'd help her? Why leave her alone, thinking no one cared?"

She lifted her chin. "I thought there was more time. The baby was about three weeks early.

And, as I said, I had no idea what Tyler was planning."

"Hannah may be arrested for Tyler's murder," Paavo said. "Evidence points her way; evidence I can't ignore. I don't want to take her in, but if I find her, I don't have a choice. Inspector Mayfield has a warrant for her arrest. I'd have to honor it."

"You can't do that to her!" Gail cried.

"She's a suspect in a murder."

Gail bowed her head, shaking it from side to side. "She's no killer! Damn, why didn't I talk to her, have her come to me? I'd have helped her."

Her cell phone began to ring. She glanced at the number. "It's the restaurant."

She stepped out to the sidewalk as she hit the talk button. "Hello?" Her eyes, wide with surprise, met Paavo's. "What? She is? . . . All right. . . . Yes."

She snapped her phone shut and put it in her purse. "I've got to go."

He cupped her elbow. "What's going on? You're in this too deep to walk away, you know. You can talk here or at the Hall of Justice."

She opened her mouth to protest, but then shut it. He let go as she walked away from the Buena Vista, across the street to the Aquatic Park, her breathing heavy the entire time. Paavo stayed with her, giving her time to sort this out in her mind, and hoping she'd make the right decision on her own, without him having to make it for her.

She stopped just past the cable car turntable, facing the water.

"If it's about Hannah," he said, "let me talk to her. The safest thing for her is to give herself up, to tell her side of the story. She needs to work with us. You know that, Mrs. Leer. Do what's right."

She nodded, and then her shoulders sagged in defeat. "The call was from my husband," she began in a soft and tremulous voice. "This morning, I told him I was leaving. That I couldn't believe he'd planned to sell Hannah's baby, that the FBI was lurking around—everyone on the dock saw them the other night—and that I couldn't sit back and watch him in silence any longer. Then I called Angie. I wasn't only calling about Hannah, but for myself as well. I'd hoped she'd be a go-between, that she'd talk to you and tell you my side of the story so I wouldn't be thrown into jail."

"Yes," he said, urging her to continue.

"Eugene called now to say Hannah's at the restaurant looking for me. She needs my help." Tears filled her eyes. "He asked me to come back, to help Hannah—and him. He said he'd been wrong; that he'd give everything up if I'd go back to him."

"Do you believe him?" Paavo asked.

"He's my husband."

Outside the Athina, the sign in the window said CLOSED. The front door was locked. Gail used her key to go inside. Paavo waited in the doorway, his gun ready.

The restaurant was empty. Even the kitchen.

"Eugene?" she called. She went into the kitchen. "No!" she cried.

Paavo hurried after her, gun drawn. Eugene Leer held her, a gun to her head. "Drop it," Paavo ordered.

"Wrong, Inspector." Eugene nodded behind Paavo.

He glanced quickly over his shoulder. Michael Zeno stood a few steps behind him, also holding a gun.

Chapter 29

When Angie returned from the hair-dresser, she called Paavo's cell phone and pager, but he didn't answer. She tried the Buena Vista with no luck. She then phoned Homicide. Yosh was no help, so she left a message for Rebecca Mayfield.

Fear and anger warred. Anger that he did anything at all, including his job, on this important Saturday. Why couldn't he wait? Why ruin their engagement party? But much stronger was fear that something terrible had happened to him. She could think of no other reason for him not to answer his cell phone. For him not to be home by now.

He was simply going to talk with Gail Leer, then head home and get ready for the party. He'd convinced Angie he wouldn't confront Gail, that she wasn't a threat to him and their meeting wouldn't be dangerous in any way. He'd question her about Tyler and Lance Vandermeer, and suggest she turn state's evidence for the FBI.

It wasn't even supposed to take an hour.

Where was he?

* * *

Paavo tried to move his wrists and loosen the rope that bound them, but they'd been tied too tight, so tight they were feeling cold, as if the blood supply had been cut off. He relaxed, trying to stop the tingling sensation from continuing.

As he'd suspected, saying Hannah had arrived was simply Eugene Leer's ploy to draw Gail back. They were afraid she might talk, and when they saw Paavo, their fears were confirmed. Gail was a liability now, wife or not.

He and Gail had been taken to the boat docked behind the restaurant. Belowdecks was an eating area with beds on one side, and on the other what was obviously a nursery set up for transporting babies. Beyond the living area were tables filled with charts, maps, and radio equipment. Toward the bow of the boat was an engine room. He and Gail had been led in there, and their wrists and ankles tied. He could hear footsteps as the two men walked around on deck and he wondered if they were getting ready to leave the wharf.

If so, to where?

He couldn't allow himself to think of Angie waiting for him. It had been all he could do to convince Leer and Zeno he'd go with them quietly—for them not to fire their weapons. Each man had looked nervous and scared, and that was the most dangerous type to face.

Gail stared at the wall, tears trickling down her cheeks. She knew these men, and her reaction was chilling.

"The worst part," she said softly, "is thinking of all that I should have done, and didn't."

"You mean when they held the guns on us? There wasn't much we could do."

"No. That's the least of it. I'm thinking of earlier. I'm thinking of Hannah. She always considered me her boss—a kindly boss, I hope, but nothing more. To me, though, she was a daughter. Everyone thinks I never had a child, but that's not true. I did have a child once, and I gave her up for adoption. She was born a month before Hannah.

"People always talk about the adopted child, how they wonder who their mother was and why she gave them up. No one talks about the mother. Do they really think it's possible to carry a child for nine months and then simply forget it was ever born? Do they think the mother picks up her life and goes on as if those months never happened? Do they think there's no heartache involved?"

He didn't respond; he didn't need to.

"For a while," she said, "I fantasized that Hannah was that daughter—both girls were born in Los Angeles, after all. I looked into it. Hired a private eye. I learned my daughter had died. She'd gotten in with a bad crowd in L.A. A gang. She was murdered. No one was ever charged; no one ever will be.

"Her adopting parents were good people, but apparently they never understood Cindy. From the time she turned thirteen, she was rebellious, and over the years it only grew worse. By age seventeen, she was dead."

"I'm sorry," Paavo said.

"I could see that Hannah was a good girl, but she had no one to help her when she was down. I tried to be there for her, but at the same time, I held back. Afraid to open myself, to get too close, you know? And now . . . now it's too late."

He didn't want to hear that. "Don't give up, Gail. We'll get out of this."

She shook her head. "We aren't the first ones this has happened to. I know what my husband is capable of. I've always known, I'm afraid. There are others who were never heard from again. Fish food I think is the term they use."

Paavo needed to stop her despair, to give her a reason for fighting. "You watched Hannah and Tyler together. How did you feel about him?"

"I didn't trust him. He was too smooth, too charming. I'd seen him with lots of women, and Hannah, frankly, wasn't his type. She was nice, quiet, and plain."

"Plain?" Paavo said. That wasn't the impression he had of her. Strangely, he'd never actually met her despite knowing so much about her.

"Yes." Gail smiled. "But she has a sweet honest innocence that can be charming to some men. Michael Zeno was one. Before meeting her, all he'd wanted to do was run his restaurant and cook. That's what he loved. He got involved with Eugene because of Hannah, wanting money to impress her, to win her love. I feel worse about him than anyone else."

Angie paced. She couldn't remember the last time she'd been so worried about Paavo. Early in their relationship, he'd often told her she wouldn't be able to handle him being a Homicide inspector—

not with the long hours, the danger, the need to be on call 24/7. She swore he was wrong, that she could not only cope, but also accept it because he loved what he did, was the best cop in the city, and she was proud of him.

Now, though, she wondered if she'd spoken too soon. What if he was hurt? Or worse?

She could scarcely breathe. If something happened to him, could she ever forgive this city and the people in it for putting him in danger—or herself for having him take a phone call meant for her?

She had already dressed in her yellow Dior, matching high-heeled sandals, her hair and makeup perfect. She kept thinking, *When I finish this task, he'll be here.* But he never was.

Her parents arrived. They were early, but wanted to spend a little time with her and Paavo before taking them to the party.

Finally, she'd find out where it was going to be held. Right now, though, it didn't matter.

"So," Salvatore said, looking around as he followed Serefina into the apartment, "where's the happy groom?" At Angie's forlorn expression, he asked, "What's the matter? Has he got cold feet already? It's not even the wedding yet."

"He . . . he's late," Angie said.

"Late? I don't believe it!" he bellowed. "And here I was trying to like him!"

"So he's a little late," Serefina chastised Sal. "It's no crime. Is it, Angelina?"

Angie's throat seemed to close and she couldn't answer.

Seeing her expression, Sal proclaimed, "Nobody jilts my little girl. Not when I've got anything to say about it!"

"I'm not being jilted," Angie cried. "It's just a party. Paavo had some business to take care of. I'm sure he'll be here as soon as he finishes it."

"Are you?" Sal eyed her closely.

She fought tears. "No."

He opened his arms and she ran to him. "What happened? A fight?"

She shook her head. "I'm afraid something's happened to him. He wouldn't do this. He'd call. I don't understand it."

"Madonna mia!" Serefina pressed her hands together as if in prayer. "If he could, he'd be here. I know it in my heart. Salvatore, do something!"

"Me?" He gasped.

Angie took great, gulping swallows of air, trying to keep her head clear, trying to stop the tears that threatened. *Where is he?* The question came from deep inside her. *Where?*

She left Sal's side and went to the windows, trying to think. He went to see Gail Leer; they were near the Athina . . .

She must have been right—that Gail was the so-called "mastermind" of the whole operation, and now she had Paavo.

Hannah knew Gail and the others well. Angie needed to talk to her.

She knocked on Stan's door, but no one was home. Of course not—they were going to get a babysitter and go out so Stan could lay it on the line with Hannah if he kept his nerve. Maybe they changed their minds and took the baby with them.

She went back to her apartment.

"We'll help you look for him, Angelina," Serefina said. "Just tell us where to begin."

"I have no idea," she said morosely.

She tried Paavo's home and cell phone again, then watched the minutes slowly tick by as she paced.

Her father tried to put his arms around her and hold her the way he did when she was a little girl and upset or frightened. But she was a woman now, so instead of curling up on his lap, after a while she squared her shoulders and stepped to the window, lost in thought.

A knock sounded on her door. It was Stan and Hannah. His apartment door was also open. "Did Kaitlyn cry so much the babysitter brought her to you?" Stan asked.

"What are you talking about?" Angie looked from one to the other.

He paled. "The baby. She's here, isn't she?"

Hannah's ashen face peered over his shoulder. "No."

"They've taken her!" Hannah cried, growing more hysterical with each word. "Someone must have been watching us, and when they saw us leave without the baby, they knew they could easily take her. God, what shall we do?"

He gripped her arms. "Take it easy. The babysitter might have just decided to go for a walk, for some reason." He didn't sound convinced. "Did you see or hear anything, Angie?"

"Nothing. But something else has happened,"

she said, as Sal and Serefina joined her. "Gail Leer phoned. Paavo went to see her, and now he hasn't returned, either."

"They're on the boat," Hannah cried. "They're taking my baby!"

Chapter 30

As Angie drove toward the Athina with Stan and Hannah, she spotted Paavo's Corvette parked not far from Jefferson Street. "We're on the right track!" she cried, then screeched to a halt just past his car, pulling into a red zone.

A set of his car keys lay in her purse, just as he kept a set of hers. She used them now to open his trunk.

In it was a case with an AR-15 assault rifle. Since crooks in the city were now heavily armed, some in the police department thought the cops should be as well. Snipers and SWAT team members always had semiautomatic weapons, but the idea of similarly arming other members of the police force didn't sit well with the heavily anti-gun populace of the city. The SFPD took the task on as a "pilot program" and only armed those few inspectors and officers who were most likely to come across desperate criminals. Like murderers.

Angie had seen where Paavo hid the key to the gun case, and slipped it out from under the car's ashtray. She unlocked the case. The semiautomatic was in several pieces.

Angie picked up two and studied them.

"What are you doing?" Hannah asked, eyeing the steel.

"I saw a program about these on the Discovery Channel. They showed how to put them together and how they worked. I was interested because I knew Paavo had one." She tried putting one piece onto the other, and when it didn't fit she turned it around and tried again.

Stan's eyes bugged out. "You don't know how to use such a thing!" He jumped back when she began to bang two pieces together on the sidewalk.

"There's a first time for everything, Stanfield," she said. "If I have to use this, I will."

"Are you sure?" Hannah asked.

"Whoever ruined my engagement party is toast!" As much as she tried to make a joke and told herself Paavo was fine, she couldn't keep it up. Her voice turned low and deadly, her eyes glistened, even as the words caught in her throat. "And if some bastard has hurt Paavo, God help him . . . or her."

"I've never seen a gun that looks like that," Stan said nervously.

She held up her handiwork. The AR-15 looked like a gun, sort of. One piece was left over and after studying it, she gave up and slipped it into the pocket of the long black wool coat she'd put on over her party dress. She'd chosen the coat to protect her dress. Somehow, she was going to find Paavo and get to their party, no matter what. She refused to think of any alternative.

"It's good enough," Angie said as she shoved the ammunition magazine into the chamber and tucked the rifle under her coat, hidden yet snug against her side.

Watching her, Stan turned several shades of green. Hannah seemed fascinated.

"It's too dangerous, Angie," Stan cried. "Call the police and let's go home."

"Don't be scared, Stan."

Both Angie and Hannah spoke at the same time, then glanced at each other, stunned.

They marched toward the restaurant, Angie, Hannah beside her, and Stan lagging at the rear. Angie watched Hannah warily—a flicker of suspicion about her still lingered. Hannah might have six inches on her, but Angie had determination.

They decided to check out the Athina first. Hannah unlocked the front door and, leaving it wide open, went inside. In moments, she was back out. "No one's there, but the fishing boat is docked."

Staying close to the restaurant, they tiptoed toward the wharf. Angie was the first to peek around the building to the boat.

"I see movement on the boat," she whispered.

"Oh, my!" Stan looked ready to faint.

Hannah peeked. "It's Michael Zeno. He won't hurt me. I'll go talk to him and see what I can find out. Paavo, Gail, and Kaitlyn are here somewhere. I know it."

"Be careful, Hannah!" Stan cried.

"I will," she said simply.

"We'll be here watching and listening," Angie said. Her plan was that as soon as she knew where Paavo was, she'd call Yosh to bring in the SWAT team. Angie pressed her back to the restaurant, the AR-15 heavy at her side, her heart pounding. Stan huddled beside her. She could feel him shaking. Or was that her own body?

Serefina was in tears.

"You'll have to go to the party, explain to everyone why Angie and the cop aren't there," Sal said. He was so angry he worried that he'd damage his heart again. "I'll admit he's a good cop, but if he's stiffed the party because he's working, I'll kill him with my bare hands!"

"Me? What are you going to do?"

"I'm going to help Angelina. It sounded like there's danger and I don't want her to get hurt. I should be there to protect her."

"You?" Serefina cried. "Are you crazy?"

He stood tall. "I've done some police work with Paavo. I know all about it. The only problem is, I don't know the restaurant or boat they were talking about."

"I do. Angelina told me. It's near the Aquatic Park."

"Ah, that's right near . . ." Sal had gotten so used to not uttering the name in case Angie happened to walk in on them he stopped himself even now.

"That's right. Why is this happening today, Salvatore?" Serefina did cry now. "The party looks so beautiful! It's so different, so unique, so . . . clever! I've dreamed of how thrilled and surprised Angelina will be when she sees it, and now . . ."

"My little girl will get to her party," Sal muttered. "I'll take care of everything."

* * *

Hannah casually strolled along the wharf to the ladder that led down to the boat. "Hello? Michael?"

He stepped onto the deck. "What are you doing here? Get away."

"No." She grabbed hold of the ladder's banister. Holding on tight, she climbed down and jumped onto the boat.

He grabbed her arm. "Are you crazy? Don't let him see you."

"Where's my baby?" she asked. "Who took her?"

He looked at her, shocked. "She's not here."

"I don't believe you!"

He pushed her back toward the ladder. "You'd better—and go now or I won't be able to save you. Trust me, Hannah."

"Not on your life!" She pulled her arm free. "Where's Gail?"

His demeanor changed, and he stepped menacingly toward her. "If you want to live, get far, far away from here. It's out of control. Remember what happened to Tyler—and Shelly Farms."

"Shelly?" she asked, stunned.

"He's dead. Murdered." Zeno reached out to grab her arm and drag her back toward the ladder. She stepped into him, kneed him in the groin, and when he doubled over in sudden, surprised pain, she twisted his arm behind his back and pushed him headfirst toward the railing. He went over, into the water.

Wow, Angie thought. She and Stan ran from their hiding place toward the boat. Zeno caught his breath and was now yelling for help.

Eugene Leer ran out from the boat's cabin to see

what the yelling was about. Angie pointed the AR-15 at him. He froze in his tracks, gawking at the weird-looking thing she pointed at him. His eyes widened as if he were trying to decide if it was a joke or some new high-tech instrument of torture. Hannah stepped behind him with an iron block and hit the back of his head.

He dropped like a sack of sand.

Zeno was in the distance, swimming away from the boat toward a far berth.

On the boat, Angie took Leer's gun and put it in her pocket, then stayed back, rifle ready, as Stan climbed into the hold.

"Anybody here?" he called.

"Hey! In here!"

Angie scooted past Stan at the sound of Paavo's voice, just as Hannah recognized Gail's. "Thank God!" Angie cried. They broke through the lock using the back of the AR-15 and Hannah's iron block.

The door sprang open. Angie couldn't tell if she was more shocked to see Paavo tied up, or he was more shocked to see her in a full-length formal carrying an assault rifle. Literally, dressed to kill.

"What are you doing here?" he asked.

"Saving you," she replied with a smile as she dropped to her knees beside him to make sure he was all right. Then she noticed Gail tied up as well. Her face fell. "She's not the mastermind?"

"Get a knife," Paavo said.

Hannah ran into the galley and screamed. Michael Zeno stood before her, a gun in hand.

At the sound, Angie scurried behind the doorway, and pushed the nose of the rifle out to point at him. "Don't move! Drop it, or I swear I'll fire."

She didn't know if it was her tone, the look in the one eye that peeked out at him from the safety of the doorframe, or the size—or bizarre shape—of the AR-15, but as his gaze darted from her to Hannah, he seemed to shrink. He tossed aside his handgun and raised his arms, his eyes locked with Hannah's. "I'm sorry," he murmured. "I never meant for this."

Hannah picked up his Glock and handed it to Paavo as she cut off his bindings, then Gail's. As soon as the blood returned to Paavo's hands and legs, he took the rifle from Angie.

"I did good, didn't I?" She swaggered like Rambo as she pointed to the rifle and handed him Leer's gun as well.

"Great. They must have looked at this thing and were stunned into silence." Paavo made sure Zeno's gun was loaded, then handed it to her and told her to keep it aimed at Zeno while he quickly pried apart and corrected the rifle section she'd put on backward. She handed him the extra piece in her pocket. It was needed. "Thank God you didn't try to fire it," he muttered, then took back the Glock.

As he motioned Zeno into the engine room, Angie found Stan unconscious in the first room of the cabin. His face wasn't bloody or battered. It was probably one good punch.

Hannah filled a cup with water and splashed it on him. He woke up, much worse for it.

While Gail and Stan tied up Zeno, Paavo and Angie woke up Leer and secured him in the engine area as well. Paavo handed Stan the Glock. "If they try to break free, shoot."

Stan looked ready to cry, but he swallowed hard and nodded.

"Kaitlyn's not here!" Hannah shouted, after searching the hold. She headed up to the deck.

"Wait!" Paavo ordered, but she didn't listen. He turned to Angie. "Come on. We've got to get you off this boat."

"Me?" Angie stared at him, confused.

They reached the deck a little behind Hannah. She stood stock-still, staring at the wharf, her voice strangled. "That's my baby!"

Angie followed her gaze, and while she recognized the lacy pink blanket and bonnet she'd bought Kaitlyn, her attention immediately went to someone else. "Oh, no," she cried. "That's my father!"

"And that," Paavo said as the last puzzle piece dropped into place, "is the woman Gail called 'Nadine Nadler.'"

Chapter 31

 Serefina had stopped on Jefferson Street, let off Sal, and then continued in the direction of Aquatic Park.

Right behind her Rolls, a taxi had stopped.

Sal watched as a woman got out, a bundle in her arms. She was dressed in dated hippie-style clothes—a long skirt, an overblouse, and a loose-fitting jacket over that. She had long brown hair that reached halfway down her back. Sal would have ignored her except for the fact that the bundle was held like a baby, and he remembered Angie's neighbor asking about a baby.

The woman reached back into the cab, pulled out a huge diaper bag, and slung it over her arm.

She paid the taxi driver and walked down the narrow side street that Serefina had told him led to the Athina Restaurant. Sal did the same.

Paavo pulled Angie to the stairs that led belowdecks. "Go down there. Stay with Stan and Gail. You'll be safe." He then faced Hannah. "I know you wouldn't leave your baby anyway, so you stay behind me." He gestured toward the woman talking to Sal and holding the baby. "She's already responsible for two deaths. We aren't going to let her add to the total."

"Nadine Nadler?" Angie repeated, studying the woman, from her shabby clothes to ... She paused. The woman's boots were distinctively styled, with a logo that showed them to be very expensive Louis Vuitton. "My God—Dianne Randle! Her name's an anagram!"

Paavo's eyebrows lifted. "I won't even ask. Okay, now—downstairs before she sees you."

Paavo and Hannah stood inside the wheelhouse and waited until Sal and Randle were near the ladder to the boat.

"Freeze! Police!" he called, AR-15 pointed at them as he stepped toward them. "Sal, step away."

Dianne Randle stopped walking, as did Sal. To Paavo's surprise, though, he didn't move.

"I don't think so," she said with a smug smile. Then she turned, and he was able to see the gun she had leveled at Sal.

"I'm sorry," Sal said.

Paavo didn't answer, but he didn't drop his gun, either. "Put it down, Randle. Or should I call you Nadler? You can't get away with it."

"Where are the others?" she asked.

"Leer and Zeno are under arrest. Put away your gun. It's all over."

"Is it?" she asked with a smile. "We'll see, won't we. Get off the boat!"

"No," Paavo said.

She nudged Sal to the edge of the wharf. Standing beside him, she swung the arm holding the baby out over the water. "Get off, or I let go. That water is black with filth. The bottom is muddy. The chance is great you won't be able to find her soon enough. You'll stop me, but the baby will be dead. And so will your girlfriend's father. If that's what you want to see happen, shoot me."

She waited.

Paavo didn't move, didn't put down his gun, but neither did Randle.

She stepped even closer to the water.

"No!" Hannah screamed, running out of the wheelhouse. "How could you? You were my friend! How can you do this? How can you threaten my baby?"

"Stop!" Randle shrieked, her gun to Sal's temple. "Or I'll shoot him!"

Dazed, Hannah did as told.

"She's not your baby," Randle cried. "She's mine, to do with as I wish. Everyone knows it now."

"Shelly Farms came to recognize that you believed that, didn't he?" Paavo said. "That was why, when Hannah told him about the pressure she'd been under to give up her baby, you realized he had to die. He was getting too close to your scheme."

"You're crazy," she said.

"You used Tyler Marsh to get rid of Shelly and then convinced Lance Vandermeer that Tyler was scamming him—that he never planned to give him the child. You knew about Vandermeer's violent temper and used it to your benefit."

"What about the knife with Hannah's finger-prints?" Randle asked arrogantly. "They're on the murder weapon. You can't get around that."

"Interesting you mention that, since it wasn't public information," Paavo said. "You took it during a secret meeting with Leer and Zeno, then told Vandermeer to use it on Tyler."

Randle looked ready to burst with fury.

Paavo continued. "Your plan would have gotten rid of Tyler and Hannah both, and gotten Vandermeer off your back. I'm sure you had some way planned to sell him the baby besides. But then the FBI showed up and too many questions started being asked. You decided to take the baby and run."

"Very clever, Inspector," Randle sneered. "If it were true."

"It's true, all right," Paavo said. "And we can prove it. Faced with the death penalty, do you really think Vandermeer won't talk?"

She snorted, head high. "I don't know what you're talking about."

"Don't you? Every day women come to you who don't know how they'll care for an unwanted baby. Many of those same days, you see couples who want to adopt and can't due to a problem with their health or background, or because there simply aren't enough babies for all the couples who want one. To both, you offered a solution. A disgusting solution."

Her face reddened with fury. "How dare you!"

"You're despicable," he sneered.

"Despicable! There was need for a service, and I

provided it. Both sides were happy. I've done nothing wrong."

"Illegally selling children? You think there's nothing wrong with that?" Paavo asked.

"What would you prefer? Abortion for the unwanted child? A childless, unhappy existence for people with love to give?"

"Those aren't the only alternatives," Paavo said. "They're the excuses you've given yourself for your greed."

"Is that so, Inspector? You know the system. You know I'm right! I won't listen to this any longer." She faced Sal. "Back up, get between me and the cop. He's going to get off the boat now, him and Hannah, then we're going aboard."

Sal did as he was told. Randle remained on the edge of the wharf, the baby out over the water.

From inside the boat, Angie saw Paavo give a slight nod. She looked all around, and suddenly Paavo's strange reaction to her rescue made sense.

He hadn't gone in blind and let himself be caught. He must have called Rebecca Mayfield with his plan, and she amassed the SWAT team, because Angie saw snipers on the restaurant's roof. Paavo had let himself be captured so Leer and Zeno would continue with their plans and somehow reveal the mastermind of the whole project.

They never expected Sal—or her—to interfere, or Kaitlyn to be in danger. With Paavo's nod, she knew what they were planning.

Still, her father was too close to Randle, as was

the baby. She was frantic watching this. She had to do something to make sure he and Kaitlyn had a chance to survive. Anything.

The way Randle held Kaitlyn, once the snipers fired, the baby would end up in the bay. Angie had seen that water—Randle was right about it being thick and murky, and that the mud churned easily. How hard would it be to find a baby dropped into it? How much damage would swallowing the bacteria and rotting garbage festering in it do to a baby even if they pulled her out before she drowned? Angie had no idea.

Her pulse pounded, her breath coming short and fast as she thought of one way to help. Randle didn't know about her. She'd have surprise in her favor . . . if she could do it . . . and if she acted fast.

Angie could sense Hannah's need to surge forward. She knew she had to act before Hannah did, or before a sniper decided to attempt a dangerous head shot. What if he missed . . . or Randle jerked her father into her place . . . ?

Without allowing herself time to think or waver, Angie slipped off her shoes and coat, ran across the deck as fast as she could, held her nose, and jumped.

The water was freezing and every bit as dark and dirty as she'd feared.

Chaos erupted above her. Gunfire, screams, the water churning wildly. Her head just broke the surface when a white blur flashed before her eyes, followed by a splash, as gunfire continued. *Kaitlyn!* She gulped for air and dived after her. The water wasn't terribly deep here, six or seven feet at most. Her eyes stung when she tried to open them, but she saw a blob of white and grabbed for it, then headed upward.

She surfaced to cheers. Paavo was on the ladder, reaching out for her. She tried to swim toward him, but it was hard holding a baby. She lunged forward and missed his hand. As she and the baby started to sink again, someone grabbed her arm. Coughing and blinking, she saw it was Sal, in the water with her. Paavo held Sal's arm and Sal held hers. Together, they hauled her and the baby to the ladder.

Paavo handed Kaitlyn up to her mother, then helped Angie and Sal onto the dock.

The area was chaotic as black-clad SWAT team members, medics, and uniformed police swarmed everywhere. Rebecca Mayfield was securing the scene and directing the arrests.

As Hannah hovered, a medic examined the crying baby. He assured Hannah it was an automatic response, not a learned one, to shut your mouth and try not to breathe when underwater. The baby was underneath just a few seconds, even though it seemed like an eternity, before Angie got her back to air.

Paavo took Angie in his arms and she saw he was nearly as wet as she was. "Are you all right?" he asked.

"I'm fine." She was shivering and he held her closer as he called for a blanket. "What happened?"

"Randle's dead. As soon as Sal saw Randle's gun turn toward you, he jumped as well. She fired wildly and tossed the baby in fury. It was over quickly."

"Thank God!" She looked around. "Where is my father?"

"A medic is checking his heart and blood pressure to make sure he's all right. He had quite a scare."

Suddenly Hannah grabbed Angie. "Thank you so much!" Hannah cried, hugging her tight, even as she continued to hold her baby. Stan came by as well and fretted over everything.

Gail placed a blanket around Angie's shoulders, then turned to Paavo. "I guess we have some business."

"Do we?" he asked. "My jurisdiction ends three miles out. We'll have to talk about our business in a day or two, but didn't you say you were taking the boat somewhere?"

She stared as his unexpected words slowly made sense. "I . . . yes!" She smiled, tears in her eyes. "Yes, I did." She hugged him and Angie. "Have a wonderful life, you two. And a wonderful engagement party! There's a shower on the boat, and a clothes dryer. Feel free to use them."

She ran to Hannah and the baby.

"The party." Paavo turned to Angie, still holding her. "I'm so sorry."

"No, it's not your fault. Anyway, it isn't over yet."

"Your dress, your hair . . . this isn't the way you wanted to appear," he said.

"It doesn't matter." Her eyes saddened. "Paavo, I'm sorry I interfered. I could have ruined everything. It's just that I was so worried about you."

"You tried to help me, as I would you. Never apologize for that, Angie."

As they kissed, Sal strolled over to them, also wrapped in a heavy wool blanket. "So, this is how my future son-in-law earns his pay. I can't say it's so boring after all. Or so easy. Are you okay, Angelina?"

It was his turn to hold his daughter as she made sure his health was fine.

"I'll go phone your mother," Sal said. "I know she's worried." Then he beamed. "When everyone hears the reason we're late, how we stopped a kidnapping and caught some baby smugglers, *Dio!* but it's going to make for one hell of a party."

He left, strutting like a peacock.

"Do you want to go home and change?" Paavo asked Angie.

"And miss another minute of my party? Not on your life. I'd go in this blanket first. We can clean up a bit on the boat, at least. I only hope the soap on board is strong enough to get rid of the fishy odor of my hair. I can't stand the way it smells!"

Paavo smiled as he took her in his arms. "You smell beautiful!" His kiss showed her how completely beautiful he thought she was in every way.

Chapter 32

Stan found Hannah sitting on the wooden bench on the wharf, the place he'd first seen her staring out at the bay. Only now, instead of being alone, she held her baby.

"How are you doing?" he asked, joining her.

She turned to him, her face calm and peaceful. "Gail has gone to pack. Paavo's letting her go. Don't tell anyone!"

"Never," he said. "But I'm more concerned about you."

She waited a long moment before she spoke. "It's hard being back here. So much has changed. Tyler and Shelly Farms dead. Eugene Leer and Michael Zeno arrested. Poor Michael! He thought he loved me, but he never knew the real me. He was kind to me, though, and I'm sorry for him."

"I'm sorry it had to be like this," Stan said.

"Me, too. But they were doing wrong—and they knew it." She took his hand and gave it a squeeze. "You're the only truly good man I know, Stanfield Bonnette."

"Hannah—" The timbre of his voice must have caught her attention because she turned to him, her face serious, as he drew in his breath to try to go on without passing out in a dead faint. Earlier that day, he hadn't been able to find the words. Now—maybe after facing guns and death—he could say them. "It's time for you to move on as well."

Her mouth opened with surprise, then she shut it, and withdrew her hand from his. "It is?"

He nodded. "You're one of the nicest people I've ever met, Hannah, and you're beautiful and kind. But you've been hiding away, and trying to live through people you think you're in love with. You love the idea of love, but you don't love me, Hannah."

She cocked her head. "I don't?"

"I'm no hero, for one thing," he said ruefully, then amended. "Not much of one, at least."

She smiled at him. "You'll always be to me, Stan." Her gaze turned to the fishing boat. "Gail's leaving as soon as possible. The boat's all set up for a baby. She told me I was welcome to join her. . . . I don't know where she's going, though. She probably doesn't, either. But it'd be someplace new." She glanced up at him. "An adventure. I've never had an adventure."

He stared at her, his gypsy girl, then nodded. "It's a great plan. A great start."

He wrapped his arms around her and Kaitlyn, holding them close. Then he kissed Kaitlyn on the forehead, stood, and stepped back. He tried to smile as he spoke, but he couldn't. "Good-bye, Hannah. Take good care of my girl, there. When you get settled someplace, I'll send you all her stuff."

"Thank you, Stan," she whispered. "Thank you for everything."

Out on Jefferson Street, he turned away from Fisherman's Wharf and headed toward the Maritime Museum. His heart was heavy as he walked beside the beach at Aquatic Park. He slid his hands into his pockets and faced the water, and as he watched the tide ebb and flow against the shore, little by little he stood straighter, and soon it felt as if the weight of the world had been lifted from his shoulders.

Or at least about a hundred twenty pounds of it.

The odd thing was, he felt good about himself, and good about having helped Hannah and Kaitlyn. More than anything else, he felt good about getting his life back again.

He took a few steps, then a few more, feeling a jaunty spring that hadn't been there for a long time.

Why in heaven's name had he ever thought his life had been lonely? Was he nuts? It was happy!

All of a sudden, his reason for happiness increased a thousandfold as he remembered Angie's engagement party. How could he have forgotten? Just the thought of it and his stomach began growling, his mouth salivating, and his body aquiver over all the great food he knew Angie's mother would be serving.

A special delivery envelope had come that morning and gave the location of the party. He looked straight ahead and smiled.

* * *

Angie wore no makeup, her hair was an unruly mass of damp curls, and her dress was shrunken, wrinkled, and carried a hint of eau de fish.

Paavo had also showered, then shaved as well and dried his khaki slacks. His beautiful new suit would have to wait for another occasion. He left Inspector Mayfield in charge of everything; he had an engagement party to go to.

Angie laughed until tears came to her eyes over what a ridiculous pair they made as the engaged couple, until she saw her father. The soon-to-be father-of-the-bride's tuxedo had shrunk. His sleeves were three-quarter length, and his trousers looked like floods.

Suddenly, though, none of that mattered. She was being lauded as a hero for saving the baby, and Sal and Paavo were not only getting along, but had worked together.

As the three of them walked toward her car for what she understood would be a short ride to the party, she looked at the two men she loved more than anything in the world, one on each side of her. She reached out and took both their hands as the memory of how close she came to losing them washed over her. She also chuckled inwardly over memories of her father and Paavo sneaking around trying to hide Sal's secret admirer from Serefina—how she would have loved to have been a fly on the wall for their conversations. Thoughts of all her sisters' stories about engagement parties past, both the good and the bad, came back to her, plus her own foolish worries about purple cakes and strippers.

The truth struck her as she walked, so simple as to be laughable, so profound as to touch her heart. It was this—Paavo, her family, her closest friends, they were what was important. Nothing else mattered. Not clothes, not job, not position, not wealth or fame. It was those you love and who love you in return.

They got into the car, Paavo at the wheel. She still had no idea where the engagement celebration was being held or what it would be like, but that was okay. Her mother had planned the entire party, details and all, with love. Wherever it was held, whatever it was like, she knew it would be perfect.

Angie's Favorite
Greek Recipes

 SPINACH TRIANGLES (*Spanakopita*)

These are wonderfully rich little triangles of buttery, flaky phyllo dough filled with spinach, onion, cheese, and herbs. They can be used as a side dish or hors d'oeuvres.

3 tablespoons olive oil
1 large white onion, chopped
1 bunch green onions, chopped
2 cloves garlic, minced
2 pounds spinach, rinsed and chopped
½ cup chopped fresh parsley
2 eggs, lightly beaten
½ cup ricotta cheese
1 cup crumbled feta cheese
salt to taste
8 sheets phyllo dough
½ cup melted butter

Preheat oven to 375°F.

Heat 3 tablespoons olive oil in a large skillet over medium heat. Sauté onion, green onions, and garlic until soft and lightly browned. Stir in spinach and parsley, and continue to sauté until spinach is limp, about 2 minutes. Remove from heat and set aside to cool. In a medium bowl, mix together eggs, ricotta, and feta. Stir in spinach mixture and lightly salt.

Cut phyllo sheets into long strips, 3 inches wide, and brush with melted butter. Place one tablespoon of the spinach mixture at the bottom of each strip and fold the corner up to form a triangle; continue folding in a triangular shape until the entire strip is folded. Continue this method until all the ingredients are used. Place the triangles on lightly oiled cookie sheets, brush each with butter, and bake at 375° for 15 to 20 minutes until golden brown.

SOUVLAKI

Souvlaki is made with tender cuts of meat cooked on a skewer. In this pork recipe, the meat is marinated in a lemony olive oil mixture. Serve with rice pilaf and a Greek salad.

1 lemon, juiced
¼ cup olive oil
¼ cup soy sauce
1 teaspoon dried oregano
3 cloves garlic, crushed
4 pounds pork tenderloin, cut into 1-inch cubes
2 green bell peppers, cut into 1-inch pieces
2 yellow onions, cubed

In a bowl, mix together lemon juice, olive oil, soy sauce, oregano, and garlic. Add pork, onions, and green pepper; stir to coat. Cover, and refrigerate for 2 to 3 hours.

Slide pork, pepper, and onion onto skewers. Turning skewers frequently, grill at medium high heat OR broil until lightly charred. Cook about 10 to 15 minutes total.

GREEK BUTTER COOKIES (*Kourabiedes*)

This is a traditional cookie—especially delicious with strong Greek coffee.

1 cup butter, softened
3¼ cups white sugar
1 egg
½ teaspoon vanilla extract
½ teaspoon almond extract
2¼ cups all-purpose flour
½ cup confectioners' sugar

Preheat the oven to 400°F. Grease cookie sheets.

In a medium bowl, cream together the butter, sugar, and egg until smooth. Stir in the vanilla and almond extracts. Gradually add in the flour to form a dough—you may have to knead it in by hand at the end. Take about a teaspoon of dough at a time and roll into balls, logs, or "S" shapes. Place cookies 1 to 2 inches apart onto the prepared cookie sheets.

Bake for 10 minutes in the preheated oven, or until lightly browned and firm. Allow cookies to cool before generously dusting with confectioners' sugar. These are often served in paper cupcake cups.

Enter the Delicious World of
Joanne Pence's Angie Amalfi Series

From the kitchen to the deck of a cruise ship, Joanne Pence's mysteries are always a delight. Starring career-challenged Angie Amalfi and her handsome homicide-detective boyfriend Paavo Smith, Joanne Pence serves up a mystery feast complete with humor, a dead body or two, and delicious recipes.

Enjoy the pages that follow, which give a glimpse into Angie and Paavo's world.

For sassy and single food writer Angie Amalfi, life's a banquet—until the man who's been contributing unusual recipes for her food column is found dead. But in SOMETHING'S COOKING, *Angie is hardly one to simper in fear—so instead she simmers over the delectable homicide detective assigned to the case.*

 A while passed before she looked up again. When she did, she saw a dark-haired man standing in the doorway to her apartment, surveying the scene. Tall and broad shouldered, his stance was aloof and forceful as he made a cold assessment of all that he saw.

If you're going to gawk, she thought, come in with the rest of the busybodies.

He looked directly at her, and her grip tightened on the chair. His expression was hard, his pale blue eyes icy. He was a stranger, of that she was certain. His wasn't the type of face or demeanor she'd easily forget. And someone, it seemed, had just sent her a bomb. Who? Why? What if this stranger. . .

As he approached with bold strides, her nerves tightened. Since she was without her high heels, the top of her head barely reached his chin.

The man appeared to be in his mid-thirties. His face was fairly thin, with high cheekbones and a pronounced, aquiline nose with a jog in the middle that made it look as if it had been broken at least once.

340

Thick, dark brown hair spanned his high forehead, and his penetrating, deep-set eyes and dark eyebrows gave him a cold, no-nonsense appearance. His gaze didn't leave hers, and yet he seemed aware of everything around them.

"Your apartment?" he asked.

"The tour's that way." She did her best to give a nonchalant wave of her thumb toward the kitchen.

She froze as he reached into his breast pocket. "Police." He pulled out a billfold and dropped open one flap to reveal his identification: Inspector Paavo Smith, Homicide.

In TOO MANY COOKS, *Angie's talked her way into a job on a pompous, third-rate chef's radio call-in show. But when a successful and much envied restaurateur is poisoned, Angie finds the case far more interesting than trying to make her pretentious boss sound good.*

 Angie glanced up from the monitor. She'd been debating whether or not to try to take the next call, if and when one came in, when her attention was caught by the caller's strange voice. It was oddly muffled. Angie couldn't tell if the caller was a man or a woman.

"I didn't catch your name," Henry said.

"Pat."

Angie's eyebrows rose. A neuter-sounding Pat? What was this, a *Saturday Night Live* routine?

"Well, Pat, what can I do for you?"

"I was concerned about the restaurant killer in your city."

Henry's eye caught Angie's. "Thank you. I'm sure the police will capture the person responsible in no time."

"I'm glad you think so, because—you're next."

Henry jumped up and slapped the disconnect button. "And now," he said, his voice quivering, "a word from our sponsor."

Angie Amalfi's latest job, developing the menu for a new inn, sounds enticing—especially since it means spending a week in scenic northern California with her homicide-detective boyfriend. But once she arrives at the soon-to-be-opened Hill Haven Inn, she's not so sure anymore. In COOKING UP TROUBLE, *the added ingredients of an ominous threat, a missing person, and a woman making eyes at her man, leave Angie convinced that the only recipe in this inn's kitchen is one for disaster.*

 She placed her hand over his large strong one, scarcely able to believe that they were here, in this strange yet lovely room, alone. "But I am real, Paavo."

"Are you?" He bent to kiss her lightly, his eyes intent, his hand moving from her chin to the back of her head to intertwine with the curls of her hair. The mystical aura of the room, the patter of the rain, the solitude of the setting stole over him and made him think of things he didn't want to ponder—things like being together with Angie forever, like never being alone again. He tried to mentally break the spell. He needed time—cold, logical time. "There's no way a woman like you should be in my life," he said finally. "Sometimes I think you can't be any more real than the Sempler ghosts. That I'll close my eyes and you'll disappear. Or that I'm just imagining you."

"Inspector," she said, returning his kiss with one that seared, "there's no way you could imagine me."

Cold logic melted in the midst of her fire, and all his careful resolve went with it. His heart filled, and the solemnity of his expression broke. "I know," he said softly, "and that's the best part."

As his lips met hers, a bolt of lightning lit their room for just a moment. Then a scream filled the darkness.

Food columnist Angie Amalfi has it all. But in COOKING MOST DEADLY, *while she's wondering if it's time to cut the wedding cake with her boyfriend, Paavo, he becomes obsessed with a grisly homicide that has claimed two female victims.*

 "You've got to keep City Hall out of this case. As far as the press knows, she was a typist. Nothing more. Mumble when you say where she worked." Lieutenant Hollins got up from behind his desk, walked around to the front of it, and leaned against the edge. Paavo and Yosh sat facing him. They'd just completed briefing him on the Tiffany Rogers investigation. Hollins made it a point not to get involved in his men's investigations unless political heat was turned on. In this case, the heat was on high.

"Her friends and coworkers are at City Hall, and there's a good chance the guy she's been seeing is there as well," Paavo said.

"It's our only lead, Chief," Yosh added. "So far, the CSI unit can't even find a suspicious fingerprint to lift. The crime scene is clean as a whistle. She always met her boyfriend away from her apartment. We aren't sure where yet. We've got a few leads we're still checking."

"So you've got nothing except for a dead woman lying in her own blood on the floor of her own living room!" Hollins added.

"We have to follow wherever the leads take us," Paavo said.

"I'm not saying not to, all I'm saying is keep the press away." Hollins paced back and forth in front of his desk. "The mayor and the Board of Supervisors want this murderer caught right now. This isn't the kind of publicity they want for themselves or the city. I mean, if someone who works for them isn't safe, who is?"

"Aw heck, Paavo." Yosh turned to his partner. "The supervisors said they want us to catch this murderer fast. Here I'd planned to take my sweet time with this case."

Paavo couldn't help but grin.

"Cut the comedy, Yoshiwara." Hollins stuck an unlit cigar in his mouth and chewed. "This case is number one for you both, got it?"

In COOK'S NIGHT OUT, *Angie has decided to make her culinary name by creating the perfect chocolate confection:* angelinas. *Donating her delicious rejects to a local mission, Angie soon finds that the mission harbors more than the needy, and to save not only her life, but Paavo's as well, she's going to have to discover the truth faster than you can beat egg whites to a peak.*

 Angelina Amalfi flung open the window over the kitchen sink. After two days of cooking with chocolate, the mouthwatering, luscious, inviting smell of it made her sick.

That was the price one must pay, she supposed, to become a famous chocolatier.

She found an old fan in the closet, put it on the kitchen table, and turned the dial to high. The comforting aroma of home cooking wafting out from a kitchen was one thing, but the smell of Willy Wonka's chocolate factory was quite another.

She'd been trying out intricate, elegant recipes for chocolate candies, searching for the perfect confection on which to build a business to call her own. Her kitchen was filled with truffles, nut bouchées, exotic fudges, and butter creams.

So far, she'd divulged her business plans only to Paavo, the man for whom she had plans of a very different nature. She was going to have to let someone else know soon, though, or she wouldn't have any room left in the kitchen to cook. She didn't want to start eating the calorie-oozing, waistline-expanding chocolates out of sheer enjoyment—her taste tests were another thing altogether and totally justifiable, she reasoned—and throwing the chocolates away had to be sinful.

Angie Amalfi's long-awaited vacation with her detective boyfriend has all the ingredients of a romantic getaway—a sail to Acapulco aboard a freighter, no crowds, no Homicide Department worries, and a red bikini. But in COOKS OVERBOARD, *it isn't long before Angie's* Love Boat *fantasies are headed for stormy seas—the cook tries to jump off the ship, Paavo is acting mighty strange, and someone's added murder to the menu . . .*

Paavo became aware, in a semi-asleep state, that the storm was much worse than anyone had expected it would be. The best thing to do was to try to sleep through it, to ignore the roar of the sea, the banging of rain against the windows, the almost human cry of the wind through the ship.

He reached out to Angie. She wasn't there. She must have gotten up to use the bathroom. Maybe her getting up was what had awakened him. He rolled over to go back to sleep.

When he awoke again, the sun was peeking over the horizon. He turned over to check on Angie, but she still wasn't beside him. Was she up already? That wasn't like her. He remembered a terrible storm last night. He sat up, suddenly wide awake. Where was Angie?

He got out of bed and hurried to the sitting area. Empty. The bathroom door was open. Empty.

The wall bed was down. What was that supposed to mean? Had she tried sleeping on it? Had she grown so out of sorts with him that she didn't want to sleep with him anymore? Things had seemed okay between them last night. He remembered her talking . . . she was talking about writing a cookbook again . . . and he remembered getting more and more sleepy . . . he must have . . . oh, hell.

Angie Amalfi has a way with food and people, but her newest business idea is turning out to be shakier than a fruit-filled gelatin mold. In A COOK IN TIME, *her first—and only—clients for "Fantasy Dinners" are none other than a group of UFO chasers and government conspiracy fanatics. But when it seems that the group has a hidden agenda greater than anything on the* X-Files, *Angie's determined to find out the truth before it takes her out of this world—for good.*

 The nude body was that of a male Caucasian, early forties or so, about 5'10", 160 pounds. The skin was an opaque white. Lips, nose, and ears had been removed, and the entire area from approximately the pubis to the sigmoid colon had been cored out, leaving a clean, bloodless cavity. No postmortem lividity appeared on the part of the body pressed against the ground. The whole thing had a tidy, almost surreal appearance. No blood spattered the area. No blood was anywhere; apparently, not even in the victim. A gutted, empty shell.

The man's hair was neatly razor-cut; his hands were free of calluses or stains, the skin soft, the nails manicured; his toenails were short and square-cut, and his feet without bunions or other effects of ill-fitting shoes. In short, all signs of a comfortable life. Until now.

*Between her latest "sure-fire" foray into the food in-
dustry—video restaurant reviews—and her concern
over Paavo's depressed state, Angie's plate is full to
overflowing. Paavo has never come to terms with the
fact that his mother abandoned him when he was
four, leaving behind only a mysterious present. But
when the token disappears in* TO CATCH A COOK,
*Angie discovers a lethal goulash of intrigue, betrayal,
and mayhem that may spell disaster for her and
Paavo.*

The bedroom had also been torn apart and
the mattress slashed. This was far, far more
frightening than what had happened to her
own apartment. There was anger here, perhaps hatred.

"What is going on?" she cried. "Why would anyone
destroy your things?"

"It looks like a search, followed by frustration."

As she wandered through the little house, she realized he was right. It wasn't random destruction as she
had first thought, but where the search of her apartment
had appeared slow and meticulous, here it was hurried
and frenzied.

"Hercules!" he called. "Herc? Come on, boy, are
you all right?"

Angie's breath caught. His cat . . . He loved that cat.

"Do you see him?" she asked, standing in the bedroom doorway.

"No. They better not have hurt my cat," he muttered, his jaw clenched. They looked under the bed, in the closets, and throughout the backyard.

She was afraid—and for Hercules, more afraid that they'd find the cat than that they wouldn't. If he had run and was hiding, scared, he should return home eventually, but if he was nearby, and unable to come when called . . .

They couldn't find him.

Finally, back in the living room, Paavo bleakly took in the damage, the ugliness before him. "Who's doing this, Angie, and why?"

For once Angie's newest culinary venture, "Comical Cakes," seems to be a roaring success! But in BELL, COOK, AND CANDLE, there's nothing funny about her boyfriend Paavo's latest case—a series of baffling murders that may be rooted in satanic ritual. And it gets harder to focus on pastry alone when strange "accidents" and desecrations to her baked creations begin occurring with frightening regularity—leaving Angie to wonder whether she may end up as devil's food of a different kind.

 Angie was beside herself. She'd been called to go to a house to discuss baking cakes for a party of twenty, and yet no one was there when she arrived. This was the second time that had happened to her. Was someone playing tricks, or were people really so careless as to make appointments and then not keep them?

She really didn't have time for this. But at least she was getting smart. She'd brought a cake with her that had to be delivered to a horse's birthday party not far from her appointment. She never thought she'd be baking cakes for a horse, but Heidi was being boarded some forty miles outside the city, and the owner visited her on weekends only. That was why the owner wanted a Comical Cake of the mare.

Angie couldn't imagine eating something that

looked like a beloved pet or animal. She was meeting real ding-a-lings in this line of work.

Still muttering to herself about the thoughtlessness of the public, she got into her new car. A vaguely familiar yet disquieting smell hit her. A stain smeared the bottom of the cake box. She peered closer. The smell was stronger, and the bottom of the box was wet.

She opened the driver's side door, ready to jump out of the car as her hand slowly reached for the box top. Thoughts of flies and toads pounded her. What now?

She flipped back the lid and shrank away from it.

Nothing moved. Nothing jumped out.

Poor Heidi was now a bright-red color, but it wasn't frosting. The familiar smell was blood, and it had been poured on her cake. Shifting the box, she saw that it had seeped through onto the leather seat and was dripping to the floor mat.

With a pinch of pernicious and a dash of dastardly,

JOANNE PENCE

**cooks up a scrumptious banquet of murderous fun
in the Angie Amalfi mysteries**

COURTING DISASTER
0-06-050291-6/$6.99 US/$9.99 Can
There's already too much on the
bride-to-be's plate . . .
and much of it is murderous.

And don't miss these other titles

TWO COOKS A-KILLING
0-06-009216-5/$6.99 US/$9.99 Can
Nothing could drag Angie away from San Francisco—except
for a job preparing the banquet for her all-time favorite soap
opera characters during a Christmas Reunion Special.

IF COOKS COULD KILL
0-06-054821-5/$6.99 US/$9.99 Can
When Angie's friend Connie Rogers' would-be boyfriend
is sought by the police in connection with a brutal
robbery/homicide, the two friends set out to find the real killer.

BELL, COOK, AND CANDLE
0-06-103084-8/$6.99 US/$9.99 Can
When Angie is called upon to deliver a humorous confection
to an after-hours goth club, she finds herself
up to her neck in the demonic business.

Coming soon!

Eye of the Needle: For the first time in trade paperback, comes one of legendary suspense author **Ken Follett**'s most compelling classics.
0-06-074815-X • On Sale January 2005

More Than They Could Chew: Rob Roberge tells the story of Nick Ray, a man whose addictions (alcohol, kinky sex, questionable friends) might only be cured by weaning him from oxygen.
0-06-074280-1 • On Sale February 2005

Men from Boys: A short story collection featuring some of the true masters of crime fiction, including Dennis Lehane, Lawrence Block, and Michael Connelly. These stories examine what it means to be a man amid cardsharks, revolvers, and shallow graves.
0-06-076285-3 • On Sale April 2005

Now Available:

Kinki Lullaby: The latest suspenseful, rapid-fire installment of **Isaac Adamson**'s Billy Chaka series finds Billy in Osaka, investigating a murder and the career of a young puppetry prodigy. 0-06-051624-0

First Cut: Award-winning author Peter Robinson probes the darkest regions of the human mind and soul in this clever, twisting tale of crime and revenge. 0-06-073535-X

Night Visions: A young lawyer's shocking dreams become terribly real in this chilling, beautifully written debut thriller by **Thomas Fahy**. 0-06-059462-4

Get Shorty: Elmore Leonard takes a mobster to Hollywood—where the women are gorgeous, the men are corrupt, and making it big isn't all that different from making your bones. 0-06-077709-5

Be Cool: Elmore Leonard takes Chili Palmer into the world of rock stars, pop divas, and hip-hop gangsters—all the stuff that makes big box office.
0-06-077706-0

Available wherever books are sold, or call 1-800-331-3761.

Don't miss the next book by your favorite author.
Sign up now for AuthorTracker by visiting
www.AuthorTracker.com

An Imprint of HarperCollins*Publishers*
www.harpercollins.com

DKA 1104